Life Comes to the Archbishop

by

George Eppley

E & D Productions: eppleybooks04@cox.net

Eppley Files: http://www.csnmail.net/~eppley/

In memory of Vincent P. Haas and James Gill, SJ, MD

Two priests who mirrored the compassion and love of Jesus

and profoundly influenced my life.

ACKNOWLEDGEMENTS

First and foremost, I would like to thank my wife, Anita Dixon Eppley, for the moral, critical, and technical support she has given me since I began this project three years ago. Were it not for her insights and for her infinite patience with the computer, something I sorely lack, this novel would still be an idea in my mind.

So many other people have contributed to the writing of this novel that I am reluctant to name them lest I inadvertently omit some who helped bring this work into existence.

In one of the chapters of the novel, Archbishop Edward Foley offers the Gaelic toast—*Sláinte*—to a longtime friend and classmate. On the Internet I found this translation of the toast:

May you live as long as you want and never want as long as you live.

To my wife and to all the friends who helped me in any way with this novel, I offer a toast—

Sláinte!

CHAPTER 1

At eleven o'clock on a bitterly cold Wednesday night in January, two police cars, lights flashing, roared into the driveway of a bungalow on Hampton Street in Forest Park. The older officer, a sergeant, red faced and overweight, drew his revolver and ran to the rear of the house. The other officer, a patrolman, younger, taller and more athletic, drew his gun, bounded up the front steps, and pounded on the front door, shouting, "Police! Open the door and come out with your hands over your head!"

"Don't shoot," a trembling voice shouted, "I'm coming out. Just wait a second till I find my bathrobe."

The door opened and a young barefoot girl in a blue bathrobe came out of the house with her hands over her head, which was wrapped in a towel. She was trembling and shivering from fright and the freezing January air that whipped around her.

"What's wrong? Has something happened to my mother?" she screamed.

Ignoring her questions, the younger officer at the front door asked, "What's your name?"

"Toni Vincent. I live here with my mom and—and—her husband—Randy Smith."

"Anyone else inside?"

"No, just me. My mom and Randy went out about three hours ago. What happened to them? Where are they?"

Just then the other officer returned from checking out the rear of the house. The officer at the front door turned to Toni as he shut off his cell phone. “Toni, I think your mom and her husband may be at the Justice Center.”

“The Justice Center! You mean the jail, don’t you? Why are they in jail?”

Before the officer could answer, the couple who lived next door hurried down their steps, drawing their coats over their shoulders. Toni ran to them as the officer looked on. “Mrs. Kolar, something’s happened! My mom and Randy are at the Justice Center.”

The sergeant said to Mrs. Kolar, “Could you take the girl inside? It’s too cold out here for the way she’s dressed. My partner and I need to search the house.”

“Search the house? Why?” screamed Toni.

“Routine. We’re looking for drugs. Toni, have your folks been using drugs?”

Hank Kolar stepped forward, showing no sign of being intimidated by the police. “Officer, you have no right to ask her that question. Do you have a warrant to search the house?”

The sergeant, hands on his hips, got into Mr. Kolar’s face. “Sir, we are trying to do a job here. Don’t make it more difficult than it has to be. Are you a lawyer?”

Kolar narrowed his eyes but remained calm. “No, Officer, I’m Hank Kolar—investigative reporter for the Forest Park Sentinel. I don’t like druggies any more than you do. But I have seen too many get off because the police were too lazy to do their jobs. Now, once again, Officers, do you have a search warrant?”

“No, we don’t, but we can easily get one.”

Kolar glared at them and said sharply, “Then, dammit, get it!”

The officers glared back at Kolar. But they knew they were wrong and did not want this newspaper guy writing about them in the morning paper. After a quick exchange that only they could hear, the sergeant said, “I’ll secure the house, and Officer Williamson will be back shortly with a search warrant.”

A small crowd of curious neighbors had gathered outside but

quickly dispersed when the police sergeant directed them to clear the area.

"Folks, go back to your homes. We're just trying to locate this young lady's parents. Nothing's going to happen, so you would be smart to get out of this freezing cold."

Realizing that Toni was probably an innocent victim, the sergeant encouraged her to go into the home of the Kolars. He asked the Kolars, however, if Toni had any relatives they should contact.

"Toni's grandmother, Mrs. Lacey, lives at Haley House," Mrs. Kolar said. "She's housekeeper for Archbishop Foley—he's retired. Is it all right, Sergeant, if I call her and tell her what's happened?"

"Sure. Tell her she might want to go to the Justice Center. I doubt that she can see her daughter tonight, but she can try. If she doesn't have a ride, we can drive her there in about a half hour."

"She doesn't drive, but my husband can pick her up at Haley House and drive her to the Center, if that's OK."

"Certainly," the sergeant said. "Toni's mother and her husband are high on something. There's going to be a lot of questions asked, and somebody should be there to give some answers."

Mrs. Kolar put her arm around Toni and led her through the yard to her home. "Just sit down, honey, while I get your grandmother on the phone." She reached Mrs. Lacey at Haley House, briefly told her what happened, and said that her husband Hank would be there in ten to fifteen minutes to drive her to the Justice Center if that was all right with her.

As Toni warmed up and stopped shivering, she began to sob. "Oh, God," she said, covering her face with her hands. Her worst fear had come true—her mother and Randy had been arrested on drug charges. Empty beer and liquor bottles, which she hauled out to the trash every week, were proof that they were heavy drinkers. She hoped that the hypodermic needle she found in the trash last week was Randy's, not her mother's.

Toni detested Randy and for some time had suspected that he

might be using drugs or even selling them. She recalled looking out of her bedroom window one night and seeing Randy in the driveway handing an envelope to a man she had never seen before that night. She concluded she was watching a drug deal. But she was afraid to voice her fears to anyone, not even her mother or Mrs. Kolar, whom she liked.

Mrs. Kolar put a kettle on the stove. "Toni, let's just have some hot tea while we wait for word from Hank and your grandmother. A little hot tea always helps me when I'm upset."

When Hank Kolar drove up to Haley House, he could see Mrs. Lacey at the lighted front entrance. By the time he was out of the car, she was half way down the walk. He greeted her and helped her into his car. It was obvious this event had unnerved Mrs. Lacey, so Kolar did not try to engage her in conversation as they drove to the Justice Center. He had met her once before, and he felt sorry for her. Julia Lacey was probably in her mid-sixties and did not need this aggravation. Kolar and his wife got along fine with Helen, Mrs. Lacey's daughter, but they thought Randy was a real loser. Not very friendly and foul mouthed and abusive when he was drinking. The Kolars had sympathy for Helen, but they avoided as far as possible any contact with Randy.

Kolar assured Mrs. Lacey that Toni was in good hands. "Toni's with my wife. She can stay all night with us if the police won't let her go back into her mom's house."

"Thanks, Hank, you two have been very kind. I hope my daughter realizes how fortunate she is to have neighbors like you." They rode in silence the rest of the way.

The Justice Center was about a ten-minute drive from Haley House, but Kolar shortened the time by exceeding the speed limit. He knew how important it was for Mrs. Lacey to be with her daughter.

When they arrived at the Justice Center, Kolar identified himself and Mrs. Lacey and then asked the desk sergeant, "What are the charges against Helen and Randy Smith?"

"Well," the sergeant said, "I don't know all the charges. But evidently the Smiths robbed a Convenience store at gun point. A security camera caught it all. The clerk in the store managed to trip a security alarm and the Smiths were stopped by the police as they were pulling away from the store. They're busted."

Mrs. Lacey was stunned and feeling faint. For a while she could not catch her breath. Kolar suggested she sit down and helped her to a bench. When she had a drink of water, which the desk sergeant brought to her, she said to Hank, "I can't believe they would do something that crazy! Taking drugs is bad enough, but using a gun to rob a store? That's stupid! How could my daughter use drugs—especially with Toni in the house. Helen and Randy must be insane!"

Kolar didn't dispute that. Mrs. Lacey sat shaking her head in disbelief. She turned to Kolar. "Helen's in real trouble, isn't she?"

"Mrs. Lacey, she could be, but we don't have enough information right now to make a judgment, so let's not jump to conclusions. She and Randy will appear before a judge tomorrow morning and we'll know more about the charges."

"Could I see her now?" Mrs. Lacey asked.

"I'm sorry, Ma'am, you can't," the sergeant said respectfully. "Her lawyer could see her, but she's in no condition to talk to anyone right now. I suggest that you call in the morning to find out when she's going to be arraigned."

"Thanks, Sergeant," Kolar said. "You've been very helpful."

On the way to the parking lot, Hank asked Mrs. Lacey if she would like to see her granddaughter before returning to Haley House.

Mrs. Lacey brightened at the suggestion. "Hank, that would be wonderful. It's very late, so I'll just stay a minute."

Ten minutes later there was a brief and tearful meeting of Mrs. Lacey and Toni. "It's OK, honey," Mrs. Lacey whispered as she held Toni close. "Things will work out all right. I couldn't see your mom tonight, but I'll be there tomorrow morning." She kissed Toni goodnight, and Kolar drove her back to Haley House, passing Saint Joseph Cathedral, a magnificent presence in the heart of the city.

CHAPTER 2

That unfortunate event involving the family of my housekeeper, Mrs. Lacey, was the beginning of a drama that unfolded over several months. I am not sure that the events in the story happened exactly as I describe them or in the order I tell them. But from interviews with others who witnessed these events, and from notes I recorded in my daily journal, I have reconstructed as best I can the characters and their conversations. Writing the story was my way of dealing with the trauma in the months following the events.

The stately Gothic cathedral that Hank Kolar and Mrs. Lacey passed on their way to Haley House, where I, Archbishop Edward Foley, lived at the time, stands on a downtown city block called Gilmour Square. Built with Tennessee crab orchard stone, one of the most durable of stones, the cathedral has the look of a building completed yesterday and not nine decades ago. Its spire rises 300 feet into the sky. At night a green light burns brightly at the top of its steeple. When it was first built, sailors in their ore boats on Lake Perry got their bearings from the steeple light as they steered through choppy and treacherous waters and into the mouth of the river. Tug boats helped the freighters negotiate the bends and turns in the river until they were safely docked at the steel mills in the Flats.

So many skyscrapers now dominate the city's landscape that the cathedral can no longer be seen from the Lake. But since it is at the corner of one of city's busiest intersections, it is central to the lives of many Catholics who stop there to attend Mass or pray for strength to help them through their work days. The steeple's green light continues to be a beacon for the discouraged, the frustrated, the forgotten, and the lonely.

The cathedral, however, shadows my life not only because I was archbishop there for twenty-five years but because of a tragic event that happened there—an event that is part of the story that began that cold January night.

Other structures also stand on Gilmour Square: a chancery building where the business of the large archdiocese is conducted, and a rectory where I lived when I was archbishop, with living quarters for the priests assigned to the cathedral and to the chancery. Within easy walking distance of Gilmour Square is a University, which occupies twenty acres of prime downtown property. It began as a small liberal arts college, but over the years diocesan officials added a graduate school for students seeking advanced degrees in music, art, law, nursing, teacher education, business, psychology, and social work. It is now a University generously subsidized by Catholic parishes, by businesses and corporations, and by people of all religious denominations in Forest Park. The faculty is primarily Catholic, but Protestant and Jewish and Muslim scholars give the University an ecumenical dimension. I regard this as one of the most significant achievements of my twenty-five years as archbishop.

When I retired at age seventy-five, I lived for a time in Haley House, an elegant mansion owned by the diocese. But when that structure was sold to downtown real estate developers some years ago, I moved to a condominium across the street from Gilmour Square. From my 20th floor suite, I can look down on the cathedral and those adjacent buildings with their beautiful stone facing and think of that complex as a well constructed theme having the elements of unity, coherence, and emphasis. Sometimes I think of it as a little island where people are striving for peace, for truth and for harmony. The people on Gilmour Square are not saints–maybe some are–but most are sinners like me. They are people with fears and anxieties and feelings of guilt for promises broken and for dreams deferred, and for friends disappointed or perhaps betrayed.

My love affair with this cathedral began some years ago after I visited the Chartres cathedral in France. Henry Adams wrote that the cathedral of Chartres represents the noblest and the best in medieval man—the highest aspirations of the human spirit. My cathedral has neither the magnitude nor the beauty and elegance of Chartres. Nevertheless, it stands in my city of Forest Park as a symbol of the hopes and aspirations of a significant segment of the population. But it is more than a symbol. Because of its proximity to the University, it is a reminder that life to be truly human is an endless journey of the mind toward truth.

The archbishop who built the liberal arts college in 1910 was a lover of Renaissance art. Not surprisingly, he filled the library and galleries of the college with paintings and art objects he had bought over the years. Some pieces were originals, but most were reproductions of famous paintings that hang in the Vatican Museum or the Louvre or the Metropolitan in New York. At noontime office workers from nearby buildings come to the University to eat in the cafeteria, to browse in its library, or to sit in the gallery and admire the works of art.

At the entrance to the gallery there stands a handsome oak table that dates back to the early 18th century. Prominently displayed on the table is a reproduction of unfinished figures, which Michelangelo called "The Prisoners."

As someone who has long admired the genius of Michelangelo, I knew that these unfinished figures vividly illustrate the sculptor's view of human life. He once wrote that there is in each of us a person who is struggling to be free. God is the sculptor who is working not with inert stone but with a more resistant substance called human freedom. "The Prisoners" seems to be saying that some people will never emerge because they prefer the bondage of the lust of the flesh, the lust of the eyes, and the pride of life. Such people remain unfinished and in the deepest sense unborn.

Why would these unfinished figures guard the entrance to the University art gallery? One day I asked the curator of the gallery to explain why "The Prisoners" had such a prominent place. Was this by accident or by design?

"By design," she said. "The late archbishop built this college to prepare teachers, nurses, and social workers. When he was alive, he often talked to the faculty about this piece of sculpture. He would say that it is one thing to fashion a sculpture of these prisoners as Michelangelo did. But it is quite another to form truly professional teachers, nurses, and social workers who can liberate bodies imprisoned by sickness and minds imprisoned by ignorance or fear."

I have often thought about her words, especially since those momentous events at the cathedral. Until now, I have kept the story to myself. And so there is a story imprisoned within me. It is struggling to get out so that I can be free. It is not always a nice story. It is a story of very human people and very weak people, some extraordinarily good people, and sometimes very sinful people. I have been loathe to tell that story because I did not want to hurt the Church, which I dearly love, and I did not want to hurt some of the people involved in the story.

In some ways, I would like to erase this story from my mind and pretend that it never happened. But I know that writing about it, difficult as that may be, is the only way I can bring closure to this tragic episode in my life.

I must try to see what God has seen in that cathedral event, and I must tell the story about some people who are imprisoned in my mind, especially myself.

The chain of events that make up the story began with the Convenience store robbery. At the time—just five years ago—I was 75 years old, living in the spacious mansion called Haley House. Mrs. Lacey, my housekeeper, lived in a suite on the third floor.

I'll start by telling a little about myself.

CHAPTER 3

I have been in excellent health all my life and have never been hospitalized in my 80 years. I gave up smoking when I was in my thirties, almost fifty years ago. But I still enjoy a Scotch before dinner and a glass of wine with my dinner. I am six feet tall and weigh175 pounds. I take long walks or swim three or four times a week in the University pool. Although I have a full head of gray hair, friends tell me I look much younger than eighty, more like a man of sixty-five. I seldom lose my temper. I like people, and I think most people like me because I try to be gentle and easy going.

A few months before my 75th birthday, I sent a handwritten letter to the pope tending my resignation as required for bishops who have reached that age. The pope did not have to act on it immediately, and I was aware that he had permitted others to stay on for as many as five years beyond their retirement age. Although Rome was reluctant to admit it, the priest shortage was beginning to be a serious concern. Naturally I thought the pope might ask me to stay active beyond retirement age, as long as I was in good health.

The pope's reply to my letter came three weeks later. It read: "His Holiness with deep regret accepts Archbishop Foley's resignation and wishes him health and happiness in his retirement years."

"Bullshit," I fumed to myself in my study. "The old man in Rome didn't retire when he reached seventy-five. Why must I?"

Deep down I knew why. I had become something of a *persona non grata* with the Vatican. I thought the Curia had too much power and, not too subtly, said so. I believed the Second Vatican Council wanted to give national conferences of bishops more authority over decisions that affected their countries and their dioceses, but the Curia fought that. I was made a bishop after the Second Vatican Council concluded, so I did not attend any of its sessions—to my great regret. I would have joined those bishops from all over the world who had often questioned during sessions of the Council why everything must be cleared through the Vatican.

In my columns for the archdiocesan newspaper, I wrote that the Church must be open to the possibility of married priests and women priests. These columns did not endear me to the rich and powerful in the archdiocese, some of whom belonged to Opus Dei, a right-wing organization of Catholics in medicine, law, education, banking, journalism and the media. I suspect some of these people wrote to the Vatican complaining about their archbishop because soon I was getting letters from Rome asking me to clarify my remarks. I did so by using vague and obscure language, imitating the tongue-in-cheek style of many encyclicals and rescripts that came from the Curia.

I once read *Journey into Russia* by Laurens Van der Post, a South African writer who said that the people of the Republic of Georgia survived with their dignity intact after they were conquered by the Russians by making "creative uses of irresponsibility." It was their way of refusing to give deference to their conquerors.

I adopted this creative tactic when dealing with the Curia. I would use arcane language, *non sequiturs*, and convoluted sentence structures to confuse and obfuscate—in other words, I put into play the creative use of irresponsibility.

This was not a strategy designed to win me a red hat and membership in the College of Cardinals. But I did not care. At least that's what I told myself at the time. I knew I had more talent and ability than some men who were chosen, so I must admit I was hurt when I was overlooked. Hell, I said, our Church doesn't need more company men. It needs men who have the guts to tell the pope and the Curia when we think they're wrong.

Even though I was disappointed that the pope so quickly

accepted my offer to retire, I was glad that I could look at myself in the mirror and know that I had tried my best to be true to my convictions. I hope it can be said of me that I did not put expediency over conviction, which is an easy thing to do in the church, in business, in academics, and in politics.

After my retirement, I moved from the cathedral residence to Haley House, a mansion owned by the archdiocese. It was (until recently when it was razed) in the heart of the city not too far from Gilmour Square. Built in the early twentieth century, it was an architectural gem overlooking Lake Perry. The mansion had a basement with spacious paneled meeting rooms, three floors and an elevator. Four suites of rooms occupied each floor.

I wanted to live in a smaller house, but Cardinal Thomas Mohr, the man who replaced me as archbishop, wanted me to live in Haley House, which was named in honor of a previous archbishop who bought the property forty years earlier. Edward Haley had come from Chicago, where he had been an auxiliary bishop to a cardinal who thought that as a prince of the church he should live an elegant and almost regal lifestyle. So when Haley became archbishop of Forest Park, he thought that he too, like his mentor, should live like a prince. Ironically, Haley's parents were poor Irish immigrants. His father, a shoemaker, through hard work and thrift, managed to own a shoe repair shop in south Chicago.

When Haley became archbishop, he bought the mansion with diocesan funds and then traveled abroad, most notably to Italy, buying art objects to enhance the place. Haley lived in the mansion for twenty years, entertaining influential prelates, especially the Apostolic Delegate Antonio DiNardo, who vacationed at Haley House during the summer months. Because he was a close friend of DiNardo's, Haley was often consulted on who should be named bishops.

I didn't try to ingratiate myself with Haley. As a young priest I was once pressed into service as Haley's master of ceremonies at a parish confirmation. After directing the vesting ceremony in which

Haley put on the surplice, stole, cope and miter, I stood next to Haley at the episcopal throne temporarily erected in the sanctuary. Suddenly Haley grabbed my arm and said, "Stand back, Father, the people want to see their archbishop."

As I took a few steps back, I realized that I had indeed been obstructing the view of the people in the pews. Haley is a pompous ass, I thought. It's not as if the people will have no other opportunity to see their archbishop during the hour-long ceremony. I filed that incident in my memory.

Years later Haley, in his late sixties, suffered from dementia and was rarely seen at public events. His chauffeur took him for long drives every day. Once when I was making a retreat at the Jesuit Retreat House, the limousine drove into the grounds and passed an area where I was standing with a group of priests gathered for a procession. Haley was sitting in the back seat. He looked as if he had shrunk a foot or more. He was wearing a sweat shirt and a baseball cap and was pounding a baseball glove on his left hand. I felt sorry for him. Sadly, I could not help thinking, "Step back, Father. The people want to see their bishop." *Sic transit gloria mundi.*

Haley built churches, elementary and secondary schools, hospitals, retreat houses, and a minor seminary for high school and college students. He was a kind man, but he was not a reader, a thinker, or intellectual who kept abreast of theological and scriptural trends. Consequently, in his public appearances, he always seemed to be giving the same talk. After he died, clerics, journalists and lay people were hard pressed to remember anything of substance or significance that he uttered.

I was uncomfortable with the affluence of Haley House, but I had no choice but to live there. A caretaker (who doubled as a chauffeur) and his wife lived comfortably in another house on the property that had once been a carriage house for the millionaire industrialist who owned the property and built the mansion. When the industrialist fell upon hard times during the Depression and had to sell the mansion, Haley offered to buy it at a greatly reduced price, and the industrialist accepted.

Mohr offered me the use of a Cadillac and a driver. I reluctantly accepted because my eyesight was slowly failing from macular degeneration. I loved driving my Olds Toronado, but I realized that the time had come for me to give up the keys lest I cause a serious accident or kill someone. That prospect was a real one and it frightened me.

I tried to age gracefully. Like the Welsh poet Dylan Thomas I wanted "to rage, rage against the dying of the light." I loved to read and made use of the library in the mansion. I was a regular at the concert and often visited museums in the area. The University nearby offered a senior scholars program every semester. Professors would talk informally about their disciplines and answer questions from the participants. In my first five years of retirement I enrolled in these mini courses in music, gerontology, dance, architecture, nursing, theology, Islam, Eastern religions, and wars of the 20th century.

At first I wore my Roman collar and pectoral cross to the classes. Because I was well known, program participants recognized me and called me by my title of archbishop. One day I surprised (and delighted) the scholars by wearing gray slacks, a turtle neck, and a navy blue jacket. I quietly told everyone I preferred in this setting to be called Ed, not archbishop. Some uptight types could not, or would not, honor my request and still called me archbishop. To my amusement.

Although I am an excellent speaker and story teller, after my retirement I refused all invitations to speak at public meetings, conventions, conferences, and commencement exercises. I politely refused to be interviewed by television and radio reporters, not wanting in any way to upstage my successor, Cardinal Mohr.

Such an attitude was good form, but it gradually removed me from the public eye. I am an extrovert, a showman, something of a ham. Now the spotlight was on someone else, and it made me a lonely man. Every day I felt–and still feel–that loneliness. I feel somewhat like the patriarch of a large family who is dusted off and brought out on occasions such as first communions, confirmations, weddings and funerals.

At Haley House I did not lack for the wonders of modern technology. I had a first-class stereo system, a stack of recordings of world class orchestras, a late-model computer, and a cell phone. With e-mail and a fax machine (which I have trouble operating), I could be in contact with the pope and with bishops and priests throughout the world, and with friends I had made over the years.

But still I am lonely. My own parents, who were married for almost sixty years, enjoyed a very simple lifestyle. After they emigrated from Ireland, they never traveled to another state, much less another country or continent. But they had family—children, grandchildren, and great grandchildren. Obviously they had intimacy, which I do not have.

When I was in the seminary I was told that there were substitutes for the intimacy of marriage such as prayer, the Divine Office, travel, friendships with priests who liked concerts, sports, movies, art. All these things are indeed good and worthwhile, and I can attest that they have added to my happiness and to the happiness of other men and women who are leading single or celibate lives, but I have concluded that in the priesthood there is no substitute for the intimacy of marriage.

Some might want to argue this point, and I respect their views. But I would ask them why then did God say in the dawn of creation, "It is not good for man to be alone. Let us make a partner for him"?

Too bad retired priests aren't invited to have frank and honest discussions with seminarians about some of the ways celibacy affects a priest's life, especially in later years.

CHAPTER 4

As events unfolded, the pope could have saved himself the trouble of naming Cardinal Mohr as my successor. Mohr died suddenly after officiating at the groundbreaking ceremonies for a new hospital for the archdiocese of Forest Park.

His death at age 63 took everyone by surprise, although observers noted that labor disputes between the nurses and the administration at Holy Cross Hospital had drained his spirits and energy. He was ordinarily upbeat about life, but the acrimonious negotiations with the unions had depressed him. Close friends noted that occasionally his remarks were rather sharp, sometimes sarcastic—so out of keeping with his smooth, diplomatic style.

Mohr began his tenure as archbishop of Forest Park with zest. He had announced plans for an extensive renovation of the cathedral and had spent months meeting with architects, contractors, and committees. The actual work, however, was scheduled to begin in August and was to be completed by November before cold weather might slow the work. With Mohr's death, the renovation would become someone else's problem—and achievement.

Cardinal Mohr's televised funeral was held the day after the incident involving Mrs. Lacey's daughter and granddaughter. I had slept late the day of the funeral because I had a severe viral infection that had persisted for two weeks. I wanted to attend the funeral, but Dr. Meyer, my personal physician, advised against it. Meyer, medically conservative, feared the cough and cold might turn into pneumonia, which could mean a stay in the hospital. Moreover, the weather that January morning was frigid. Meyer recommended that I write out an expression of sympathy to the people of the archdiocese and stay away from the services. Reluctantly, I followed this advice.

I was unaware of the events of the previous night involving Mrs. Lacey. She intended to inform me of her daughter's and Randy's arrest for armed robbery of the Convenience Store but hadn't found an opportune time that morning.

As I settled in to watch the funeral procession for Cardinal Mohr, I called out, "Mrs. Lacey, would you mind bringing me that sweater hanging in the hallway–the one I brought from Ireland last year?" Mrs. Lacey brought it in, picking the lint off as she handed it to me.

"Don't worry about that," I said. As I slipped it over my head, my glasses fell off and slid to the floor.

"I'll get them," said Mrs. Lacey, as she stooped to pick them up.

"No, No. They're right under my chair. I can reach them."

But still she waited, as if she had something more to say. She looked troubled.

"Mrs. Lacey, is there something you want to tell me?"

"Well, yes," she said. "I. . . I. . . there is something. But I know you want to watch the funeral. I don't want to detain you."

"Mrs. Lacey, please sit down and tell me what's bothering you. The funeral will last all morning."

"What I have to discuss with you can wait until after the funeral," she said. "I have some things to take care of right now, but I do need to see you then."

"Fine. But only if you prefer to wait. I'll see you in the sitting room right after lunch."

"Thanks, Your Grace." She nervously straightened the magazines on the end table as she left the room. Something was really bothering her. She was a godsend, and I hadn't told her enough how much I appreciated all she did. I resolved to change that. I had tried to get her to stop calling me "Your Grace" without success.

Sitting back in my reclining armchair, I turned on the television, quickly zapping a commercial that featured middle-aged would-be macho types guzzling beer.

"What?" I said aloud to the television screen as I read a bulletin flashing across the bottom of the screen: "Technical difficulties. Only the procession into the cathedral will be televised. WCKR apologizes for the inconvenience." WCKR was the local station.

If this were the opening game of the baseball season, I thought, the station manager would have brought in the best technicians to make sure his station covered the entire event. "I just can't imagine them showing fans singing the national anthem before a baseball game," I mused, "and three hours later showing fans leaving the stadium after the last out. Too bad Cardinal Mohr didn't have a good batting average."

The doorbell rang, and a minute later Mrs. Lacey ushered in Jack Raleigh, a priest friend of mine. Raleigh was a big bear of a man whose former muscular frame had softened for not having exercised as his doctor had ordered. We were classmates at the University of Notre Dame. I was delighted to see Raleigh and welcomed him warmly. We were both ordained on the same day and had kept up our friendship for over half a century.

"Jack, good to see you. Take off your coat and sit down. I was about to watch the funeral service for the cardinal. Join me." I paused, then said, "Say, why aren't you there?"

"Couldn't find a parking spot," Raleigh said, "and I didn't think I could walk four blocks to the cathedral. Besides I have prostate problems and knew you wouldn't object to my making a pit stop here."

"Certainly not. Will you stay for lunch?"

"Sure," Raleigh said, "but I hope I'm not inconveniencing you, Mrs. Lacey."

"Not at all," Mrs. Lacey said, "we're having soup and sandwiches. Can I bring you gentlemen something to drink?"

"What a good idea!" I said. "Bring us two Rusty Nails, you know that drink you told me will cure me or kill me? We can sip them as we watch the procession."

"All right, your Grace, I'll be right back," Mrs. Lacey said. She soon returned holding a pitcher. Turning to Raleigh she said, "This drink is called a 'Rusty Nail,' a mixture of Scotch and Drambuie. My friend Ellie Seligman told me it will cure a sore throat and cold." She smiled.

We graciously thanked her and began sipping our Rusty Nails as we watched TV.

The television commentator introduced a clip on the life of Cardinal Mohr. Both Raleigh and I admired him. He had a good sense of humor and a keen intelligence that enabled him to go quickly to the heart of an issue. And he was accessible to the people. Most clergy agreed that Mohr was the right man to succeed me.

I used the remote to mute the sound as the procession began. A television commentator and a tall thin priest had begun the commentary on the funeral procession, but I suggested we could do without these talking heads. Raleigh agreed.

First came a large group of Knights of Columbus. When the cameraman panned the group, Raleigh spotted his former stockbroker among them. "That crook should be wearing an orange prison jump suit," he said. "How the hell did he become last year's Catholic Man of the Year?"

"Jack, you're being too hard on him," I said. "He told you that high tech stocks were very volatile and they were not a safe investment. Your trouble is that you're afraid you'll outlive your money. You got greedy, Jack, and got burned."

Raleigh did not respond. He knew I was right.

We watched as images of the clergy appeared on the screen.

"Who's this guy?" Raleigh asked. "Don't think I ever met him."

"That's because he's not from this diocese. "He's Jim Kelley, a priest psychiatrist. At lunch I'll tell you more about him."

Next to appear on the television screen was Carroll Miller, the respected scripture scholar, who was teaching that semester at the seminary.

"Is Miller gay?" Raleigh asked.

"Hell, no. But he does minister to an AIDS community. He has great compassion for gays and lesbians. He once said that he believes Jesus was condemned to death because he preached that all people—even gays and lesbians—were welcome in God's kingdom. He also advanced the position that the Bible was written by the elite for the elite."

"No wonder the Chancery took a dim view of him! Look," said Raleigh, pointing to the screen. "There's Harry Burns, the peace activist who went to Vietnam with some other college chaplains and chained themselves to the gates of the United States Embassy in Saigon to protest the war. Made headlines all over the world. I forget what diocese he's from. Somewhere out West. His bishop got so much flak from pro-war Catholics that he sent Harry to the University here for doctoral studies. Burns earned his doctorate and never went back to his own diocese. Can't say I blame him."

We sipped our Rusty Nails in silence as we watched the long line of priests walking solemnly by.

We caught sight of Paul Hart, a much loved theology professor at the University. Religious women and lay people came in great numbers to his lectures on the theology behind the Second Vatican Council, but relatively few priests attended. I suspected that many were terrified of the changes brought about by the Council.

I reflected on the men as we watched them parade by on the TV screen. They came from solid, hardworking families of various ethnic backgrounds—Irish, German, Polish, Hungarian, Slovak, Slovenian, Croatian, Bohemian, English.

Few of their parents were college educated. Like my parents, many of them had not completed high school. The mothers stayed home and reared the children. The fathers worked as policemen, firemen, truck drivers, managers, salesmen, craftsmen, steel workers, laborers. They believed education was the key to success in America, so they worked long hours to give their sons and daughters at least a high school education in a Catholic school. Many of their sons left high school and entered the seminary. Some of the young women graduated and entered religious congregations.

For the most part these men did not go into the priesthood to enrich themselves or to escape a bad home environment—maybe some few did—but to follow in the footsteps of Jesus.

I felt a sense of sadness. "I should have thanked them more," I thought, "and their parents, as well."

At the end of the procession came the bishops and cardinals. I never envied the cardinals their red hats and titles. But I have to admit I would like to have been asked. Mohr was made a cardinal after just two years here as archbishop. I was an archbishop here for twenty-five years, but I was ignored. Inwardly I seethed when someone was appointed who lacked the intelligence, experience and leadership skills I possessed. Despite the hurt, I was always courteous to them, but what I didn't like about some of them was their total submission to the Curia in Rome.

The National Conference of Bishops in the United States had crafted some good policy statements on the economy, capital punishment, nuclear war, but the conference bishops were—and still are—fearful of saying anything on the subject of optional celibacy and the ordination of women.

Bringing my wandering thoughts back to the procession, Raleigh said, laughing, "Look, there's old Brandy—that jerky little bastard." That was Raleigh's favorite putdown.

Bishop Thomas Alessandro, whom the clerical types nicknamed "Brandy Alexander," was a great entertainer and story teller, and loved to mix drinks. In his residence he had three sets of china, expensive linen table cloths, a wine cellar, and more than one set of fine silverware.

What a comedy, I thought. I had worked with Alessandro on

some committees, and I didn't like his style. Alessandro always worried how our position statements would be viewed in Rome. Having studied in Rome for five years, Brandy adopted a style called *Romanita* which means he had a style of living and a way of speaking that must have greatly surprised his parents, who took to heart Jesus's admonition about plain speaking.

Alessandro's father, a foreman at a steel plant, and his wife had lived frugally and had saved enough money to put a down payment on a modest home in a new development after WW II. They were good people who never adopted regal airs. Yet suddenly they had a regal heir. Prince of the Church? Absurd, I thought.

Archbishop Paul Halligan came into view. Raleigh and I liked him because he was genuine. He was intelligent and had a down-to-earth manner and a sense of humor that endeared him to the priests and people in his diocese. And he was not angling for a new diocese. Nor did he want a red hat.

Halligan was dying of a liver ailment, and that helped him put everything in perspective. A year earlier he had gone with a group from his office to a restaurant to celebrate his secretary's birthday. His entree was a seafood plate of shrimp, crabs, and mussels. Later in the evening he had such a violent reaction that he had to be hospitalized for weeks before a team of physicians determined that he had contracted hepatitis. I knew that within a year Halligan would be dead, and it saddened me.

I said, "Jack, I believe Halligan could have been the first American pope. And if he had, we would have women priests by now."

"Ed, what makes you think that?" Raleigh asked.

"Well, Jack, before the Council ended its final session, Halligan called for the ordination of women, if not to the priesthood, at least to the deaconate. I have close friends who were present when he said that."

The television camera focused on Cardinal Edward Monroe, not one of my favorites. He was a seminary rector at one time.

Seminarians called him "Alpine Ed" because he was always trying to climb to better positions in the Church.

Raleigh said, "He would have been a nice guy if he had just had a heart."

I suddenly stood up. "Come on, Jack, let's have lunch. We can always come back to the TV after we have eaten. I'm taping the rest of the procession."

"That's OK with me, Ed. I'm starved."

After we said grace, Mrs. Lacey brought to the table a tureen of chowder. When she returned to the kitchen, Raleigh asked me what I thought of the procession.

"Rather impressive, Jack. Church funerals of bishops and cardinals are good theater. Holds people's attention. Too bad the station didn't include the Mass with the music. The cathedral choir does a great job with parts of Beethoven's Missa Solemnis. I was looking forward to hearing the choir."

"And the homily?"

"No," I said. "I'm not sorry I missed it. Hugh Farley's a good man, but preaching is not his forte. Rather than writing out his homily, he wings it with the result that he often speaks for a half hour or more. Today he should give Mohr his fifteen minutes of fame and get out of the pulpit. But I'll bet he will go on for at least thirty minutes."

"I wouldn't take that bet," Raleigh said. After a short pause, Raleigh said, "Ed, you know what concerns me about the procession we just watched?"

"No. What?"

"Well, it's the absence of a younger clergy. Ed, most of the guys there are not old farts like us, but they're getting there. They're in their fifties, sixties, and seventies. And they're tired. You can see it in their faces."

"I know. And there's not much we can do about it."

"Not true, Ed," Raleigh said. "The Church could start by ordaining women, or if they don't have the guts to do that, they could at least ordain women deacons. Hell, most women religious are light years ahead of priests in current theology and scripture. Some of them could run IBM or General Motors. We could reinstate men who have left the active ministry to get married. We could ordain married men."

"You'll get no argument from me, Jack. But that is not going to happen anytime soon. The powers in Rome will not permit it."

We were both reflective for a moment until Raleigh broke the silence. "Ed, you promised to tell me about this Kelley guy. Who is he and how do you know him?"

"He's a Jesuit from San Francisco. Was a fighter pilot in World War II. Joined the Jesuits and then earned his MD at Saint Louis University. He earned a degree in psychiatry at the Institute of Living in Hartford. He teaches in the Harvard Medical School.

"I met him about twenty years ago when I was looking for help in dealing with priests who were pedophiles. He advised me to notify the civil authorities immediately, which I did.

"I also had regional meetings with our priests and told them how angry and saddened I was that some few of them had broken their vows. I let them know that we would not move them to other parishes and would not hire lawyers to defend them. If convicted, they would go to prison."

Raleigh said, "I recall those meetings, Ed. I have never seen you so angry. And so were the priests who heard you reveal that some were preying on little kids, boys mostly. They too felt betrayed. What else happened? Can you tell me?"

"Well, Jack, at Kelley's direction I met with the parents of the youngsters who had been abused, apologized for these crimes, and offered to pay for all legal and medical expenses for counseling. I also told the parents of these youngsters that if and when they sued in civil court, the diocese would not assemble a team of high powered lawyers to cover up incriminating documents which the plaintiffs would need at trial."

"Wasn't that pretty risky?"

"Not really. Kelley convinced me that the risk was going to trial and losing. Jack, look at how some dioceses have covered up their cases of priest pedophiles. They moved these guys to different parishes instead of getting them the professional help they needed to control their sexual urges and making sure these pedophiles never had contact with youths again. Dioceses that tried to sweep these cases under the rug have lost in the courts and have paid out hundreds of millions of dollars to the victims. The public has zero tolerance for priest predators. Thank God. And I thank God I met Jim Kelley."

"Do you think he's here because some new scandal is about to break involving some priests who are sexual predators?" Raleigh asked.

"I don't think so. I think he's here to pay his respects to the cardinal."

"Let me ask you, Ed, do you think there's a crisis in the priesthood? And I don't mean just a sexual one."

"Jack, we both know there is. Some priests are writing about it and we know what they are writing is true. But even if we didn't read their books, we know their conclusion is correct," I said. "We haven't lost our ability to count."

I looked at my watch and said, "We will have to discuss the priest shortage sometime soon. I forgot that I told Mrs. Lacey that I would meet with her right after lunch."

"Of course," said Raleigh, always the gentleman. "I'll see Mrs. Lacey and thank her on the way out. Hope you get over that cold. I'll call you in a couple of days."

CHAPTER 5

I walked as briskly as I could down the hall to the sitting room where Mrs. Lacey was waiting. "I'm sorry to keep you waiting. Father Raleigh and I got carried away talking about Cardinal Mohr's funeral. Time just got away from us."

"That's all right, your Grace."

"No, it's not. Etiquette also applies to the clergy although sometimes we clerics think it doesn't. Now, tell me, what is it that is going on with you? And how can I help you?"

"It's my granddaughter I'm worried about—Toni. She's just 16 and—I'm ashamed to tell you this—but her mother—my daughter – and her husband were arrested last night for—Oh, God—for doing something very stupid." Her eyes filled with tears.

"Something stupid?" I asked. "I can see this is very hard for you, Mrs. Lacey. Just take your time. Why don't you start by telling me about your granddaughter—Toni is her name? I don't think I have ever met Toni. Tell me about her."

"Well, her name is Toni Vincent, a wonderful girl. Maybe I'm prejudiced because she's my granddaughter, but she's very bright. Exceptional."

"How so?" I asked.

"Well, she spoke in complete sentences before she was three. She remembered songs she heard on the radio and could sing them for us. She read not only children's books but some stories in the newspaper. Every night, David Vincent, her dad, read to her. Bible stories, fairy tales, stories about Helen Keller, Joan of Arc, and people like that."

"What a wonderful father! Tell me about him."

"Dave died very suddenly. One evening he was playing

basketball with some college friends at a YMCA gym and he went into cardiac arrest. The paramedics couldn't revive him."

"How old was Toni when her dad died?"

"She had just celebrated her fourth birthday."

"How tragic for your daughter and Toni—and for you. I am truly sorry."

"It was quite a blow," she said. "Toni never got over it. She really missed her daddy—and still does. My daughter had to go to work. I took care of Toni."

"That was generous of you. It must have been tough."

"Well, your Grace, it wasn't that tough. Toni was such a wonderful child. That made it easy. The tough part came when some years later my daughter married Randy Smith, a man she met at work."

"What is he like?"

"Almost the exact opposite of her first husband Dave. He drinks a lot. Gets so loud and mean at times that my daughter has had to call the police. He's a high school dropout. Got expelled because he was caught shaking down younger kids for money, and he traveled with a gang that got arrested for stealing cars. He never was into books. Has a hard edge to him, too. And he has always resented Toni. My daughter—Helen—thought Randy would like Toni when he got to know her, but that didn't happen. So there was no adoption. I'm glad about that."

"How old was Toni when her mother and Randy married?"

"She was ten or eleven, I think," Mrs. Lacey answered.

"Did this affect her at school?"

"No. She loved school. It was a place where she could read, write, and study. In school she was free of Randy and her mother and their drinking. The teachers and the kids love Toni because she's so bright and friendly. She must be embarrassed that her mother and her stepfather are so mixed up, now more than ever."

"What do you mean?"

"Oh, your Grace, they have a terrible police problem. They're into crack and drinking—and I don't know what else." With that she started crying. I said nothing. I felt there was therapeutic value to her tears. She needed to talk to someone about this situation.

"I'm ashamed of my daughter. How could she marry a man she knew was an alcoholic?"

"Happens often," I said. "I've known people like that. They get involved with an alcoholic and think marriage will solve the drinking problem. More often than not, it doesn't. The situation gets worse and the wife especially feels trapped."

"That's what happened in my daughter's case. And now she's in a lot of trouble."

"Tell me about it, Mrs. Lacey."

"Well, yesterday she and her husband needed money—to feed their habit." She paused as she choked up. Quickly regaining control, she said, "They robbed a Convenience Store last night. The security camera caught them on tape. The film shows Randy pointing a gun at the clerk while my daughter is cleaning out the cash register. The clerk managed to trigger an alarm, and the police were there in minutes and took them to jail."

"Are they still there?"

"Yes, I was there this morning for their arraignment."

Somewhat surprised by her response, I asked, "When did you find out about their arrest?"

"Last night about eleven o'clock," she replied. "Mrs. Kolar, my daughter's neighbor, called me and told me that Helen and Randy were arrested. Her husband Hank drove me to the Justice Center."

"Why didn't you call me?"

"Your Grace, you've had a severe infection. You need your rest. Besides, I didn't want to involve you in my family's problem."

"I want you to know that you can call upon me at any time, Mrs. Lacey." After a pause, I asked, "What happened at the hearing this morning?"

"The judge set a time for the trial, but he won't release them on bail. He thinks they're a flight risk. He's probably right."

"What about Toni?" I asked.

"Well, the judge assigned her to me until the trial next month. Right now she's staying with Mrs. Kolar and her husband. They like Toni and have been good to her. But I asked the judge to name me her guardian."

"Well," I said, "I don't know what we can do for your daughter Helen. She could do some time in prison. The authorities in this district are tough on people who use a gun to commit a crime. They're not sympathetic to people who commit armed robbery."

"I know," murmured Mrs. Lacy, shaking her head in dismay.

"Right now, my concern—and yours, of course—is for Toni," I said. "I think we can persuade the judge to name you guardian. I'll talk to a lawyer friend of mine, if that's all right with you."

"Oh, thank you, your Grace. That would mean a lot to me."

"Did you have the opportunity to talk to your daughter this morning?"

"Yes, briefly. She's embarrassed and promised that if she gets out, she'll kick the drug habit. But she's often said that about her drinking."

"Mrs. Lacey, if she's into crack or cocaine, she's got a habit that's not easy to break. A couple of our priests were addicted to cocaine. We sent them to some first-class treatment centers and had a team of doctors, psychiatrists, and social workers evaluate them and prescribe therapy. It cost the archdiocese thousands of dollars, which we were willing to pay."

"Did the treatment work?"

"It helped them stay clean for a while. But they both got back into drugs."

"Where are they now?"

"I don't know. They both left the diocese. I heard that one was living in a flop house in another city. They might even be dead."

"How awful," Mrs. Lacey said.

"I don't want to frighten you, Mrs. Lacey. But I don't want to tell you that it's going to be easy. Your daughter is facing some rough days, maybe years, ahead. And so are you."

"If I could just get her back to church and get her to pray, especially the rosary, I think she would be well again."

I didn't say anything. I didn't want to question her piety. She's a good person who was probably having a lot of guilt feelings about the way she raised her daughter. Probably too much religion and not enough instruction about men and about sex. I suspect that Mrs. Lacey's late husband was an alcoholic, but I didn't ask. There would be time to go into that at a future date.

"I'm concerned about your daughter, Mrs. Lacey," I said. "But I'm even more concerned about Toni, your granddaughter, who is facing the prospect of having to live with foster parents. I'm sure that you don't want that to happen. Do you have any ideas about what to do about her?"

"Well, Your Grace, I've been thinking," she said. "I need more help in keeping up this place. I was wondering whether I could bring Toni here to work with me. She could come on Saturdays and maybe one or two afternoons a week after school. She's a good worker."

"I am sure she is," I said. "And you do need help. So, of course, bring her along. I don't think I'll have any trouble clearing it with the diocesan financial office. We could start her at the minimum wage and increase it if she works out all right. Would that be fair?"

"Yes, your Grace. Very fair. Thank you."

I have always had great sympathy for those who work for the church, especially women like Mrs. Lacey. In her mid-sixties, she was a tall, stately woman with lovely gray hair. She had worked in rectories since her husband died twenty-five years earlier. Pastors for whom she worked liked her because she was discreet. She was a good housekeeper and an excellent cook. Cardinal Mohr arranged it so she would be my housekeeper.

In the past I had some heated arguments with personnel in the financial office who seemingly had never heard that even people who work for the church are deserving of a living wage. Mohr was not like that, so he saw to it that Mrs. Lacey was paid a decent wage—probably the best salary she ever had.

"When do you want to bring Toni here?" I asked.

"Saturday morning."

"Fine. I look forward to meeting her. Does she know about her mother and Randy?"

"Yes, the police came to their home last night and tried to question her and search the home for drugs, but Hank Kolar, my daughter's neighbor—the one who drove me to the Justice Center—insisted that they get a search warrant. He's a newspaper reporter, you know, so he knows what procedures should be followed. I guess the police finally got the search warrant this morning, so they have probably searched the house by now. And they questioned Toni about what she knew about the robbery. She is frightened to death."

"Poor kid," I said. "What a way to get that kind of news. How is she taking it?"

"All right, I think. She's tough. Had to be, living in that home. You'll find her to be a good girl. She's not had much training in religion. She's been baptized, but I don't think she goes to church. And recently she has become rather moody. She sometimes loses her temper. What I'm saying, your Grace, is that Toni has some rough edges."

"Mrs. Lacey," I said, "so do all of us. So don't worry about her. She and I will get along just fine."

"Thank you. You don't know how much this meeting has meant to me."

"Have a good afternoon, Mrs. Lacey. I look forward to meeting Toni."

I retired to my study and called Bill Danko, one of the best lawyers in the city. Danko was out of town but would return that evening. The secretary promised that he would call me first thing in the morning.

I went to my room to lie down. I removed my shoes and the heavy Irish sweater, lay on the bed, and pulled a blanket over myself and thought about Toni and what her grandmother said about her. Good personality. Outgoing. Curious. Extremely intelligent.

But there was something else that I learned about Toni, which Mrs. Lacey had not mentioned. Maybe did not even suspect. *Toni, I thought, has to be a very angry young girl. She's angry at God, the Church, her mother and stepfather. How could she not be? It won't be easy dealing with Toni. She's a walking time bomb.*

After a few minutes I was asleep.

CHAPTER 6

The only newspaper in Forest Park is *The Sentinel*, which I read daily. It has won some prizes for outstanding journalism. However, it has never won a Pulitzer, but I think that some year it will. During my tenure as archbishop, its coverage of the Church was, in the main, objective and unbiased. About a week after Mohr's funeral I got a call from a reporter.

"Archbishop, this is Hank Kolar from the Sentinel."

"Hello, Hank, we have never met, but I look for your byline in the Sentinel. You write good stuff. How can I be of help?"

"Thanks. Well," Kolar replied, "I want to do a rather lengthy story on you. The Sentinel has never done one, and my editor thinks it's about time we get moving."

"Hank, excuse me while I laugh. What you really want to do is write my obituary. I suspect that when Mohr died, you didn't have one filed away. So you had to scramble around in the City Room and come up with something. Your editor then asked to see my obituary and there is none. Right?"

"Archbishop, now excuse me while I laugh," Kolar said. "You're half right. We haven't written your obituary, and we need to do that. But the editor thinks you're good copy. He needs something while waiting for the new archbishop to be named. What do you say?"

"Hank, I'm agreeable but I won't promise to answer all of your questions."

"Fair enough, but I'd like to get started as soon as possible."

"I'm free this afternoon," I said. "How about three o'clock?"

"OK," Hank said, sounding surprised that he could get an appointment so soon. "See you then."

Kolar came to Haley House right at 3:00, ushered in by Mrs. Lacey, who introduced him to me.

"Your Grace," she said, "Mr. Kolar is the person who drove me to the Justice Center the night I learned that my daughter Helen and Randy had been arrested. Remember I told you about the Kolars who were so good Toni that night?"

"Hank, thanks for that," I said. "You and your wife are real friends." I motioned Kolar toward the living room and asked Mrs. Lacey to bring us some coffee. She told me she anticipated that request, so the coffee pot was already there.

Kolar was about forty-five years old and balding and had strong facial features. He had the look and demeanor of a true professional. When we were seated, he asked me how I got to be a bishop.

I parried his question with one of my own. "Hank, you don't think I should have been made a bishop? Right?"

"Well, I don't know your history," Kolar said, "but you have a reputation of being someone who didn't always agree with the company line. I've read some of the stuff you wrote in your diocesan newspaper. Your writing implied that you thought the pope's encyclical on birth control was a mistake and that the Church should at least be open to a discussion about a married priesthood. Doesn't Rome usually select men whom they know won't rock the boat?"

"Yes, I wrote those things, but that was after I was made a bishop," I said. "I've often wondered myself why I was appointed. Even as a young priest I was a social activist. I deplored segregated schooling and segregated housing. I supported the worker's right to form unions and I fought for a minimum wage. Some of my friends warned me that I'd be banished to the boondocks if I continued on the path I was going. They were right. Quite early in my priesthood I was appointed pastor of Saint Peter Claver."

"Where is Saint Peter Claver?" Kolar asked.

"It was a storefront church for African Americans in

Bridgetown. You know Bridgetown—about 40 miles south of Forest Park, which of course is the see city of the archdiocese. At the time Bridgetown had a population of about 300,000. It was a blue collar city with industries that made parts for the automobile industry. Since the end of World War II, it had increased its population significantly every year. The workforce of the city was dominated by blacks from the South and whites from Appalachia."

"So, your bishop banished you from the see city?" Kolar asked. "But something tells me that's not the end of the story. Tell me what happened."

I relished the opportunity to relate the story to someone new, especially to someone who seemed truly interested in hearing it:

"When Vincent Lagrange, a nationally known Jesuit sociologist, read newspaper accounts about my appointment to this newly created store front parish, he was greatly disturbed. After his ordination in the early 1930's, Lagrange had devoted himself to implementing the Church's social justice issues. He fought for a living wage for workers and tried to raise the consciousness of Catholics on issues affecting the family. He was often on the picket line and for that became a hero to workers.

"Lagrange vehemently opposed what was then the practice in some Catholic churches of segregating the congregation by having a separate area in the church for blacks. He thought this was an obscenity, a mortal sin, he called it, which did not endear him to many rich white Catholics and their bishops who condoned the practice. What appalled him most was the ignorance of many priests and bishops on papal teachings and social justice issues."

I paused to offer Kolar more coffee. "This is a long story. You'd better get comfortable."

"No, thanks. I had a couple of cups just before I left the City Room. Please go on."

"OK," I said as I rearranged my legs in my comfortable leather chair. I told Kolar about Lagrange calling me from his office in Washington, D.C. I vividly remember the conversation because I was so surprised and pleased that a man of Lagrange's stature would call me—a relative rookie of the diocese.

After Lagrange introduced himself on the phone, I told him that although we had never met I always looked for his articles in *America,* and I congratulated him for having the courage to take on some tough issues.

He thanked me and told me he wished he could congratulate me on my appointment as pastor of Saint Peter Claver, but couldn't. He said he thought I would know why—that he found it repugnant that we now have a segregated parish church.

I agreed and told him that was why I hesitated about accepting the pastorate. I decided to take it when I heard rumors that the bishop wanted to build a grand edifice for blacks. I didn't want that to happen because, as Lagrange knew, it was only a thinly disguised way to continue segregation in the church. I had no intention of building that church. In fact, I told Lagrange, I wanted to see the present structure torn down and the parishioners instructed to worship in any of the churches in their neighborhood.

He was glad to hear me say that. He planned to be in Bridgetown the following Monday for a meeting with some labor leaders and asked if we could meet for an early dinner sometime on Monday afternoon.

We agreed to meet in the lobby of the downtown Sheraton that Monday. I suggested that we could have a drink and then go to the restaurant. He liked that arrangement and said he looked forward to meeting me.

When we met at the hotel's restaurant, I was surprised at Lagrange's small stature. I expected him to be a tall man, not someone just a little over five feet. He did, however, have a strong handclasp and penetrating eyes. There was a kindly look about him, but I could see that this man was no pushover. Years of labor negotiations had given him a strong will, a sense of humor, and a quiet manner that probably disarmed his adversaries.

There was a story that he once negotiated a labor contract with some hard-nosed executive types who thought Lagrange would see things their way. When the negotiations concluded with a contract that labor leaders liked, one of the executives said to his assistant, "If you ever again put me in the same room with that pious-looking priest, I'll break your goddamned neck."

Over drinks in the bar, I asked Lagrange how the meeting went with the labor leaders, and he filled me in on what had transpired, but at dinner he came right to the point.

"Ed, this storefront church where you are pastor is a disgrace to the Catholic Church in the United States. Blacks should worship in the parish churches in their own neighborhoods. In the name of all that is decent, I want you to promise me that you will do everything in your power to close this church."

He also wanted me to promise that I would never resign as pastor because I would be replaced with someone who thinks the way the chancery people do. Then he asked me to do something which, he said, would be extremely hard. The powers in the chancery, he said, would do everything to get me to resign. He said, "Some of them are not nice people, especially when they think they are doing the work of God." He looked directly into my eyes and said, "Ed, you might have to stay at Saint Peter Claver for ten or fifteen years. But you cannot resign."

I didn't argue with him. "I will not resign," I said, "but some very wealthy white Catholics in the area are going to insist that I do."

I told him again that I had heard there was a move afoot to build an entirely new church for Negroes. Some rich whites were all for it and they would contribute substantially.

He wasn't surprised. He said something like, "Point out to these myopic sons of bitches that the Supreme Court has ruled that separate but equal facilities in schools are unconstitutional." He wondered why they couldn't read the signs of the times. He said, "Don't they know that segregated facilities for worship may not be unconstitutional but morally they are wrong?"

I told him he would get no argument from me, and I assured him that I would do what I could to educate them.

He told me to feel free to call him if he could help in any way. After we had dinner, Lagrange picked up the check, left a generous tip, shook hands with me and left the restaurant. His train for Washington was departing in ten minutes.

"What happened next," I said to Kolar, "is my favorite part of the story."

A few weeks Lagrange's visit, I got a call from Monsignor Maytin of the chancery office. This young chancellor with ambition to match his monumental ego told me that he would be there the next morning at ten to discuss a very important matter. I knew what was coming.

At precisely ten o'clock the next morning, I looked out the window of the storefront church and saw Monsignor Maytin reaching into the back seat of his Cadillac for some blue prints. I met him at the door and greeted him professionally.

"Hello, Monsignor," I said. "Nice of you to come here for a visit. Let me help you with those blueprints you're carrying."

Maytin was tall—about six-feet-four—and carried 190 pounds on his athletic frame. He wore a well tailored black suit and his shoes were highly polished. Just below his white Roman collar was an inch of red thread which was sewn in his rabat, the clerical vest worn by some priests. Having the red thread sewn into the vest was not something that was required, but the practice was eagerly adopted by monsignors who wanted to let people know they were "prelates," members of the papal household.

Maytin had a rugged face and good looks, but his very serious demeanor hid them. Had he learned to laugh at himself, he would have endeared himself to the clergy who worked under him. He seemed, however, to delight in using his height and his stern attitude to intimidate clerics. Maytin was wise enough, however, to know he could not frighten me.

After the monsignor entered the rectory, I laid his three rolls of prints on the kitchen table. He said to me, "I know you will want to see these, Ed. This is a project that is very important to His Grace and also to you."

Wearing an expression of an innocent child, I feigned ignorance. "What project is that?"

'These are the plans for the new Saint Peter Claver Church," responded Maytin, smiling as if he was about to confer a great gift upon me. "We have hired a nationally known architect who we believe is the best. These are his plans. It's going to be a Gothic structure and His Grace said we will spare no expense in making it an outstanding edifice. We want the Negroes to feel that this is a special church for them."

I managed to control the rage slowly rising within me. "Do you really think we should build a segregated church?" I asked. "Why not let these black people attend the churches that already exist in their areas?"

"His Grace thinks they will be more comfortable in a church they can call their own."

"With all due respect, that's bullshit," I said, "and you and His Grace know it. You are being pressured by wealthy white Catholics to keep the blacks out of their lily white churches. If His Grace is not a eunuch, he'll tell them all to go to hell."

"Ed, if you don't like the decision," Maytin said, "you can resign the parish." Maytin was the typical cleric who can be found in most chanceries—men who have risen in the ranks because they always obey orders. Rarely do they challenge authority. The only thinking most of them do is about their careers.

I was surprised when Maytin said, "We can appoint someone to take your place. In fact, we have someone in mind."

"That'll never happen. I am not resigning," I said. "I'm staying here until they tear this place down."

"Fine," Maytin said, "we have ways of dealing with your kind. We'll hang you out to dry."

I would like to have punched out this clerical lackey. I thought that I could ice him with just one punch to his jaw. But I kept my temper under control and said in a dangerously quiet voice: "Monsignor, if you take one move to remove me, I am going to call the newspapers, especially the New York Times, and the radio stations in our city and in New York and Chicago. I am going to tell them that you people in the chancery office don't think Negro Catholics are good enough to worship alongside white Catholics. I'll tell them that at a time when schools are being integrated, the Catholic church in this diocese is to be segregated. How will that story play on the front page of the New York Times?

"And, Monsignor, what quotes will they get from His Grace? Something to the effect that the Catholic Church wants to build a new church for black Catholics because they might be uncomfortable worshiping next to white Catholics? Will you have some pompous super wealthy white Catholic utter some inanities about wanting to make black Catholics feel comfortable? Do you realize how stupid you are going to look in the national press? Reporters and news photographers from every state in the nation will descend upon the archbishop. So, if you want to play hardball, Monsignor, go ahead. But I am telling you that your career will come quickly to an end. Hang me out to dry? You little shit, get out of here before I throw you out."

I picked up the blueprints and handed them to the monsignor. "Have a nice day," I said. "Drive carefully going back and give my regards to His Grace."

"Foley," the Monsignor said, "you've got a lot of nerve."

"No," I said, "just a lot of testosterone. It's in short supply in many monsignors. Wouldn't you agree?"

His face red with rage, Monsignor Maytin picked up the blueprints, left the room, slammed the rectory door, marched to his Cadillac, and roared off with a screech of tires. I barely managed to suppress a laugh.

I didn't hear from the archbishop, which did not surprise me. But I thought that eventually I would hear from Maytin, a vindictive man. The archbishop was media savvy and also knew that I was not the type to make idle threats. If he removed me and brought in someone else to build the church, he knew that I would deliver on my threat, and he would be savaged by white and black liberals all over the country. He decided to put the blue prints on the shelf and visit the issue at a more opportune time.

Those plans remained on the shelf for five years. I continued the pastorate at the storefront church and was not visited again by the arrogant Monsignor Maytin. Nor did I get any telephone calls or letters from the archbishop.

Then one night the archbishop had a stroke, was rushed to the hospital and died the next day. After he was buried, the people of the archdiocese waited, wondered, and worried about who their next shepherd would be.

It was a time of great civil unrest in the country. Blacks were demanding more authority in the government. And in the church. But there were only a few black priests, and most of them were in their seventies. My name was mentioned as a possible successor, but most thought I would be passed over. A very long shot. Too independent.

But I was appointed to be archbishop, much to the delight of the people and to the chagrin of Monsignor Maytin. I was fifty years old when I was ordained a bishop.

"Hank," I said with great intensity. "One of the first things I did when I visited the chancery building was to find those old blueprints. When they were brought to me, I personally supervised the shredding of the plans for the Gothic church for Negro Catholics."

"I was never one to cultivate the right connections and the right people, nor did I schmooze those in authority. I detested sycophants and brown nosers. I would like to have had these words emblazoned on my coat of arms: *Annulum solum faveas osculari.*

"I never took Latin, Archbishop," Kolar said. "What does that mean?"

"It means 'Please kiss only the ring.' However, I thought that might stretch the Vatican's patience beyond the breaking point."

Kolar laughed hilariously. His laughter was interrupted by a call on his cell phone. His editor wanted him back in the City Room to cover a breaking story—a scandal involving a local stockbroker. I escorted him to the door, and we agreed to meet again soon.

CHAPTER 7

On Saturday I awakened at 4:00 AM, restless and unable to sleep. At first I thought it was my cold and sore throat, although the "Rusty Nail" seemed to be working. Was it Cardinal Mohr's death that made me confront my own mortality? Perhaps. From my early days in the priesthood, however, I realized that I could die at any time and the Church would go on fine without me.

Was it the meeting later in the morning with Mrs. Lacey's granddaughter? Hardly. I was looking forward to meeting her. I had considerable pastoral skills and was looking forward to helping this young girl whom life had seemingly dealt a losing hand.

Suddenly I thought I could identify the cause of my restlessness. It was the procession of the clergy that had come to pay their respects to the dead cardinal. My thoughts over the past two days kept coming back to that televised event. Many of these men had worked under me when I was in charge of the archdiocese. Raleigh was right. Most of them looked tired. The shortage of priests meant that some had stayed on long past retirement age and were probably working two jobs.

Not only did many of them look tired; they also looked unhappy, maybe demoralized. I thought back to my own ordination at the cathedral over fifty-five years ago. What a happy and joyous occasion for me and my parents. I remembered standing in that sanctuary with twenty-five other young men who were being ordained. Most of them were in their mid-twenties, but seven were a few years older. All in my class had survived eight years of intensive training in the seminary. We had taken classes in scripture, moral and dogmatic theology, philosophy, Greek, Hebrew, and the humanities. We had studied under some very good professors and some mediocre ones.

We were for the most part bright, talented, creative. We looked forward to daily recreation periods when we could compete against other teams vigorously, sometimes even brutally. We lived in rooms of Spartan simplicity—a desk, chair, lamp, bed, bookcase, and a clothes closet. There was a strict daily regimen of Mass, communal prayer, spiritual reading and meditation.

We were permitted to smoke but not inside the building. At ten o'clock a prefect for the week pulled a switch and all the lights in our rooms went out. At six the next morning, the prefect pulled the switch again and like the first day of creation there was light.

My classmates and I thought it absurd to obey rules designed to protect us from an "evil" world. So we defied the rules forbidding us to listen to the radio or read secular newspapers and magazines. On afternoons when we were free to take walks in the park or visit a museum, we would visit drug stores and load up on magazines and newspapers to read far into the night. Some bought a new invention called a transistor radio. If the administration thought it could shield us seminarians from the world in the name of holiness, it did not know the caliber and ingenuity of the men under them.

My classmates and I didn't want to perpetuate a system that was sick and dysfunctional. We were convinced that we would bring a new Pentecost to the Church. So when the ordaining bishop asked us this question in Latin—"Do you promise to give me and my successors obedience?"—all twenty-five, eager to be sent forth to minister to the community, almost shouted the Latin answer *"libenter"*—gladly!

Libenter. Gladly. We were about to embark upon a journey as celibate priests. For me it was a journey that brought me as a young curate into contact with lay men and women who were on a journey of a different kind, that of trying to rear their children in the teachings of Jesus and in a Church that had some definite restrictions about sexuality in marriage.

It brought me into contact with Monsignor Lawrence Newton,

my first pastor. Newton had earned a doctorate in scripture in Rome and had taught me in the seminary. He was a tough and demanding teacher whom we nicknamed "The Fig." Newton left the seminary when he was assigned pastor of a large parish in a small city in the diocese. That's where I was sent on my first assignment. I went to that assignment with some fear of Newton, but I soon found "The Fig" had a wealth of stories and a great sense of humor.

At table he would often regale us with stories of the tough neighborhood of Irish immigrants where he grew up at the beginning of the 20th century. The neighborhood was close to the center of Forest Park, the see city of the archdiocese. It was here that a twisting, crooked river brought ore boats from the lake into the city. It was here that Irish immigrants fleeing from the famine in Ireland came in great numbers to settle in along the river banks. Poor, illiterate and unwanted, the Irish had to fend for themselves.

Newton would tell us, "That neighborhood was so tough the canaries sang bass!" To prepare for their first communion he and the other boys in the class at St. Malachi School gave up chewing tobacco.

The girls there were taught by the Ursuline Sisters and the boys by the Christian Brothers. Occasionally, Newton told us, a brother would beat a young boy within an inch of his life. The kid would go home and tell his family, and later that afternoon the kid's brothers would lie in wait for the Christian Brother and beat him within an inch of his life as he left the school. When Newton became a pastor, he made it clear that there was to be no corporal punishment in the school by priests, nuns, or lay teachers.

An old 200-bed general hospital was located at a major intersection about a mile from the parish. Since Newton had three curates in the rectory, it was his responsibility to provide spiritual service to the Catholic patients in the hospital day or night. I had been there only a few days when the telephone rang at three in the morning. I was on duty so I answered it. When I hung up, Newton met me in the hallway.

"What happened?" Newton asked.

"That was a nurse at the hospital," I said. "They have a railroad worker in the emergency room who's been in an accident. Both his legs have been cut off and he's bleeding profusely. He's asking for a priest."

"I'll take this call," Newton told me. "Go back to bed." I didn't protest. I didn't relish being part of that scene although I would have gone gladly had not Newton intervened.

Newton was a man of the Book. Every night at nine o'clock he would finish his office calls and retire to his room where he would read and study the Bible. Only he did not read the Bible in English; he read the Old Testament in Hebrew and the New Testament in Greek.

He encouraged me to interrupt his Bible reading if I had some pressing pastoral problem. For example, what was I to do about the eighteen-year-old-girl whose father had died unexpectedly? The family came to me distraught because she would not visit the funeral home where her father was being waked. In a state of denial she insisted that her father was still alive. Her mother, brothers and sisters asked me to talk to her. I asked Newton what I could say to her to bring her out of this state of denial.

Newton pondered the question for a moment, looked up from his Bible and said, "Just tell her that dead or alive, her father is being buried after the ten o'clock Mass tomorrow morning." He then continued to read his Bible. Fortunately, later that evening the daughter on her own accepted the reality of her father's death, so I didn't have to deliver Newton's comments.

Although Newton was a brilliant biblical scholar, he was a humble man. One Sunday afternoon he answered the rectory door bell and found standing before him a tall elderly black man who introduced himself as Son Allen Brown. He told Newton that he wanted to be baptized a Catholic. Newton thought it strange that this man had never been baptized.

Son Allen explained that his parents were Catholics who lived in a part of Mississippi where there were few, if any, Catholics and no Catholic church. And no priest. His mother made him promise that if he ever got up north, he would go to a Catholic Church and asked to be baptized. That's exactly what Son Allen did after he stepped off the bus at the Greyhound station in Kingwood that Sunday afternoon in August 1952. Newton made arrangements to give Son Allen instructions.

Newton soon found that Son Allen had minimal skills in reading and writing, so he didn't give him a catechism. Instead, Newton and Son Allen would spend an hour each week talking about Jesus. Son Allen knew and loved Jesus. The morning after an instruction Newton would come to the breakfast table and tell his curates some profound truth that Son Allen had spoken the night before. Son Allen was not only Newton's student but his teacher as well.

When Newton asked Son Allen his ideas about prayer, Son Allen responded that at night he would lie in his bed and begin what he called his "Open Prayer." It went something like this:

"Dear Jesus, I thank you for this day. I thank you for the gift of life. I thank you for my mother and father who raised me, I thank you for my sisters and brothers and relatives and neighbors who loved me and cared for me, I thank you for my eyes that I can see, my ears that I can hear, my tongue that I can speak, my mind that I can think, my legs that I can walk, my arms and hands that I can work. Thank you Jesus for the air I breathe, the flowers I smell, the sun that rises and sets, the birds that fly, the fish that swim, the water that cleanses me, the food that feeds me."

"That's a beautiful prayer," Newton said, "but why do you call it your Open Prayer."

"Because," Son Allen replied, "I never close it with Amen. I fall asleep, but some night when my soul leaves my body and I enter into heaven, all the angels and saints will shout Amen. And that will close my Open Prayer."

When it came time for Son Allen's baptism, Newton asked him what his baptismal name would be.

"Son," Allen replied.

"But, Son Allen, you have to take a saint's name for baptism."

"Monsignor," Son Allen replied, "have you never heard of the Son of God?" Here was a poor migrant worker with minimal skills questioning a renowned biblical scholar.

Newton laughed, "Son Allen, you are absolutely right. Jesus is certainly a saint."

Son became his baptismal name. In the registry of baptisms kept in the safe at the parish rectory is this entry in Newton's handwriting—*Son of God Allen Brown.*

I have often thought of Newton and Son Allen Brown and the Amen that ended his open prayer. I thought, too, of the friendship I developed with Son Allen. Newton had asked me to look in on Son Allen at least once a week. Son Allen would always welcome me graciously. He was living in a black section of the city and the people who lived there were dirt poor.

I was appalled at the living conditions of these blacks. Their homes were in desperate need of major repairs and coats of paint. I tried to get them better jobs and better welfare benefits, but I had little success. Almost daily I would write to authorities and express my concern. I often went to council meetings and described the miserable living conditions of the Negroes to the annoyance of councilmen, one of whom was a rather prominent Catholic.

After one meeting the councilman walked out with me and told me to get off my soapbox.

"Father Foley," he said. "Those aren't our people. Very few of them are Catholic."

I looked at him and said, "Andy, that's the same attitude that many German Catholics used when the SS was hauling Jews to death camps to be incinerated. Damn it, get your head on straight. And have your fellow councilmen do the same." I then left, leaving Andy speechless.

I knew that the councilman would complain to Newton. Which he did.

Newton approved of my efforts and recommended that I be appointed pastor of the newly established St. Peter Claver, the storefront church that to me was a stark symbol of segregation and white supremacy.

As I told Hank Kolar when he interviewed me for the daily newspaper, it was a journey that brought me to the realization that the wealthy in the church could sometimes try to dictate policy. It was a journey, however, that put me in the right place at the right time.

Ironically, when the archdiocese finally closed that storefront church with great fanfare and hype, they gave the impression that it came about because of the vision and courage of top churchmen. Pure bull, I mused.

Soon after the closing, for political and public relations reasons, I became archbishop. In that role, I came into contact with women religious who taught in parish schools with burgeoning enrollments and did it for the most part gladly (*Libenter*). And it brought me into contact with older priests who shared their experiences and knowledge with me and did it for the most part gladly (*Libenter*).

I met important people in the city, the state, the nation. I had been to dinners at the White House on several occasions. Every five years I went to Rome, as required by Canon Law. There I met the pope and cardinals and bishops. I occasionally vacationed in the Alps and in the south of Italy. The journey for me had indeed been a very good ride.

For some who began that journey in the cathedral that ordination day, the ride was not as eventful. Most were curates for fifteen years or more before becoming pastors. For the most part they performed admirably. I was proud of my classmates, but I regretted I had not called them more often, visited them in their rectories, written them notes of support, met them at restaurants for lunch or dinner.

Had my classmates and I brought forth a new Pentecost? I

didn't think so. But maybe I was more to blame than my classmates because I was in a leadership position. Was I too timid, too cautious, too conservative, too fearful of the heavy hand of the Roman Curia? Perhaps I was and that made me anxious and angry. This was not helping me get to sleep. On that night and other nights when sleep did not come easily, I would think of my friend Son Allen and his Open Prayer. I silently began my own Open Prayer.

Dear Jesus, I thank you for my fifty-five years in the priesthood.

I thank you for my mother and my father and my sisters.

I thank you for the nuns who taught me in grade school and the brothers who taught me in high school, and for the lay teachers who were committed to Catholic education, even though they were greatly underpaid.

I thank you for "The Fig" and his example.

I thank you for Son Allen Brown and his great love of you, The Son of God.

I thank you for my classmates and the work they did in your vineyard, most of it known only to you.

I thank you. . . . . .

I don't know when I dropped off to sleep, but a couple of hours later my alarm clock rang summoning me to a new day. I reached over, turned it off, got up and said, without knowing why, "*Libenter.*"

CHAPTER 8

I awoke Saturday morning feeling rested despite my having awakened earlier at 4:00 AM. I dressed in my black cassock with red buttons down the front and red piping on the sleeves, blessed myself, knelt down and read the Roman Breviary for a half hour. When I arose, I put on my violet zucchetto, better known as a skull cap, and went down to eat breakfast. Mrs. Lacey wanted to prepare my breakfast, but I insisted on making my own. She thought that pouring orange juice, poaching a couple of eggs, toasting a couple of pieces of bread and making coffee was beneath my dignity, but I finally convinced her that I had been doing that all my life. She had enough to do with housework and preparing dinner in the evening.

I greeted her warmly and said, “Oh, by the way, I might not be here tomorrow morning. Dr. Meyer is coming at eleven this morning. I’m hoping he says I’m healthy enough to celebrate Sunday Mass at St. Thomas Aquinas. I’ll let you know what he says.”

“That will be fine, your Grace.”

After I finished breakfast and read the morning paper, I asked Mrs. Lacey what time Toni would be coming.

“She should be here any minute. Mrs. Kolar called and said she had a hard time getting her up. Toni went to a school dance last night and didn’t get home until one. I told her to be in by twelve at the Kolar house, but she doesn’t like curfews.”

“When I was her age,” I said. “I didn’t like curfews either. And, Mrs. Lacey, I don’t think you did either.”

She only smiled. Just then, the doorbell rang. “That must be Toni,” she said. “I’ll get the door.” But Toni was already in the rectory.

"The door was open," she said, "so I just walked in. Nice place you got here, Bishop."

"Thanks."

"Toni," Mrs. Lacey said, "didn't you wash your face this morning?"

"Yes, I did, Grandma. But I couldn't wash away the black eye I got last night at the dance," Toni said.

"Heavens, what happened, Toni?" her grandmother asked.

"Well, this born-again freak outside the dance hall made a crack about my mother being arrested, so I popped her," Toni said. "Some of her friends jumped me and one of them gave me this shiner. But I'll get her. I'm not one to turn the other cheek."

Somewhat embarrassed Mrs. Lacey said, "Your Grace, as you probably guessed, this is my granddaughter Toni."

She was rather tall and slender for a fifteen-year-old, a brunette with long hair that came down to her shoulders. She had a nice complexion and intelligent deep blue eyes. Not a teenage beauty but attractive. She had a casual attitude about her—respectful, but not afraid.

"Hello, Toni," I said, standing and extending my right hand. "Your grandmother has been telling me good things about you. I'm glad you can come and help her out a few times a week. Toni, why don't you take off that parka you're wearing?"

She shook hands with me and said, "Good idea. It's rather warm in here." As she took off the parka, Mrs. Lacey's face turned crimson. On Toni's sweatshirt that hung loosely over her jeans was written: "Last year I got scrod at Cape Cod."

Fortunately, Mrs. Lacey did not ask Toni where she got the shirt with the double entendre message it conveyed. I was quietly amused. As a college student I once worked as a lifeguard at a beach in Chatham, a lovely town on Cape Cod. Many times I could have gotten "scrod," but fortunately I didn't yield to the temptation. How different my life might have been if I had.

"Well, make yourself at home, Toni," I said.

"Thanks."

"Come on, Toni," Mrs. Lacey said, "we've got a lot of work to do."

"In due time, Mrs. Lacey. As Toni's employer," I said with a twinkle in my eye, "I need to interview her. Diocesan regulations, you know. And don't worry. She will get paid from the time she entered the rectory this morning. So come back and rescue her in about thirty minutes."

"I will, your Grace." She left, obviously worried about what her precocious granddaughter would say or do to embarrass her further before an archbishop.

"Please sit down, Toni." I said. "Have you had breakfast?"

"Before I left this morning to come over here, I had some cereal, milk, and toast."

"How about some more toast and juice?"

"No, just a diet Coke," Toni said.

I went into the kitchen to the refrigerator, opened the coke bottle and poured some into a glass, and brought it to the dining room table.

"Grandma says you're a nice guy for an archbishop."

I laughed. "Did she? Well, I am complimented. I do know some bishops and archbishops who are pretty good guys too. You'll probably meet some of them."

Toni made no reply.

"Your grandmother has high praise for you," I said.

"She's always been very good to me," Toni said. "I hope the court says I can stay with her if my mom and that jerk Randy go to prison."

"I hope so too. In fact, I have a lawyer from juvenile court looking into the possibility of having your grandmother become your guardian in case your mother is sent away."

"Do you think that will happen?" Toni asked.

"It could. But I don't want to build your hopes too high. Someone in the court system may say your grandmother is too old and that you should live in foster care with a husband and wife who are much younger."

"I don't want to do that."

"I understand," I said, "but that's a little way down the road. Let's see what my lawyer friend says. OK?"

"OK."

"In the meantime let's just assume your grandmother will be your guardian. Now tell me something about yourself, Toni."

"Not much to tell. I'm almost sixteen. Good student—good athlete. I'm a sophomore at Hayes Public School not too far from here. Do you know where it is?"

"Yes. It's at the corner of Grant and Euclid."

"Right. It's a pretty good school."

"Your grandmother tells me you're a very good student."

"Yeah, but just a B student. I mean I could be on the honor roll, but I missed too many days."

"Were you sick?"

"No, last September I ran away from my parents because one night they decided to get high on drugs and started doing all sorts of crazy things. Anyway, the principal said I was a truant."

"No you weren't, Toni. You did the right thing," I said.

"Yeah, well, I mean, come to the school and tell the principal that."

"All right, I will sometime within the next two weeks, if that's OK with your grandmother and you."

"Really?" Toni asked.

"Really," I answered.

I could see that the girl was somewhat skeptical. She had little trust for anyone in authority, and even though I was no longer in charge of the archdiocese, I was still an authority figure to her. The skull cap, the pectoral cross, the ring on my finger. I realized immediately I should not have worn those trappings of authority. Why did I? Force of habit. However, this kid doesn't fear me. I like that.

"Your grandmother told me that you read the Bible almost daily. That's good."

"Yeah, I mean, but don't get the idea I'm into religion," Toni said. "I mean I'm Catholic but last Christmas was the first time I was at Mass in six months or more. I only read the Bible to find passages I can quote to argue with my friends."

"Do they read the Bible?"

"They sure do. They're born again Christians. Ever hear of them?"

"Yes, I have," I said.

"Do you like them?"

"Why do you ask? Shouldn't I?"

"No, I mean they sure don't like you and most other Catholics. They think I'm going to hell because I haven't been born again. They think I'm a lost soul, or a lost sheep. They've really been on me to accept the Lord Jesus into my heart."

"And have you?"

"No. Not the way they want."

"What way do they want?"

"They want me to attend a Campus Crusade and confess to the minister and the congregation that I have accepted the Lord Jesus into my heart. I went to a revival meeting once and will never go again."

"What happened?"

"Once, you know, when I was twelve years old, I went with my friends to a meeting that was in a big tent. I remember I was wearing a white dress. I sat, you know, in the front seat with my friends, and I remember looking at my finger nails and listening to the preacher—Brother Buddy Burke was his name.

"Even at age twelve I knew I was the only sinner in the church and I was Brother Burke's only hope for the 'call.' He made his call and then came and knelt in front of me. He said, 'Toni, do you want to go to heaven?' Then he started describing what heaven was like. Lots of joy, angels, and eternal life. Did I want to come and accept

Jesus as my personal savior and be guaranteed a place in heaven?"

"What did you say?" I asked.

"Well, I thought about everything I heard and asked him, 'Would my family, my mother and grandmother go to heaven?'"

"No," he said, "they're not saved." He took my hand and asked if I was ready. I stood up, pulled my hand back, and said, "Heaven would be hell without my family." Then I sat right back down."

"That's quite a story," I said. "How did your friends react?"

"They were real mad. Wouldn't even talk to me for a long time."

"How did you connect again?"

"Well, I'm a good athlete. Good at basketball and volley ball and good with my fists when I have to. And I'm tall. They asked me to come out for the basketball team and I did. Sports, you know, are more important than religion to a lot of kids."

Or ethics, I thought. Winning is all important. My fervor for my alma mater Notre Dame cools when I think the athletic department is bending rules to keep outstanding athletes eligible. But I didn't go into that with Toni. It was time to bring closure to this meeting.

"Toni, I enjoyed this conversation. We must talk again. Would that be all right with you?"

"Sure, Bishop, but there's something you gotta know."

"What would that be?"

"Well, you know, if this job means I've got to go to Mass every Sunday, I'm outa here."

"Toni, your job here puts you under no obligation to attend Sunday Mass," I said.

"Will you tell Grandma Lacey that?"

"I certainly will. Promise."

"Here she comes now," Toni said.

"How did she do?" Mrs. Lacey asked.

"Just fine," I said with a smile. "She's hired."

CHAPTER 9

Later that morning, my lawyer Bill Danko phoned me. I told Mrs. Lacey I would take the call in my office. A minute later I picked up the phone. "Good morning, Bill, thanks for returning my call."

"You're welcome, Archbishop. I have an urgent meeting shortly, but I do have a few minutes to talk."

I quickly filled him in on what had happened to Toni's mother and her husband.

Bill took it in without interrupting. "Now," he said when I finished. "I need to know where Toni is living since her parents were jailed."

"Bill, she's staying with a neighbor couple, the Kolars, right next door to where she lives with her mother and stepfather. But I know her grandmother doesn't like that arrangement."

"Is there a relative with whom she could live?"

"Yes, she could stay here at Haley House with her grandmother. You remember Mrs. Lacey, my housekeeper? She's Toni's grandmother, and as I understand, she's the only close relative in the area. It would work a great hardship on Mrs. Lacey—and on me, I might add—if the court required her to move out and live with Toni in her daughter's house."

"Archbishop, would it work a great hardship on you if Toni moved into Haley House with her grandmother?"

"Not at all." I replied without hesitation. "We certainly have enough room here. She could have a suite of rooms on the same floor as her grandmother. But I'm not sure Toni would like to move into a house she probably thinks is a rectory or convent."

"She may have no choice," Danko said. "If I can convince Toni's mother and the juvenile authorities that Toni is in a good, healthy and stable environment at Haley House, the more likely it is that the court will let her grandmother be her guardian. Tell Toni to be in my office after school on Monday, say about four o'clock, and I'll lay out the options she has. Better that I do this rather than you or her grandmother."

I was happy that Danko had volunteered to do this. "Bill, thanks much. I'm sure Toni will accept this solution. She might not like it, but I think her living here will be good for her, her grandmother, and me. And it will certainly take a load off her mother's mind. She must be worried about what's going to happen to Toni."

"Archbishop, I'll encourage Toni to keep you informed about our meeting. We need to respect this girl's privacy, so I won't tell you what we discussed. That's up to her."

"Bill, you are absolutely right. Thanks again."

After I hung up, I called in Mrs. Lacey and told her what Danko had suggested. She was happy with the solution but wondered whether Toni would be happy.

"I think she will be, Mrs. Lacey. Danko has been through similar situations many times. And he knows how to talk to kids her age. In time, I think Toni will be happy living here. But it's your decision."

"Well, your Grace, if Toni moves in here, I'm going to set down some rules. And that sweat shirt from Cape Cod will have to go.

"Mrs. Lacey, as a celibate male who never reared children, may I offer some advice?" I asked.

"Of course. What advice do you have for me?"

"Let Toni be Toni. Don't think that everything in this house has to be perfect because an archbishop lives here. In time, Toni will do what is appropriate."

Mrs. Lacey was dubious, but she didn't want to displease me, so she said, "I certainly won't. Thank you, your Grace."

"Let's keep our fingers crossed and keep this matter in our

prayers. We have a long way to go, but we've taken an important first step."

On the following Monday evening I was having dinner when Mrs. Lacey came into the dining room with Toni in tow.

"Your Grace," Mrs. Lacey began, "I'm sorry to interrupt your dinner, but Toni insists on seeing you right now."

"By all means. Toni, please sit down."

"Thanks, Bishop." She then sat at the other side of the table facing me. I could see that she was angry. Her face was flushed and her eyes looked as if they were on fire.

"I went to see that Mr. Danko today," she said, "and I'm damned mad about what he had to say. I think he's doing what you want, and I don't like that."

"Then we should discuss that. But before we talk about your meeting with Mr. Danko, let me ask—have you had anything to eat?"

"No," Toni replied. "I'm going out to McDonald's for a hamburger later on."

"Good. I wish I could join you. I like Big Macs, but your grandmother has prepared a wonderful Irish stew. Why not eat here and save yourself a buck or two?"

Caught off guard and somewhat short of money, Toni reluctantly agreed to stay for a bowl of Irish stew.

When her grandmother placed the bowl of stew before her, I decided that I was going to give focus and direction to the conversation. Toni's meeting with Danko had upset her and I wanted her to tell me why.

"Toni, your meeting with Mr. Danko this afternoon upset you. Right?"

"Right. He's a nice man. I can tell he's pretty smart."

"Very smart," I added. "I've known Bill for thirty years or more. He's a good guy and a straight shooter. Don't you think so?"

"I suppose. But, well, you know, I didn't like what he suggested." She hesitated.

"Which is?" I asked.

"Like he wants me to live here with my grandmother for the time being. But you already know that because I'm sure he wouldn't dump me on your doorstep without clearing it with you."

"And why, Toni, does he want you to live here with your grandmother?"

"Because Mr. Danko thinks I'll have a better chance of not going to a foster home if we can prove to the courts that I'm in what he called a 'stable environment.'"

"Do you have a better idea?"

The question caught her off guard. After a moment's pause, she answered, "No, I don't. What bothers me, I mean, is the kids at school."

"How so?" I asked.

"Well, I mean how is it going to look when they find out that I'm living in this place called Haley House? They'll think I'm becoming a nun. They'll mock me out."

"So, you're worried about what others might think?"

"Sure I am. Wouldn't you?" she asked rather testily. I could almost hear the time bomb ticking.

"Yes, if I were your age, I would care about what others thought or said." After a short pause, I continued, "Toni, you are no different from me and the vast majority of older and younger folks out there. Most of us worry about what other people think or say. I was the same way when I was your age."

"You were?" Toni asked doubtfully.

"Yes, I was," I reached over to pour some tea and asked Toni if she wanted a diet Cola, but she declined.

She watched me as I slowly sipped the tea." Would I bore you, Toni, with a story from my early college days?

"No," Toni said, with genuine interest in her voice. "I'd like to hear it."

"When I was away in college," I began, "my folks came by train to visit me on Freshman Day. They were not wealthy people.

Far from it. I was worried about how they would look and what my friends would think.

"Fortunately, a popular senior named Bob Mayer was from the same parish back home. He was a big personable guy. Very popular on campus. He knew my family and he liked me. Took me under his wing. When my parents came to the campus, he was with me when they got off the train. He stayed with us all day and introduced me and my parents to everyone as if they were celebrities. After my parents returned home by train that evening, I thanked him for his attentiveness. He then told me something I have never forgotten."

"What was that?"

"He said, 'Ed, when I was a freshman, my parents came to visit me and I was ashamed of them because they were not dressed elegantly. So I avoided crowds and places where I would have to meet a lot of people. That night when they boarded the train for the trip back home, I felt ashamed of myself. How could I be such a snob? Right then and there I resolved never to give a damn about what others think. And neither should you, Ed.'"

I paused and looked at Toni. "And, Toni, neither should you."

We sat silently for a long time. For the first time Toni seemed to realize that I was someone who had been vulnerable and who was willing to share that vulnerability with her. Finally, I said, "Toni, you are welcome to stay here. But don't think we're going to put up a sound system and announce: 'Now hear this, neighbors of Haley House. Toni Vincent now lives here.' And you don't have to make any announcement at school. All your friends need to know is that your grandmother needs your help. Period."

"You make it sound so easy," Toni said, staring down at her hands in her lap.

"Well, it's not easy, but let's not make it harder by worrying about what others think. Toni, you can stay here one day or one month or one year. Just remember that all the doors on the ground floor open from the inside. This is not a prison. You can come here or leave here at will. Let me know what you want to do. Now you'll have to excuse me. I need to write some letters this evening that must be in the mail tomorrow morning. Good night, Toni."

"Thanks, Bishop, and good night."

Her grandmother was in the next room and overheard the end of the conversation between Toni and me. When she entered she said to Toni, "Let's go up to the third floor. I want to show you your rooms."

When they got off the elevator, Mrs. Lacey stopped off at her own suite, which Toni had seen on visits to her grandmother. It was nicely decorated. Good solid furniture on hard wood floors. Crucifix on the wall and a Mona Lisa print on the wall along with a print of Chartres Cathedral, Saint Paul's in London and Monmarte in Paris.

They walked some ten paces down the hall to another suite. Mrs. Lacey switched on the light in the sitting room. Again, good sofa and chair on hard wood floors. The bed was made and the bathroom had a shower stall. Nothing fancy. No pictures or religious objects graced the walls. Mrs. Lacey told Toni that she could decorate the rooms to her liking.

"Really?" Toni asked, eyes wide and looking very pleased. She saw a wall where she could put up her posters. Toni sat on the chair, turned on the faucet over the sink in the bathroom, tested the bed and leaned back on the pillow. "This is a real nice bed, Grandma. Would it be all right if I stayed here tonight?"

Mrs. Lacey hugged her granddaughter. "Toni, I'm delighted that you want to stay."

"What are the rules for this place?" Toni asked. "I suppose there are many so I better start to learn them."

"Let me ask you, Toni, what rules you would have for me if you were in charge of this place and I was a fifteen-year-old girl?

Toni was taken back by this reversal of roles. She thought for a moment. "Well, I would want you to make your bed, clean your room, and do your own laundry. On school nights you would have to do your homework and on weekends you couldn't be out past 11:00 PM. And I'd want to know who your friends were."

"Good, Toni. And those are your rules too. Just one other thing. We are here at the invitation of Archbishop Foley, and we must respect his privacy on the second floor. That's his space. If you want to see him, he has an office on the first floor."

"I suppose the kitchen is off limits too," Toni said mischievously.

"Not at all. It's open from seven in the morning and closes at nine every night."

"Grandma, it might take a little time, but, you know, I think I might like living at Haley House."

"And, Toni, Haley House and everyone in it is going to love you."

CHAPTER 10

When I came down for breakfast the next morning, I was met by Mrs. Lacey, who told me that Toni stayed at Haley House that night. She was obviously pleased that Toni had made the decision on her own to move into the residence. So was I.

As I entered the dining room, Toni stopped short to avoid running into me, dropping her book bag and a sweet roll she had grabbed to eat on the way to school.

“Well, good morning, Toni.”

“Good morning, Bishop. Sorry.” Embarrassed, she stooped to retrieve her book bag and roll.

“Your grandmother tells me you stayed here last night. How did you sleep?”

“Good,” Toni said.

“I’m happy you’re going to live here. I think you’ll like it.”

Toni nodded and said, “Well, I’m off to school. Can’t be late for my geometry test first period.”

“Good luck, Toni, we’ll see you this afternoon.”

“OK. See you, Grandma.” She picked up her books, clambered down the steps and out the door.

When I was having breakfast, I spoke to Mrs. Lacey about Toni.

“Mrs. Lacey, this afternoon when Toni returns from school, would you and she like to drive over to her mother’s house and collect the things she wants to bring back here? I’ll tell the driver to be ready about 3:30 this afternoon if that’s all right with you. You should be able to get everything in the car, don’t you think?”

“I’m not sure. She has clothes, a stereo, basketball shoes, roller blades, posters and a whole lot of other things. I hope they can all fit in the car.”

"Well, if they don't, the driver can make another trip. It's only a few miles away."

"Thanks, your Grace. I'll be ready."

"Good. There's something else I want to prepare you for."

"What's that, your Grace?"

"Late yesterday afternoon, I talked to my lawyer friend, Bill Danko. He wants Toni and you to meet with her mother at the Justice Center tomorrow afternoon. Toni's mother wants to see her, but her stepfather doesn't. Do you know why?"

Mrs. Lacey was silent for a moment. Then she said, "I think so, your Grace. He has never liked Toni. He's a very immature man who is jealous of the affection that my daughter Helen gives to Toni. He's always putting Toni down. Criticizes just about everything she does. Never compliments her. That has caused a lot of tension between my daughter and him."

"It's too bad that he's taking it out on Toni," I said. "It's important that her mother and Toni meet."

"I agree, your Grace, but I'm not sure Toni will want to see her mother. She ran away from that home, you know. She's very angry at them both."

"I know, and I can't say I blame her. But we all make mistakes, including mothers. Toni could help rehabilitate her mother through forgiveness. That's not an easy thing to sell, but I think we need to try."

"I'll leave that to you, your Grace. For me, talking to my daughter about her life style is like talking to a brick wall. But I'll do whatever you think will help."

"Fine, Mrs. Lacey, have you thought about what you're going to say to your daughter when you see her this afternoon?"

"Not really, but I know what I'd like to say to her," Mrs. Lacey replied.

"And what would that be?"

"Well, I would like to tell her that if she had said the rosary every day and went to Mass every Sunday, she wouldn't be in this terrible mess."

"Do you think that would help?"

"No, it wouldn't, so I'll bite my tongue and not say that."

"I think you're right," I said. "Just tell her that you love her and will not abandon her—or Toni. That's what she needs to hear."

"You're right, your Grace. I certainly do love my daughter and I do love Toni. They both need my love now more than ever."

"They surely do, and you can be very helpful in bringing healing to this family wound."

She asked me, "Would you tell Toni about the visit to her mother in the Justice Center?"

"Yes. I can do that. Tell her I'd like to see her in my office after dinner this evening. I want to ask her how things went in school today. Then I'll tell her about the visit to the jail to see her mother."

"What if she doesn't want to visit her mother?" Mrs. Lacey asked.

"Well, we can't force her to go. If she refuses, then you will have to go to the jail alone. Your daughter is expecting visitors. We can't disappoint her, can we?"

Mrs. Lacey was waiting for Toni when she came home from school. She told Toni they were going to drive to her parents' home so that she could get the things she would need at Haley House.

"Cool," Toni said. "I was wondering how I was going to get all my things over here. When do we leave?"

"Right now, Toni," Mrs. Lacey answered. "The driver is waiting for us by the garage." They went out the back way and got into the car, which was parked near the garage. Toni gave directions to the driver, and five minutes later they were in front of her home.

Toni insisted on going in alone and bringing her possessions out to the car. Fortunately, they were able to get everything into the trunk, so only one trip was necessary. When they parked at Haley House, Toni, Mrs. Lacey, and the driver used the elevator and carried everything up to Toni's suite of rooms. By the time they were finished, it was almost 5:30.

"Toni," Mrs. Lacey said, "I'll have everything ready for dinner a little after six. So why don't you wash up and come down in a half hour? Oh, by the way, the archbishop wants to see you in his office about seven."

"Why? What'd I do?"

"Silly girl," said Mrs. Lacey as she put her arm around Toni. "You haven't done anything. He probably wants to find out how things went at school."

"They went fine. There's nothing to tell."

"Fine," Mrs. Lacey said. "That's all you have to tell him. Then you can leave and finish your unpacking. But, Toni, please be courteous to him. He has certainly been nice to you."

"OK," said Toni, "I'll try to be nice."

"Good."

After dinner, Toni came to my office and knocked on the door.

"Come in, Toni, I've been expecting you. Please sit down."

She was surprised to find me not wearing my black cassock, cross and ring. I was wearing gray slacks and a navy blue turtle neck sweater, and loafers. She knew that clerics didn't play golf in their robes, but her expression told me she didn't expect to see an archbishop dressed so informally.

"Gosh, Archbishop," she said. "You look like a regular person!"

"I'll take that as a compliment, Toni. Did you finish unpacking?" I asked.

"Not yet. When I leave here, I'll go up to the third floor and finish."

"Do you need anything up there? If you do, tell Mrs. Lacey and she'll get what you need."

"Thanks a lot. I have a lot of homework tonight and I have to finish unpacking. Is there anything else, Bishop?"

Sensing that she was uncomfortable in this setting, I got right to the point. "Far be it from me, Toni, to interfere with your school work. But last night you were quite worried about how your friends at school were going to take your moving into Haley House. Did they mock you out by saying that you were going to become a nun?"

"No, they didn't. I mean they were glad that I was getting out of that house where my mother and Randy live."

"Do they know your mother and her husband?" I asked.

"Yes. Once they were at the house when Randy caused a terrible scene, yelling and calling my mom and me—well, calling us awful names and kicking my friends out. He was drunk and so was my mom. I was so embarrassed I could have died."

"Of course you were. I would be too. Fortunately, my parents didn't drink. When they were young kids in Ireland, they both belonged to the Saint Matthew Society. To join it, they had to pledge they would never in their life take a drink. And neither one of them did."

"I suppose you joined that club and want me to join it too," said Toni.

I found it difficult to contain my amusement at her remark. Reaching into my desk drawer, I brought out a stack of index cards. "Oh sure," I said, "please fill out this card, Toni. It will make you a teetotaler for life." I handed her the card.

"This is just a blank card, Bishop. Are you playing a joke on me?"

"Of course, I am, Toni. As far as I know, there is no St. Matthew Society in this archdiocese. At least, there wasn't one when my parents came here; and even if there were I wouldn't have joined. We don't recruit young people your age to swear off drinking for life as they once did in Ireland—and may even be doing now."

"So I don't have to join the St. Matthew Society?"

"Of course not. However, if your parents are alcoholics, you might at some time want to join Al-Anon, which helps children cope with this disease."

"I'll think about it."

"Fine. There's one other thing I want you to think about," I said.

"What's that?"

"Well, your grandmother is going to the Justice Center

tomorrow afternoon to visit your mother. Mr. Danko has obtained permission for you to come if you want to."

"Well, I don't want to," Toni said rather sharply.

I expected that response. Quietly I said, "Toni, I hope you'll change your mind and go. Your mother wants to see you."

"Well, I mean, you know, I don't want to see her."

"Toni," I said, "when I first met you, your grandmother thought you hadn't washed your face. Remember that?"

"Yeah. I had to tell her that I got into a fist fight at the dance the night before with some born again who kept ragging on me because my mom got busted."

"You were angry, weren't you?" I asked.

"Sure, I was damned mad—excuse me—darned mad because she was mocking out my mom," Toni said. "I didn't like that."

"Was it because you had some feeling and love for your mother?"

"I don't think so. I always wanted to pop that girl, and what she said about my mother gave me the chance."

"I can understand that. But you might want to talk about the jail visit with your born again friends," I said.

"Bishop, why would I do that?"

"Well," I said, "I think they would give you a quote from Scripture that might change your mind."

"What quote is that?"

"I was in prison and you visited me."

The words stunned her. As she rose to leave, she said, "I'll think about it. Good night, Bishop." She rushed out of the room so fast that she didn't hear me say goodbye.

CHAPTER 11

Mrs. Lacey spent most of Wednesday morning in a state of anxiety. She worried about the afternoon visit to the Justice Center. She did not know if Toni would accompany her, and at breakfast Toni said nothing about it. After she had eaten, she gathered her books, put on her coat, kissed her grandmother, and was out the door in a hurry to get to school on time.

I knew Mrs. Lacey had a heavy heart, but I said nothing to her about the forthcoming visit to the Center. I felt great compassion for her, a sixty-six-year-old widow, who had tried to play by the rules all her life. She should be retired, either living comfortably alone or else living in a center with other seniors with whom she could play cards, go to the movies, or take bus trips to casinos, parks, theaters or museums. The salary she earned as my housekeeper was somewhat substantial, but she probably was still using used a good part of her savings to pay her late husbands medical bills. And now she is preparing to visit her thirty-five-year-old daughter in prison. Life is not fair, I thought, and it is most unfair to the Mrs. Laceys of the world.

Toni was now facing the tough choice of visiting her mother in jail or refusing to see her. I thought Mrs. Lacey would go alone to the Justice Center that afternoon. I was pleasantly surprised when Toni came home from school and said she had decided to visit her mother. I didn't know why she had changed her mind, and I was not inclined to ask.

Mrs. Lacey and Toni arrived at the Center about fifteen minutes before they were scheduled to visit. Visitors were informed that their visits would last only ten minutes unless special permission had been given for an extension.

Mrs. Lacey had been to the Center when her daughter was first arrested, so she knew the procedures. However, it was all new to Toni, who had never been in a jail. Toni and her grandmother were not the only ones visiting prisoners that afternoon. Thirty to forty people were waiting to get clearance to go in, mostly African American or Hispanic women who appeared to be in their twenties or thirties. Two men in their forties or fifties were also part of the group.

The Center had been built to replace an ugly looking jail that had served the city for more than seventy-five years. As jails go, it was a clean, well lighted facility. The guards were business like and not friendly. Mrs. Lacey and Toni checked their coats and filled out a sheet indicating the person they were to see.

Their keys, money, wallets and purses were put on a tray. The guard then inspected the contents looking for weapons and drugs. When he determined there were none, he then passed an electronic detector over their bodies. They were then cleared to enter the waiting room. Mrs. Lacey was first, so she entered the glass enclosed cubicle where she would talk to her daughter by phone. A few minutes later, her daughter Helen, in an orange prison jump suit, entered and sat down facing her mother.

"Hi, Mom," she said, in a voice so low that Mrs. Lacey could barely hear her. "Thanks for coming." She paused. "Is Toni here?"

"Yes, she is, dear. She will be in here shortly."

"Oh, I'm so glad she came. I've been dying to see her."

"Helen, there's something you should know. Toni has not been dying to see you. In fact, right up to the time we left I didn't know whether she would accompany me. She's very angry at you and Randy."

Helen was silent for a moment trying to control her tears. She covered her face with her hands. When she could talk, she said, "I can't say I blame her, Mom. I really messed up my life—and yours—and her life too. When I get out, I'm going to make it up to her."

"I'm glad to hear you say that, Helen. What does Mr. Danko say about your chances of getting out?"

"He said I could get probation because it's my first offense. But he's not too hopeful. Said the courts are not lenient when it comes to armed robbery. I could get sent away for a few years. Randy could get up to ten years."

"Helen," Mrs. Lacey asked, "is this the only time you were involved in a robbery?"

"Yes, Mom. We were so broke and desperate for drugs. Randy thought the Convenience Store would be easy."

"So, it was his idea?"

"Yeah, but I went along with it. We were both out of our heads."

"I hope you told all this to Mr. Danko."

"Yes. He took a lot of notes."

"Well," Mrs. Lacey volunteered, "Archbishop Foley says he's a very good lawyer. One of the best, he claims."

"Mom, please thank the bishop for getting Mr. Danko as my lawyer."

"I'll do that, Helen. And I'll also tell him that you are thankful that he's letting Toni live with me at Haley House."

"Yes, please do. I got your letter saying that Toni was living with you. How is she adjusting? Any problems?" Helen asked.

"No," said Mrs. Lacey, "Toni is doing just fine under the circumstances."

As soon as she uttered the words—"under the circumstances"—she wanted to take them back. It was like kicking a helpless person who's down and out. Her daughter, however, seemed to accept the rebuke without wincing.

"Helen, I think my time is just about up. So I'm going to say goodbye. Just remember I love you and I'll do my best to take care of Toni for you." They both said tearful goodbyes, and Mrs. Lacey left the cubicle.

Toni had to wait until the guard entered and made sure nothing was hidden or left behind.

When Toni entered the cubicle, her mother was overjoyed to see her. She held out her arms as if she wanted to hug and hold her daughter close to her, but the glass prevented that.

"Toni!" she said with tears in her eyes, "It's so great to see you again. How's my precious little girl?"

"Hello, Mother. I am not your precious little girl, so just call me Toni. I haven't been your precious little girl ever since you married that creep Randy. It was like I didn't even exist any more. How could you marry such a loser? You trashed what was left of our family. My dad was such a great guy."

"Toni, I am sorry for what Randy and I have done to you. Please forgive us."

"I'll try, Mother, but it will take some time. And I may never forgive you. I'm really angry at what the two of you did—not just robbing that store. I've lived in fear of him. He's mean. I hate his shouting and cursing at you and me. I hate him."

"I know. He's a different person when he's drinking."

Toni made no comment. A minute of silence was broken when Toni asked, "Do you know the real reason why I ran away, Mother?"

"Well, yes, honey, because of our drinking."

"That and something else. Randy started to put moves on me. I was afraid he would rape me."

Helen was stunned. She began to sob. "Toni, honey, oh, my God! Oh, honey, why didn't you tell me?"

"Mother, I tried to, but you were always drunk. How could I tell you?"

After a long pause, Toni's mother said, "Toni, I'm so sorry. Oh, dear God. I should have divorced him years ago."

"Why didn't you?"

"I guess because I thought I had to make it work. The Church looks down on divorce," her mother replied. "Then too, I was hoping and praying that he would change . . . and that I would change."

"Yeah! You changed all right. Became armed robbers. Mother, I know some Catholic kids at school whose parents are divorced. The Church does permit it. I asked myself if divorce is OK for their parents, why not mine? So don't use the Church as an excuse."

"You're right, Toni. I am doing that and I shouldn't. If only I had listened to your grandmother and went to Mass and said the rosary, I wouldn't be in this mess. Toni, I hope you are going to Mass and saying your rosary every day."

"Mother, don't give me a lecture on religion. Bishop Foley doesn't. He knows I'm not going to Mass and that I'm not saying the rosary, and he hasn't kicked me out of Haley House. So don't start on me."

After an awkward pause, she said, "I know the time is almost up. I hope you will come again, honey."

"I don't think so. This place depresses me."

"You mean I depress you, don't you?"

"I didn't say that. Don't put words in my mouth. Goodbye, Mother."

"Goodbye, Toni."

Toni rang the buzzer for the guard and left without even a wave to her mother.

On the way back to Haley House, both Toni and her grandmother were silent. Toni did not venture any information about the meeting with her mother and her grandmother did not ask for any.

After dinner that evening, I was in my study watching the evening news when Toni knocked on the door, which was open.

I pushed the mute button. "Hello, Toni, what can I do for you?"

"Nothing, Bishop. I just want to thank you for getting me to go see my mother. Those words of Jesus you quoted really hit me. But I have to admit I wasn't very Christian when I met with her this afternoon. I was pretty rough on her."

"I know," I said.

"How do you know?"

"Your mother told me."

"You talked to her? When?"

"About an hour after you talked to her."

"So you were spying on me?"

"Toni, if I were spying on you," I said, "you would have every reason to be resentful. I followed your visit for two reasons. First, Mr. Danko asked if I would be willing to testify at the probation hearing for your mother whom I don't know. I wanted to meet her to see how she reacted to your visit with her.

"Secondly, I thought you might beat up on your mother, who is a very fragile person. She needed someone to put her together again after you saw her. What I did, Toni, was to explain to your mother that she could resent you or that she could begin to turn her life around. You gave her something that some would call 'tough love.' She needed that, so don't go beating up yourself for what you said this afternoon. If you could re-live this afternoon's visit with your mother, you wouldn't want to change a word."

"Really?"

"Yes, really. That's probably the first time your mother realized how you felt. It was a very honest conversation, probably the first honest conversation the two of you have had since you were a little girl."

"You're right, Bishop."

After a long pause, Toni said, "Bishop, I have something to say and it's—you know—very difficult to say it."

I said nothing, just waited. Finally, Toni got the courage to say what was on her mind. "I don't think you bishops and priests know how kids like me really feel. You're not very good at listening."

"Toni, you're right. But let's admit that not many young people your age are looking to have a conversation with a pastor or a bishop. Why is that?"

Toni thought for a moment. "Well, one reason is that we're not important enough for you guys—I mean, you priests and bishops listen to people with money and influence. Like if a kid my age called the chancery and said she wanted to talk to the bishop, what would happen?"

I thought for a moment and said, "Well, the bishop's secretary would ask her why she wants to see the bishop and then make a judgment about whether she should schedule her for an appointment."

"Yeah, well, I can just imagine the secretary saying—The bishop will see you now. Just deposit your check on the way in."

I gave a hearty laugh.

She seemed surprised that I found her remark funny. She laughed and said, "Well, seriously, if I really wanted an appointment with a bishop? I wouldn't get one."

I said, "Toni, I have to admit you're right. But the same thing would happen if you walked into the offices of General Motors and asked to see the top man. Don't you agree?"

"Sure. But we're not talking about General Motors. We're talking about the Church that Jesus founded. Is it right that it should be run like General Motors?"

This kid is really a thinker! She knew she had me on the ropes so she prepared to give me a knockout punch. "OK, Bishop," she continued, let's go back to what I said before. What if I showed the secretary a check for $25,000 made out to the church—or the diocese or whatever you call it. What would happen?"

"Well, Toni, that secretary would excuse herself and go right to the bishop's office. A few minutes later the bishop himself would appear, heartily greet you, and ask the financial treasurer to come to his office and give you a receipt for the check."

We both smiled.

Toni got up to get a coke. I said, "Toni, this conversation has been good for me because it's been so honest. Do you think we could have more of these conversations?"

She didn't answer right away. After a while, she said, "Bishop, let me think about that. I appreciate your wanting to talk to me. But I don't know if I want to make that kind of commitment. I've got my studies and work around here."

"Toni," I said, "I understand. Just remember that when you want a bishop to listen to you, I'm available."

"Thanks, Bishop, I'll tell you when I need another honest conversation."

"Good, Toni. I look forward to it."

CHAPTER 12

At dinner a few nights later, Toni had asked if she could see me that evening. I told her I would be free at seven. I think she wanted to test me and to see if I was really open to having honest conversations with a kid of fifteen.

I can't really prepare for it, I thought—only think about it. She's right in saying that often we bishops and priests do not really understand what kids her age are thinking and feeling. Many of us are not good listeners. Maybe priests, ministers and rabbis who are younger or who are campus ministers understand, but old dogs like me are often not in contact with these young turks who work with kids. That situation has to change.

A knock on my office door interrupted my musings. I looked at my watch—exactly 7:00 PM—so that must be Toni. I got up and opened the door.

"Hi, Bishop," Toni said cheerily.

"Good evening, Toni. How did things go at school?"

"Fine. I got called in by the principal. I was scared, but she told me not to worry. She wanted me to know you came to see her about all those absences. She agrees with you that I did the right thing in running away from my parents' house, but she said that if something like that ever happened again, I should talk to a counselor or to her. Anyway, those absences will be removed from my record. Thanks."

"You're welcome. When you're a senior, Toni, you will probably apply to many colleges for admission. I don't want some college entrance committee to disqualify you because of those absences which could look to some like you were a truant. Those committees have so many applications that they look for reasons such as unexcused absences to drop an applicant."

"Well, thanks again, Bishop. I do want to go to college, like, you know, but I'll need scholarships to get there."

"Yes, you will, and I'm sure you will get some," I said. "But let's get down to business. The last time we met you indicated some reluctance to having more honest conversations. Why the sudden change of heart?"

"Well, I guess I wondered if you would really see the principal about those absences. But you did. That told me you were someone I could trust. So I'm here for another honest conversation."

It's been a few days since I've had one of those," I said with a wink. "So how shall we start?"

"Well, Bishop, I mean, why do archbishops have 'Most Reverend' before their names? Are there some clergy who are less reverend or not reverend?"

"That's a good question, Toni. I must admit that some of these titles make me feel uncomfortable. That's one of them. I have never used it on my documents or on my stationery. If you come across material where I have used 'Most Reverend,' please let me know and I'll change it."

"OK, Bishop. I will. This next question might seem silly. You wear a nice ring on your left hand? I mean, do you like people coming up, kneeling down and kissing your ring?"

"That's an easy one to answer, Toni. No, I don't like that custom and never have. Seems so un-American."

"Have you ever let people kiss your ring?"

"When I was in charge of the archdiocese," I said, "I let the priests know that I didn't want them kissing my ring. A lot of lay people knew that too. But many times some older people would come up to me in meetings, grab my hand and kiss the ring. I would smile and try to be as gracious as possible."

"Bishop, sorry, but I don't buy that. If you didn't want people kissing your ring, why did you wear it? What would happen, I mean, if you didn't wear it? Would you still be an archbishop?"

"Of course, I would. When I used to play golf in my younger

days, I always took the ring off my ring finger. Interfered with my grip on the club."

Toni thought about my answer. She was obviously having difficulty framing a follow-up question without being rude.

Noticing her discomfort, I said, "I think you want to ask me if my wearing the ring doesn't cause me to lose my grip on people."

"Yeah, something like that."

"Let me think about that, Toni. It's a very good question."

My answer seemed to put her at ease. After a short pause, Toni continued the conversation. "Bishop," she said, "just before I came in here, I was just surfing TV and saw this program on C-Span. A lot of cardinals were dedicating some building to honor the pope."

"Yes, Toni, that's the new Pope John Paul II Center in Washington. Quite a building, I'm told. Cost millions."

"Yeah, but, you know, I don't want to talk about that."

"Fine, Toni. What's on your mind about that ceremony?"

"Well," Toni said, "the president of the United States was there, and he was dressed in a dark blue suit, white shirt and tie. You know. Simple. Looked nice. Looked American." She then paused.

I knew what was coming, but I didn't interrupt her.

"Guys like you. . . Sorry, you're not a cardinal. I mean the cardinals were all calling each other 'Eminence.' And they all wore red beanies, black capes, black robes, and big red sashes around their bellies, I mean stomachs. Bishop, do you know what that event looked like to me?"

"No, what?"

"It looked like the president was at a Halloween Party."

"Toni, isn't that rather harsh?"

"Maybe." She laughed. "But remember, this is an honest conversation."

"You're right," I smiled. "I didn't see the ceremony so I'll reserve judgment. C-Span often repeats programs so I'll watch for it tonight. Thanks for telling me about it. Then we can talk about it some more."

"OK." After a pause she continued. "Bishop, those guys in the red beanies and belly bands must really like this pope."

"I'm sure they do. He's a very good man," I said.

"Then, Bishop, I mean why don't you have a big picture of him in this office? It would show that you like him. That picture on the wall over there is a pope, but not this one."

"Hold on," I protested. "You're jumping to the conclusion that since his picture isn't on the wall, I don't like him. Is that fair?"

"Maybe not, Bishop. I can only speak from my own experience."

"Which is?" I asked.

She was silent for a moment and then said, "Look, Bishop, I have a picture in my room of my father. He died when I was four. But I sure don't have a picture of Randy anywhere because I despise him. Do you despise the present pope?"

"Of course not!" I said emphatically. "In fact, I admire many things he has done. He's just not one of my heroes."

"Why not?"

I didn't expect the conversation to go in this direction. I didn't want to appear disloyal to the pope, so I knew I had to choose my words very carefully. After a moment of reflection, I said, "Toni, this pope has done a lot for the church. He has traveled to just about every place in the world. He has spoken everywhere of peace and justice. He has met with young people in this country and other countries and made a great impact. He has gone to the Wall in Jerusalem and apologized to the Jewish people for the sins Christians have committed against them throughout the centuries. He has reached out to the Muslim world by removing his shoes and praying in a mosque."

"But he's not one of your heroes? Why not?"

"Because it seems to me that he does not tolerate dissent very well," I replied. "He refuses to let cardinals and bishops discuss certain topics like the marriage of priests and the ordination of women."

"That really bothers you, doesn't it?"

"Yes, it does," I said. "Here is a man who grew up under a communist system where dissent was not tolerated. Then he comes to Rome and imposes silence on issues that are really important to the Church. That puzzles and disturbs me."

"So is that other pope on the wall your hero?"

"Yes. He is Pope John XXIII, who was pope from 1958 to 1963. Long before you were born, Toni, that man in five years did more to unite Christians and non-Christians than all the other popes did in the 500 years before him. People the world over cried when that little fat man died. Even the bells of some Protestant churches in Belfast, Ireland tolled to mourn his death. And cartoonist Herblock of the Washington Post drew a picture of the world with a funeral wreath around it. His title for it was *A Death in the Family.*"

"You mean it was like when Princess Diana died?" Toni asked.

"Yes, something like that. I forget that you were not born when President John Kennedy was killed in Dallas. But you certainly were alive when Princess Diana died. What a shock when the world lost that beautiful lady who did so much to aid the poor of the world. I grieved for her and the two young sons who survive her."

"I'm glad to know you liked her," Toni said. "Maybe I'll write about her and President Kennedy for my history class. I might even write about that pope, but I have to tell you that popes don't interest me. Sorry about that."

"That's all right, Toni, you have your heroes and I have mine."

Suddenly was distracted. "Un-oh, I have a report due tomorrow. I have to print it out and read it over. I'd better say goodnight."

"Goodnight, Toni. I can't see you tomorrow because a friend is coming over to visit me. But the night after that is clear. See you then?"

"OK. I'll be here. Bishop, this honest conversation has been fun. Good night!"

CHAPTER 13

About a month after Cardinal Mohr's funeral, February 22, as I recall, Tom Rinehart, a young priest who was the Cardinal's secretary, telephoned me and asked when he could stop in to see me. I learned from him later that he was hoping to see me at the funeral to tell me that he had fallen in love with Kate Green, an English professor at the University, and that they had made plans to marry after he received a dispensation from the Vatican. My viral infection, however, prevented me from attending Mohr's funeral.

I had ordained Rinehart about ten years earlier. I assigned him to a parish where he was well liked and quite successful. When there was an opening as chaplain of the Newman Center at the University, I tapped Tom for the job. Tall, handsome, intelligent and outgoing, Rinehart immersed himself in the academic, cultural, and social activities of the university. He had a master's degree in communications and was working on a doctorate. At times he had difficulty keeping his temper under control, but in the past few years he had made significant improvement.

For example, when he was in the major seminary, a couple of years from ordination, the professor of dogma announced that for the next two weeks the class would be studying the doctrine of Indulgences.

Some in the class groaned, but Tom slammed his book on the desk and said, "Father, you're going to have us waste our time studying that shit?"

"Mister Rinehart," the professor said, "it's one of the topics to be covered in this dogma course and I intend to teach it."

"Well," Tom said, "I don't intend to learn it. Nobody in this class believes in 'indulgences.' Let's be honest, Father, I don't think you do either. You know as well as I that this doctrine was one of the reasons for the Protestant Reformation. For the past 400 years we have been trying to undo the harm this stupid doctrine caused."

"Mister Rinehart, if you don't like what is being taught here, you don't have to stay."

"Thanks, Father, for giving me permission to leave. I'm out of here."

With that, he picked up his books and left the room, slamming the door on the way out.

Fortunately, the professor was a wise head, but he was greatly offended by Rinehart's behavior. He needed time to cool off, so he told the class to take a twenty-minute break, which they were happy to do.

When the class reassembled, the professor said, "In a couple of years, you men will have oral exams before ordination, and you will be questioned on everything in this book including the doctrine of Indulgences. If Mr. Rinehart had the good grace to stick around, he would have learned that I want you to have a reason why you support indulgences or reject them. I don't want some old graybeard on the orals committee to tear you apart because you know nothing about their history or their impact."

But he was not going to let Rinehart get away with his temper tantrum. He could have reported Rinehart to the rector, which would resulted in a disciplinary hearing. Rinehart could have been expelled, and the professor did not want that to happen. He recognized that Rinehart was a man of exceptional talent.

When he returned to his office, Rinehart was waiting for him and apologized for his outburst, which the professor accepted. He told Rinehart that he would like him to write a ten-page paper on why the doctrine of Indulgences should be abolished from the curriculum. The class could then discuss the paper. When Rinehart agreed to do that, the professor said the matter would go no further.

He did say this, however: "Tom, that temper of yours is going to get you into trouble some day. You must learn how to disagree without being disagreeable. If you ever pull a stunt like that again in my classroom, I'll move for your immediate dismissal from the seminary." Rinehart thanked him and said he would follow his advice. Which he did. Two years later, I ordained him.

When Cardinal Mohr succeeded me as archbishop, he tapped Rinehart as his secretary and aide, a position Rinehart did not want or like. He pleaded with Mohr to leave him at the University and to choose someone else, but the cardinal would not hear of it. So out of blind obedience to authority—something he learned in the seminary—Rinehart became secretary.

He liked Cardinal Mohr, but he did not enjoy working in the chancery office. Why, he wondered, should an ordained priest with years of pastoral education be pushing paper in the chancery office in addition to being the driver for the cardinal and acting as his master of ceremonies at confirmation and other liturgical events? Couldn't these duties be performed by someone else—a retired person perhaps who would be honored to be of service to the cardinal?

Rinehart preferred to be with college kids at the University, listening to them, going to cultural events with them, and celebrating the liturgy in small groups. Furthermore, in his new position as secretary, there was no place for his own plans to work on his doctorate. He was the cardinal's man and was expected to be on call at all times.

Independent by nature, he became depressed in this subservient role. He tried to put on a happy face, but he bristled when he heard rumors that he was on a fast track to become a bishop. He did nothing to dispel the rumors. What could he do? He knew that many bishops were at one time secretaries or chancellors. Frequently when a bishop died and a diocese became vacant, Rome promoted some chancery official to become bishop. In the process, Rinehart thought, the Vatican often overlooked pastors of parishes, guys in the trenches, working sometimes fifteen hours a day.

What galled Rinehart especially was the statement some chancery people often made when they were named bishop. At a press conference, many would say, "I am unworthy of such an honor. I am humbled by this appointment. I did not expect it."

Unworthy? Rinehart thought. Of course, you are unworthy, you dumb son of a bitch. We all know that. Humbled? Did not expect it? Pure bullshit. You've been angling for this ever since you were ordained. And even before. He remembered when, two years away from ordination, he was at his desk at the seminary studying for a final exam. Suddenly someone opened his door. A priest whom he did not know, said, "Kid, if you want to become a bishop, start kissing ass right now. Otherwise, it will be too late."

When Rinehart called me, he briefly told me about Kate and his decision to marry her. He was not asking for my advice or approval, but for my help in submitting his application for a dispensation. I took the news very calmly and suggested a Wednesday dinner two weeks away. Wednesday was my housekeeper's day off, so Rinehart and I would have Haley House to ourselves.

When that Wednesday arrived, Mrs. Lacey and Toni had gone out for an early dinner and a movie. I was glad they got along so well. Mrs. Lacey had baked a chicken that morning and, after it cooled, placed it in the refrigerator for our supper, along with a large salad, macaroni and cheese, and strawberry shortcake. I told her I had invited a priest friend in to join me, a Father Tom Rinehart, whom Mrs. Lacey did not know.

When the doorbell rang at Haley House, I went to the door and greeted Tom. "I'm glad you could come. Today is Mrs. Lacey's day off, so you and I will have to raid the fridge."

"Thanks for inviting me. It means a lot to me to discuss my decision about leaving."

"Tom, we'll get around to that soon enough. Let's have a drink before dinner. What would you like?"

"Scotch on the rocks with a few drops of dry vermouth,"

Rinehart said.

"Good choice," I said. "Rob Roys are my favorites too." I went to the liquor cabinet and removed a bottle of Dewars Scotch and a bottle of dry vermouth. I asked Rinehart to go to the fridge and remove an ice tray. I put a few cubes in each glass and poured the Scotch into them followed by a few drops of dry vermouth. We touched glasses as if giving a toast and then sat down for our discussion of Rinehart's future.

"Tom, it's too bad Cardinal Mohr didn't let you stay as chaplain at the University. You belonged there with college kids. It must have torn you up to be working in an office with us clerical types."

"Yes, it did, but in a way it was a good thing because it forced me to reexamine my life. I began to question not only whether I wanted to do desk work for the rest of my life—I definitely did not."

"There were other options, Tom. You could have gone back into youth ministry, or you could have gone to graduate school and completed work on your doctorate."

"That's true, but I began to realize that even doing those things wouldn't cure the tremendous loneliness I feel in the priesthood."

"Tell me about that," I said.

"Well, I've lived in rectories with guys who were really attuned to what was happening in the Church and in the world," Tom said. "They were readers, observers and thinkers. They were committed to their work. But some other guys in rectories where I've lived hadn't read a book since they were ordained. They couldn't have cared less about the Second Vatican Council. All they seemed to be interested in was the sports pages and the entertainment sections of the newspapers. They ridiculed the idea of continuing education for the clergy. They went to clergy conferences because they had to, but came home and bitched about what was discussed. And I'm not referring to older priests, but to guys who had been out ten years or less."

"How did you deal with that, Tom?"

"It made me mad as hell," he said. "In fact, some of us got into shouting matches at times. I felt depressed. I asked myself if I wanted to be doing this for years to come. Do I want to try to educate guys who don't want to be educated?"

I got up, went to a book case against the wall, and took out a small volume titled *On Education* by Sir Richard Livingstone. I said, "Tom, I've had this book for many years. It's a gem but it's out of print. Anyway, listen to this passage about the indifference to continuing education in all institutions:

"Are not all familiar, in parliament, in the churches, in education, in medicine, in government and municipal offices, in business, with men of forty years and over, whom the tide of their education carried some way up the shore and who are content to remain where it deposited them years before, who have found their way into directing posts by merit, by seniority, by mere efflux of time, who should be the pumps to drive the water of progress onward, and are at any rate the pipes and conduits through which it must pass, but who are in fact so furred and fossilized that they prevent its flowing at all? They may be men of ability and good will, they may have had an excellent education. But they are living in the world as it was when they were in their twenties, they have lost the intellectual and imaginative vigor which would have enabled them to move with the movement of the times; the pace is too much for them, it frightens them; routine, which is another name for action divorced from thought, gets an increasing grip on them; and the younger generation grumbles impatiently: 'When will they retire or die, so that we can get on?'"

"That's a great quote. Could I get a copy of it?" Tom asked.

"Sure, Tom, I can copy that page before you leave tonight. Just remember that quote when you start working in another institution. It goes to the essence of change or non-change in any institution. You will meet men and women—good people—who are so "furred and fossilized" that they don't want to think about continuing their education. So don't think this is just a problem in the Catholic Church. It's a problem everywhere."

"I guess I knew that. My point is that it should not be a problem in the Church. And in some places it isn't. For example, at the University, nuns and other women in great numbers take courses in theology, scripture, catechetics, psychology, and history, but the clergy stays away in great numbers. There's nothing more to learn. Ordination has made them Renaissance men, or so they think."

"Tom, you're describing the priesthood today, but I think you are painting everyone with the same brush. Don't you know men of your age or older who are thinkers, idea men, readers, questioners with whom you could develop deep friendships? Aren't there some priests your age who are into philosophy, theology, music and art? Why not develop friendships with them?"

Tom thought about this for a minute and said, "You're right. I do know many men with whom I would like to be friends. The problem is that many are in parishes miles away. The other problem is that I'm so damn busy helping the Cardinal with the paper work on his desk that I've lost touch with many of them. Then too some of these guys have avoided me since I went to work for the Cardinal. They don't want their fellow priests thinking they are "sucking up" to the Cardinal's man in hopes of getting a better job."

"I get the picture, Tom," I said. "It was probably the same when I was in charge. I should have rotated men. A few years in the chancery and then send them back to parish work. Or five years in a parish and then five years in the chancery. Then may five years as a hospital chaplain."

I rose from my chair and brought back the bottle of Scotch. I poured a jigger into Tom's glass and then my own. "What you say, Tom, about the smug attitude of some priests is true. It seems to me that most of the nuns in this county are light years ahead of the clergy in the matter of continuing education."

"Yes, isn't it sad that they can't be ordained?" Tom asked.

I replied, "You won't get any argument from me, Tom, but that's not going to happen for a long, long time." I finished my drink, then rose from the chair. "Well, let's eat. I'm starved and I think you are too. Then let's talk about Kate Green, whom you want to marry." Tom nodded in agreement.

After we said grace, I started carving the chicken, and proceeded to place the slices of white and dark meat on a platter. Tom served up the salad and spooned some macaroni onto my plate and then his own.

"How is your mother, Tom?"

"Thanks for asking," he replied. "Well, she's still taking my dad's death very hard even though she knew he would never recover from Alzheimer's."

"How old was your father when the disease began to affect him?"

"He was fifty-nine and died six years later. Those were tough years. Fortunately, my mother had the financial resources to take care of him at home."

"Tom, your mother is very lucky. I hope you understand what I am saying."

"I do. Alzheimer's is one hell of a disease. Sometimes it can last for fifteen or twenty years."

"Very true," I said, "and drain away family resources. And work a terrible hardship on care givers."

"Right. But my family, as you know, is quite affluent. So money problems aren't my worry. What I worry about is how my mother will take my wanting to leave and marry Kate."

"Tom," I said, "she will be just fine. She's a woman of faith who probably thinks you should be married."

"I wish I could be as confident as you, Archbishop."

"Tom, would I bore you if I told you a story from my own experience?"

"No, please do," Tom said.

"Well, some twenty years ago," I began, "a priest friend of mine who was ordained for a religious order in Ireland came to America and was assigned to teach at a Catholic college in the East. He fell in love with a woman on the faculty and the two decided that they wanted to get married. Mike—that's the name of this priest—went back to County Galway and told his widowed mother."

"How did she take it?" Tom asked.

"She said to her son, 'Michael, I don't have many more years to live. But I could never die in peace knowing you were unhappy.'"

"Did they get married?"

"Yes, they did and had a son whom they took to Ireland a couple of times before she died as a very happy mother and a very happy grandmother."

"Thanks for telling that story," Tom said. "It helps a lot."

Tom sipped his drink. "This whole celibacy thing bothers me," he said. "It should be optional. Why should I be forced to live a celibate life in order to be a priest?"

"I can't argue with that," I said, "but under the present pope, the Vatican will never approve such a radical change in policy. And even if the pope would die tomorrow, changing that policy wouldn't happen overnight. "

I rose from the table to get the coffee pot from the side table. As I filled Tom's cup, I said, "Tom, let's talk about you and Kate and your decision to phase out of the priesthood. I have known you a long time and I'm sure you arrived at your decision after prayer, reflection and consultation. So my only question is, how can I be of help in expediting your request for laicization?"

Tom said that the death of Cardinal Mohr complicated matters. "Whom do I see at the chancery office to expedite the paper work?" he asked. "That place leaks like a sieve. If I let someone there know I'm leaving, it will be all over the diocese before I'm ready to have that happen."

"Unfortunately, that's true," I said. "Some guys in the chancery just love to pass on confidential information like that. They ask a priest friend not to say anything. He in turn tells another priest friend and asks him to keep it secret. Soon fifteen guys are in on the secret. And so it goes."

After a brief pause, I continued. "Tell you what I've already done, Tom. Right after you called me, I asked the chancellor to send me the forms that Rome wants submitted. He might be wondering if I'm leaving and asking to be laicized so I can get married. But he didn't have the guts to ask and I didn't tell him the documents are for someone else. This is going to be fun."

"Archbishop, you're a genius. There's something Machiavellian in this, if you know what I mean."

"Yes, I do, Tom, and I take no offense in your comparing me to Machiavelli," I said laughingly. "That poor chancellor is probably having some sleepless nights wondering if at eighty I'm going to get married. I can just imagine him worrying about the headlines and news coverage. How old is Foley's bride-to-be? Will he start a family? Is she pregnant? He might like to leak this information to the press, but he wouldn't dare."

The two of us laughed like two teenagers planning a Halloween prank. Then we helped ourselves to two servings of the baked chicken. A little later I removed the dinner plates and went back to the refrigerator for the strawberry shortcake. "Would you like some Reddi-Wip on the strawberries, Tom?" I asked.

"Yes, but not too much. Have to watch my cholesterol."

"More coffee, Tom?"

"Yes, but let me get it, Archbishop."

As Tom reached for my cup, I said to him, "Tom, tell me about Kate Green. How did you two meet?"

"Well, Kate is a professor of English at the University. When I was Newman chaplain there over five years ago, Kate and I served on a few committees together. She often came to the social functions and lecture series sponsored by the Newman Center or by the University. Sometimes our students went to other colleges for cultural or social events and Kate came along."

"Did the students like her?"

"Very much," Tom said, "because she was so competent and articulate, and she respected the opinions of others. And she's very attractive. She lights up a room when she enters it."

"And those good looks are what captured you," I said with a smile.

"Not entirely," Tom said. "I admit that I was physically attracted to her, but there was one incident that convinced me that she was the kind of woman I could really be happy with."

"What happened?"

"Kate was chairing a meeting of the college-wide curriculum committee of twenty faculty members. I was a member. About a half hour into the meeting, a door opened and a little African American boy, about three years old, walked in crying his eyes out. He was lost and terrified. Kate went over to him, picked him up, sat him on her lap, dried his tears, and tried to calm his fears. Then she stood up, told the group to take a fifteen-minute break, and carried that little boy into the crowded hallway. Ten minutes later when the group reassembled, she reported that she met a frantic woman in the hall who was searching for her lost son."

"So that incident told you there was something special about Kate," I said.

"Yes, it did. She could easily have passed that little boy to someone else who could have gone out and looked for his mother. After all, she was chairing a very important meeting. But she saw there was something much more important. A little kid was lost and lonely—and terrified—and his mother had to be found. And Kate found her. And I found Kate."

"So, Tom, you think of yourself as a lost and lonely kid?"

"Well, I guess you could say that's true. Yes, I do," Tom said. "When I entered the priesthood, I thought the fraternity of the priesthood would cure the loneliness, but for me it hasn't. And I think most of the priests I know would say the same thing."

"That's very honest, Tom, but let me clarify something. You're not looking for someone to mother you, are you?"

"No, I'm not, although the example I gave might give that impression. Kate and I can relate to one another on many levels. We can discuss music, films, art, politics, sports, literature. She's multi-dimensional, and to be candid, so am I. Our marriage will be a very nurturing relationship for me, and I think, for her."

"That's great, Tom. Too often that's not the case."

"Archbishop," Tom said, "there's something I want you to know about Kate and me. It's not just physical attraction; it's sexual attraction, and it's strong."

"Tom, you don't have to tell me about your sexual intimacy with Kate."

"But I want to because it's one of the reasons why I am seeking a dispensation," Tom said. "You know that my family is affluent. I own a condominium in Lake Chautauqua which is about a three-hour drive from Forest Park. Once or twice a month, on weekends, I drive up there just to get away from the office. Kate drives up and stays overnight. But neither she nor I are happy with these secret meetings. We long for the day when we can be upfront about our relationship. That's one of the main reasons I am asking for a dispensation."

"I applaud that honesty, Tom. I know some priests who have girlfriends whom they lead along, promising that someday they will get married. They have no intention of getting married. They want to have one foot in the priesthood and one foot in the single life. I pity the women who get involved with such hypocrites."

"So do I and so does Kate. That's why I want out now."

"Well, Tom, sometimes these requests take years. Can you and Kate give it three years?" I asked.

"No. We'll give it a few months at most—maybe until the end of this year. If permission isn't granted by then, I'll resign and Kate and I will be married by a justice of the peace or by a minister."

"Tom, that's exactly what I would do. But let me move on to

another concern I have. How does she feel about this business of going to Rome for a dispensation so the two of you can be married?"

"Well, she's not thrilled. She's Catholic, but her roots in religion are different from mine. She thinks it's ridiculous to send all these documents to Rome. Why can't someone over here give me the dispensation?"

"An excellent question. As you probably know, a number of bishops, myself included, have been asking that same question for years. But the Vatican won't budge on this."

"It's about control, isn't it?"

"That's the way many would interpret it, Tom. But, tell me, what do you and Kate plan to do after you receive the dispensation?"

"Well, we'd like you to witness our marriage vows in a small private ceremony, if you will. Then we'll be off to Chicago, where I'll complete my doctoral studies at Northwestern. Kate has tenure here and could remain as an associate professor of English. But she'll resign and go with me to Chicago until I get my doctorate. There are plenty of colleges and universities in Chicago that would be happy to have Kate on the faculty."

"That's good," I said. "And, Tom, I'm honored that you asked me to be part of this great occasion. Of course, I accept. When do I meet your bride?"

"Soon, I hope, Archbishop. Kate's been so overwhelmed with correcting exams and committee reports that she's had very few nights free. But we'll set up something soon."

"Good, Tom. I look forward to that. In the meantime, take this questionnaire that I got from the chancery office. Fill it out and bring it to me along with all the documents the Vatican requests. I have some good contacts in Rome. People who know how to short cut the system. And now I'll have to cut short this conversation. I have some letters to write."

"And miles to go before you sleep," Tom said. "Good night,

Archbishop. Thanks again, and please convey my thanks to Mrs. Lacey for a great supper."

"That I will," I said. "Good night, Tom."

I retired to my office and wrote a number of letters to priests and bishops in Africa and Asia who were requesting money for projects dealing with AIDS prevention, education, human rights. I enclosed a check for a small amount in each envelope, sealed them and then went to the den to watch TV. After I surfed for a minute, I turned it off and just sat back in my chair to reflect on the day's events, particularly the meeting with Tom.

Why does the clergy have to lose a talented man like Tom Rinehart just because he wants to get married? What is more natural than that? And if Jesus wanted only celibate males in the priesthood why were all the apostles except John married? At least that's what tradition tells us. Rinehart asked if the Vatican's stance on mandatory celibacy is about control. He was nice enough not to pin me down when I evaded the question. Yes, it's about control, and I should have said so. And it's also about punishment. A priest who is laicized is told he must not celebrate Mass, must not preach, must not administer the sacraments. The Vatican is saying to him, "You're a traitor and we're going to punish you." Yet I know some priests who don't keep their vow of celibacy, or who never read a book, and utter all kinds of inanities in their sermons, and we keep them. At their funerals the choir sings "Thou art a priest forever." But the wife and family of a man like Tom Rinehart will never hear those words, all because he got married. How absurd!

CHAPTER 14

In April, a few weeks after Tom visited with me, the mail carrier delivered a new book written by Eugene Kennedy titled *The Unhealed Wound*, which I had ordered after reading a review of it in the National Catholic Reporter. I ripped off the wrapping and started thumbing through it. The words on the inside cover of the dust jacket intrigued me, made me want to read more: "The pain of the unhealed wound in human sexuality is felt everywhere. It is not inflicted by Jesus who wants us to be whole and free of sin's burden, but by Church leaders who control people by manipulating their sexual feelings. They make good people feel bad for being human and sexual at the same time." I sat back and reflected on what I had just read.

This is going to be an interesting book. I'd like to start it right now, but Toni should be here soon. A very intelligent young girl– not afraid to ask me tough questions. I wish I had her around when I was running this archdiocese. She would have been open and direct, not like some of the men I had around me. In retrospect, I believe most were afraid of me. Afraid they would lose their jobs. Afraid they wouldn't be advanced. I was at fault. Probably too businesslike. Too much Type A in me.

A knock on my office door brought me back to the business at hand. I rose from my chair, opened wide the door, and smiled a welcome to Toni. She smiled in return, but she looked a little downcast.

"Toni," I said, "I know that you called your grandmother from school earlier today and that she told you about what happened at the sentencing this morning."

"Yes, I know that my mom and Randy pleaded guilty to the

armed robbery charge, so there won't be a trial. Grandma said Randy will get ten years in the State prison without parole. And Mom got probation."

"Yes, but she'll have to spend at least a year of rehabilitation in a halfway house for women. If she gets good evaluations, she could be released in less than a year."

Toni listened attentively. Finally she said, "How did my grandma take it?"

"Well, under the circumstances she took it very well. She's glad your mother got probation since she could have been doing time in the State prison. The halfway house is about sixty miles away and it's a good treatment center. Your grandmother is also happy that Randy won't be around for ten years."

"Not as happy as I am!" Toni said. "I'll be over twenty-one when he gets out, and that means I won't have to live with him if my mother decides to stay married to him. Which I hope she doesn't. He's bad news. I think the judge should have given him life without hope of parole. That creep tried to make out with me. I was afraid he would rape me if he got the chance."

"Did your mother know that?" I asked, unable to conceal my surprise.

"Not at the time," Toni said. "I told her when I visited her at the Justice Center. She went ballistic when I laid that news on her."

"That must have been a shock to her. Maybe that explains why she seemed so mad at Randy in court this morning."

We sat in silence for a few minutes. She seemed to want to stay, but I felt she wanted to close the conversation about her mother and Randy.

Toni and I had been having our "honest conversations" for about three months now. We usually started out chatting about something inconsequential before launching into deeper issues. But sometimes we just chatted. I looked forward to her visits. It was like having the granddaughter I never had. I found myself bragging about her when I talked to friends who have children or grandchildren.

After we had sat quietly for several minutes, I said, "By the way, Toni," I said. "Have you and your grandmother seen any good movies lately?"

"Aha! Are you checking up on the kind of rating it had?" She had moved quickly into her teasing mode. "Well, it sure wasn't porn. Might have had an R rating—you know—'restricted.' Kids my age can't get in unless accompanied by an adult."

"Toni, you *were* kidding about checking up on you, weren't you?"

She made a face as if trying to decide whether she was serious.

"I had too much of that when I was your age," I said. "Church authorities and Hollywood producers established what they called the Legion of Decency. They used a rating system to evaluate current movies and printed the results in the weekly diocesan paper. My parents always checked the paper before I went off to a movie. So, is the movie you saw one that I would like to see?"

"Do you like karate, Bishop?"

"Not really, but I've only seen one karate movie; and I can't say I liked it. But I haven't closed my mind to all karate movies. What's the name of this one?"

"It's called *Crouching Tiger, Hidden Dragon*. Grandma didn't like it, but it was my turn to choose a movie. She chooses next. If a Disney movie is around, that's what we'll probably see."

"Well, Toni, I think it's great that you go to the movies together and that you can choose what you want to see."

"Yeah, but I have to be careful," Toni said with a mischievous little laugh.

"What do you mean?"

"Well, I mean—well, once I chose one with a lot of sex and heavy breathing. Grandma wasn't too pleased. She has a lot of hang-ups about sex."

I waited for her to continue.

After a moment of silence, Toni said, "Bishop, since this is an honest conversation, I mean, you know, you probably have a lot of hang-ups about sex too."

I hoped my expression did not change. I didn't want to show that her statement surprised me. I parried her statement with a question.

"Why do you say that?"

"Well, you know, Catholic kids at school talk about what the Church teaches, and it's mostly about sex."

"For example?"

"Well, I mean, they're always talking about things like having sex before marriage. Is that a mortal sin?"

"Look, Toni, I can understand how two young people can be very attracted to each other and have intercourse without intending to go that far. Sex is one of the most powerful drives in human nature. Keeps the human race going. So tell me, Toni, what should the Church tell her people about it?"

"I don't know what you mean," she answered somewhat caught off guard.

"What I mean, Toni, is this: Should the Church say absolutely nothing about sex? Should we take it off the table and not even discuss it?"

"Of course not."

"What then should we say?"

"Well, I mean, I haven't thought that much about it, so I don't know what the Church should say."

"Well, suppose churchmen like me said, 'Kids, you're high school students now and you are mature enough to have babies and start families. So go ahead and have sex, enjoy yourselves. Make babies. The more the merrier.' Should we tell them that?"

Toni thought for a minute and said, "If the Church did that, it ought to tell them to use condoms or birth control pills."

"And how effective are they?"

"Well, most of the time they work, but sometimes they don't, I guess. The girl gets pregnant and has to make some tough decisions."

"Like what?"

"Like dropping out of school and having a baby without being married," Toni said

"Is that a good thing?"

"Bishop," Toni replied rather sharply, "you know it's not, so why even ask that question?"

I decided not to let her get away with that remark. I leaned forward and said, "Toni, I thought this is supposed to be an honest conversation. So are you telling me that certain questions that are out of bounds? "

"Yeah, I see what you mean. I shouldn't have said that. Sorry."

"That's all right, Toni. But tell me, what other options does the pregnant young girl have?"

"Well, her boy friend could also leave school. They could get married—but I don't think that would be good."

"Why not, they would be together, wouldn't they?"

"Sure," she said, "but what kind of future would they have? They'd probably have to move in with her parents, if her parents would have them."

"What if her boy friend decided that he wanted to graduate and go to college so he could have a better career?" I asked.

"Well," Toni explained, "that can happen and did happen to a friend of mine. She stayed home with her parents and had a baby girl—a darling baby. Her boyfriend went away to college and fell in love with a college girl. Broke off with my friend. She was so depressed she almost . . . took her own life. A woman counselor at school got her into therapy. I think she's going to be OK."

"Good," I said. "I hope your friend gets her life together and maybe meets a young man who can be a good husband and father."

"So, do I. But what guy's going to want to marry her—with another guy's baby and all?"

"Well," I said, "maybe someone will." I paused. "There's another option for a girl who is pregnant, isn't there?"

"Yes, Bishop, there's abortion. I don't know what to believe about it. I mean, you know, part of me says it's OK. The woman should have control over her body, but the other part of me says it's wrong because it's the taking of a human life. I'm still sorting it out."

"That's good, Toni."

"Bishop, I can't believe you said that."

"You expected me to give the party line on abortion. Right?"

"I guess so," she replied.

"Toni, I'm not going to do that. I want you to figure out for yourself what to believe. So go to the library and ask for some material on the abortion issue, both pro and con. Read the material and reflect on it. I have some materials on it if you like, but I think you should start your own research."

"OK, Bishop, I'll do that."

"And, Toni, I know that at times we churchmen through our statements and our preaching give the impression that the most important and most serious sins are sexual sins, but they aren't. Abortion, sex before marriage, adultery can all be serious sins. But generally—and notice I said generally— these sins are committed not out of malice but from human weakness. People often panic, commit them in moments of great passion or great fear. For example, remember that pregnant teen-age girl in a Catholic high school who had a baby in a lavatory and then stuffed the infant in a garbage bag?"

"Yeah, I sure do. You think she did this out of weakness?"

"Yes, I do. I think she couldn't face her parents and her classmates, so she killed her child. She did it out of fear, not malice."

"Well, give me an example of someone doing something out of malice."

"All right, in the Bible Cain murders his brother Abel out of jealousy. Remember that story?"

"Sure I do, but give me some modern examples."

"All right, parents who seriously neglect their children. Companies that deceive their customers about a product that could cause serious harm. Employers who don't pay their help a living wage or fire an employee without giving the employee a hearing. Adult children who refuse to visit or to help their parents in their old age. Writers who plagiarize material that others wrote. I could go on and on. . . ."

Toni sat quietly for a moment, pondering these ideas. "Is it OK if I go back to abortion and condoms?" she asked.

"Sure, Toni."

"Well, I mean, you know, sometimes what the Church teaches doesn't make sense to us kids."

"For example."

"Well there's this girl at school who has had two abortions. She talks about it with her friends, so it's no big secret. One of her friends asked her why she doesn't use the pill or have her boyfriend use a condom. Do you know what she said?"

"No, what did she say?" I guessed what was coming.

"She said she couldn't use birth control because she's a Catholic and birth control is a mortal sin. Now, Bishop, that doesn't make sense to me."

"Nor does it make sense to me. Abortion is also a mortal sin. I think the young lady needs to speak to a counselor who knows what the Church teaches about premarital sex."

"Gosh, I wish we could keep talking, Bishop, but my history teacher wants us to watch a program tonight on the History Channel. It starts at eight o'clock. If it's OK, I'll see you the day after tomorrow. We can talk more about sex and other things at that time. Good night, Bishop." She quickly got up and left the room.

"Good night, Toni," I said.

She was almost out the door when she turned around and threw me a kiss.

Her gesture surprised me and filled me with such feelings of warmth that my eyes filled with tears. I felt envious of men my age who had granddaughters and grandsons whom they could affectionately kiss or hug. I would have loved to hug Toni as I would a grandchild—to return her affection and her love. However, that might be misinterpreted by others. That's a price that even a priest in his eighties has to pay for celibacy.

I decided to sit back and quietly reflect on this conversation with Toni. That was a good session. She certainly knows a lot about the Church's teaching on sex, or at least appears to know. I hope she reads that material on the abortion issue and comes to her own conclusion. Naturally, I hope she will agree with the Church's position. What I want her to do is to have a reason for her position. I don't want her to say I believe this because the Catholic Church teaches this. Nor do I want her to say I believe in abortion because this is the teaching of the National Organization of Women. I want her to look at the arguments advanced by those who are pro-life and those who are pro-choice.

I want her to grow up to be a critical thinker like Eugene Kennedy who in this book has the guts to challenge the official church on celibacy and the ordination of women. His book, I think, is going to help me become more of the critical thinker I should have been. I hope these sessions with Toni are good for her; they certainly have been good for me.

CHAPTER 15

Both Tom and Kate were unhappy about having to apply to Rome for his dispensation from his vow of celibacy, but Tom thought his mother, a staunch Catholic from childhood, would accept his leaving the priesthood more easily if she knew he had gone through the proper channels. He had put aside the questionnaire I had given him to complete back in March. It was almost June, and he hadn't returned it. I said nothing. Whether he returned it or not was entirely his decision.

Finally, in early June, Tom dropped off the completed questionnaire requesting laicization from the Vatican along with his baptismal certificate, parents' marriage certificate, ordination certificate, and letters from professionals supporting his request to be returned to the lay state. Included with these documents was a letter to the pope detailing his reasons for seeking laicization.

As I looked over the material, some statements in Rinehart's letter and some of his answers on the questionnaire raised red flags. "Better get in touch with Tom at the chancery office," I thought.

I had to go through two secretaries to reach Tom. "Hello, Tom. I wonder if you could stop over to see me some time. I need your advice on an important issue. Are you free for lunch today?"

"Good to hear your voice, Archbishop," answered Tom, sounding genuinely pleased that I called. "Hold on for a minute and I'll check my calendar." A minute later he was back. "I can make it if it's an early lunch. I have to be back at 1:30 for an urgent meeting on diocesan finances."

I laughed and said, "Well, Tom, I wouldn't want you to miss that meeting. Can you be here at 11:45 and stay for lunch?"

"I'll be there," Tom said. "Tell Mrs. Lacey something simple—

soup and salad, maybe—will work for me."

He said goodbye and hung up. From experience, I learned not to say too much when connected to the chancery office. Priests and secretaries there sometimes hear parts of conversations and jump to conclusions and spread rumors that are often not based in fact. I was being very discreet and knew that Tom would be discreet as well.

Shortly after 11:30 AM, Mrs. Lacey greeted Tom, who thanked her for preparing their lunch.

"I always know I'm in for a first-class dining experience when I'm invited to Haley House," he said. Genuinely pleased with the compliment, she led him to my office. I rose from my desk and shook hands with Tom.

"Tom, I know you don't have much time, so let's go into the dining room. I told Mrs. Lacey you want soup and a salad, but she thinks half of a roast beef sandwich should be included. I'll eat the other half of that sandwich."

"Good," said Tom. "Archbishop, I can't begin to thank you enough for doing an end run around the chancery office. Sorry I didn't get this stuff back to you earlier, but Kate and I wanted time to think over the entire process. As I've told you, we're not happy about it, but we'll give it a try."

Our conversation was interrupted when Mrs. Lacey brought in a tureen of chicken rice soup, the roast beef sandwich and salad. As she left, she closed the door to the dining room, picking up signals that this was to be a very private conversation.

We said grace, and as I ladled soup into the bowls, I said, "Tom, I looked over the material you left this morning. All in all, it looks good. But before I can send it to my friend in Rome, who will walk the documents over to the Vatican, there are a couple of places where the priests judging your case might have some problems."

"Such as?" asked Tom.

"Well. Tom, in your letter to the pope, you implicitly criticize Cardinal Mohr. You must never, under any circumstance, criticize a member of the hierarchy."

"Hold on, Archbishop Foley, I didn't criticize the cardinal!"

"Tom, I know you didn't, so calm down. In your letter you say that you pleaded with Cardinal Mohr not to make you his secretary, but he did."

"That's right, I did."

"Well, Tom, you're calling into question the judgment of the cardinal, and someone in the Vatican who will be deciding your case could interpret that as criticism."

Tom was stunned. When he recovered, he said, "What a hell of a system! What kind of a game is this? The guys at the top are always right and the guys at the bottom like me can never say, No you are not always right. It stinks. I don't like this."

"And, Tom, neither do I, but if you want to get laicized, you have to play the game according to their rules. Tom, you're a shrewd man. Rewrite the letter and soften that paragraph about Cardinal Mohr making you his secretary despite your objections. If you can, write a couple of drafts, and I'll be glad to review them."

Tom's anger had abated. "I'll try to do that, Archbishop. I'll drop off the drafts on my way to the chancery tomorrow. Anything else I need to change?"

"Yes, there is, Tom. Somewhere in your letter or your questionnaire, the folks in Rome want you to say you can't keep the vow of celibacy."

I was not prepared for Tom's sudden burst of anger. "God dammit. I've kept the vow of celibacy for ten years. But I now have fallen in love with a woman and I want to get married. My sex life is none of their goddamned business. If discussing it with them is what it takes to get laicized, then I say to hell with it. I won't do it."

"And neither would I." I rose from the table, went to the coffee urn and poured some coffee into the cups Mrs. Lacey had set at one end of the table. I hoped the pause would give Tom a chance to settle down. "Look, Tom, this has to be demeaning. You don't like it and neither do I. So let's strategize for a moment. Could you write that you have asked Kate to marry you and that you are unwilling to renege on your promise to her? Just put it that way, plain and simple."

"Will that work?"

"Maybe. I'm not sure. But at least you're telling the truth. Maybe some guys in Rome who are judging your case will see that you're a man of integrity. That may not get their approval but it will certainly get their respect."

"Well," Tom said rather sarcastically. "Let's not hold our breath. You mentioned there's one other item in my documents that also causes you concern."

"Yes, Tom, in your letter to the pope you state that there will be a minimum of scandal because when you go to Northwestern for your doctoral studies Kate will resign her position as an associate professor here so as not to give any scandal."

"That's right."

"Tom, what I'm going to say next might cause you to hit the ceiling, but don't even mention her in your letter except to say that you will not renege on your promise to marry her. To those men, the pope included, Kate's giving up her job is not at all important. Doesn't count."

Tom took in that information without flinching, but I could see that my friend was about to explode.

When we finished our coffee, Tom said, "Archbishop, I do have to get to that finance meeting, and I don't want to be late. I'd like a little time to sort out what you said about my rewriting part of the forms you'll be sending on to Rome. So would you mind if I stopped in later this evening to discuss it further?"

"Not at all, Tom. Why not come by around nine?"

"I'll be here, Archbishop. And don't bother seeing me to the door," he said as he left the room. "I'll stop in the kitchen to thank Mrs. Lacey and go out the back way."

After lunch, I went back to the office and resumed reading Kennedy's *The Unhealed Wound*. When I was head of the archdiocese, I had to read so much material that I became a speed reader without ever taking a speed reading course. Although I began reading the book just a day ago, I had read more than half of it. I decided to finish it that afternoon, but around four I grew so drowsy that I decided to lie down on the sofa in my office. I quickly fell asleep and slept longer than I intended. It was almost 6:00 PM when Mrs. Lacey found me stretched out on the sofa. She called out to me and I awakened immediately.

Looking at my watch I realized she would be serving dinner within a few minutes. "Mrs. Lacey, I'm sorry but I'll be twenty minutes late for dinner. I need to freshen up."

"That's all right, your Grace, just ring the bell on the dining room table when you're ready."

After a dinner of meatloaf, mashed potatoes, and a salad, I had dessert and tea. When I left the table, I went into the kitchen to apologize to Mrs. Lacey for my tardiness and to tell her someone would be coming at about nine.

"I'll answer the door. So when you're finished in the kitchen, why don't you go up to your suite and relax? You probably have a favorite TV program you'd like to watch before you retire."

Mrs. Lacey, a perceptive woman, knew I was protecting the identity of the nine o'clock visitor, so she said, "Thank you, your Grace. Yes, there is a good movie on at eight. I'll say goodnight now."

I said goodnight and went to my study to finish reading Kennedy's *The Unhealed Wound*. I had just finished reading the last page when the doorbell rang. I got up and answered it. It was Tom, as I expected.

"Come in, Tom, can I get you something to drink?"

"No, Archbishop, I won't take much of your time."

"Take as much time as you want. I'm retired. Let's not stand here by the door. Come into my office and tell me what you decided."

"Good," Tom said and followed me down the hall to my office.

When we were seated, Tom said, "After the finance meeting this afternoon, I called Kate at her office and told her I'd like to see her. We met at the college cafeteria for dinner. Kate and I have been on a number of projects at the University, so college people are accustomed to seeing us together. We would really have raised some eyebrows if we had met at a quiet corner in some restaurant. There are probably some rumors about us floating around right now. But we don't want to do anything to feed them."

"I applaud your prudence, Tom, and Kate's, too. Now tell me, if you can, what you and Kate decided."

"Sure. Well, we had a long talk about the request for laicization. We have decided to go ahead with it, but we're not going to change a word in the material I sent you."

"May I ask you why?"

"Certainly. The whole process is so demeaning. The guys over there seem to want to control my answers. Isn't it absurd that I can't write anything that would even imply a criticism of a cardinal or bishop? Have these bastards forgotten that in the Acts of the Apostles Paul severely criticized Peter?"

"They remember, Tom, but their memories are selective. Getting scriptural bothers some clerics unless it's convenient for them to be quoting it."

"I refuse to respond to that question about celibacy, Archbishop. It's like that old question—When did you stop beating your wife? I refuse to play their games. They want me to be the heavy in this scenario. They want me to admit that I have had some psychosexual disorder since birth and that I should not have been ordained in the first place. Well, I'm not going to do that."

"How did Kate take the suggestion that she doesn't count with the pope or with the priests who will be deciding your case?"

"Well, at first she was hurt and then angry. She's Irish and can really boil over at times. She's not angry at you, Archbishop, but at the whole damned system that says to women that they don't count. She's had it and wants to keep that part about her in the letter."

"All right, Tom. Tell Kate I won't change a 'jot or a tittle'—to get scriptural again. I'll send everything over just as you wrote it. Let's see how it plays out and go from there."

"Good, Archbishop. It's been a long day for both of us so I'm going to say good night. I can find my way out."

I rose from my chair, shook hands with him and said, "Good night, Tom, and God bless."

After Tom left Haley House, I decided to forego watching the late evening news. I wanted to reflect on the day's events.

After reading Kennedy's book, I can't fault Tom and Kate for their unwillingness to change anything in Tom's application. It's been over five years since I have handled a request for laicization and I'm embarrassed to admit now that I agreed to send those requests to the Vatican. Kennedy's book makes me realize more clearly that the whole process is about control. Tom saw that even without reading Kennedy's book. Why didn't I? Why did I buy into that nonsense? I admire Kate for being angry that a reference to her has to be deleted from the letter because the pope and the men over there believe she does not count. How did we as a Church of Jesus ever come to this?

After pondering that question for a couple of minutes I knew the answer. It came to this because people like me let it happen. We gave away power. We gradually turned the decision making process over to the Vatican. Why must a man like Rinehart submit his case to Rome when the matter could be decided right here by some regional office in the United States? Why can't we just honor Rinehart's request to get married and thank him for the service he has rendered to the Catholic Church? There is not a word of thanks in the rescript granting the request for laicization–just a series of petty punitive actions that attempt to lay a guilt trip on the priest who wants to exercise a basic human right, the right to marry. Is not that a greater sin than the sexual sins Toni and I discussed the other evening? And I was an integral part of that dysfunctional system. Mea culpa.

CHAPTER 16

One June evening shortly before the end of the school year, Mrs. Lacey served a picnic supper on the screened-in patio to celebrate Toni's sixteenth birthday. Kate and Tom gave her a book of poetry that she had wanted to buy in the University book store, and the Kolars gave her an attractive pair of earrings. Her grandmother, having learned that selecting clothing for a teenager is a no-win task, gave her a gift certificate to her favorite shop in a nearby mall. My gift to Toni was a beautifully bound Bible and reservations for dinner at an elegant restaurant for Mrs. Lacey and Toni.

After the guests had left and we had helped clear the table and carry dishes to the kitchen, I returned to the patio to relax. Toni said, "Bishop, mind if I join you for a while?"

"Not at all. Pull up a chair," I said, pleased that she wanted to talk. "What's up?"

"This afternoon, my born-again friends and I had a rather heated discussion about the Catholic Church. They know I'm living here and want you to answer some questions. I wrote them down so I wouldn't forget them."

"Toni, what questions do your friends want answered?"

"Well, I mean, they're in no particular order. Like why does the pope call himself His Holiness? Like, isn't only God holy?"

"Toni, we discussed that the other night with the term 'most reverend' applied to me, an archbishop. I don't like the term and I suspect the pope doesn't like the term 'his holiness,' but there isn't much he can do about it just as I can't help it if people insist on calling me Most Reverend Archbishop Edward Foley."

"Well, you know, I'm not sure the born-agains will buy that," she said, "but I'll run it by them and let you know. They also want to know why the pope has Swiss Guards to defend him. Didn't Jesus say those who live by the sword will perish by it?"

"Yes, he did, but those guards aren't part of any papal army as they once were. They're there to protect the person of the pope."

Toni frowned and wrinkled her nose. "Why? I mean, is that necessary?"

"Toni, a public person such as a president or a pope is always in need of protection. You weren't born when President Kennedy was assassinated in 1963. Then in 1981 President Ronald Reagan was nearly assassinated shortly after he took office as president. He took a bullet but survived. And a few years later President Gerald Ford escaped being killed by a deranged woman who was determined to kill him. Pope John Paul II survived an attempt on his life. He also took a bullet. It's too bad our presidents and popes need to be protected by Secret Service agents or Swiss Guards, but that's reality."

"OK. That makes sense to me but, I'm not sure my friends will buy that," Toni said.

"That's their right. I wouldn't try to argue that point."

"All right, but they've seen pictures of the Vatican on TV, like those treasures in the Vatican museum. They've seen the pope saying Mass in Saint Peter's surrounded by cardinals and bishops and priests in beautiful vestments. They see all this wealth and want to know why all these things aren't sold and the money given to the poor."

"Over the centuries, Toni, a lot of people like Martin Luther have asked the same question. He went to Rome in the sixteenth century and was simply shocked and appalled at the extravagant lifestyles of the pope and some cardinals. It's one of the reasons why he broke with the Catholic Church and started the Lutheran Church and the Protestant Reformation."

"What did the Catholic Church do about that?" Toni asked.

"They called a Council at a place called Trent and assembled all the bishops. They met over a period of fifteen years and made laws to eliminate these abuses."

"Did the Council succeed?" Toni asked.

"I think some historians would agree it did," I said. "For example, the bishops made some strict laws about the education of priests in seminaries. They wanted to weed out those who were morally and intellectually unfit for the priesthood. And I think the Council of Trent did that."

"OK," Toni said, "but that was then and this is now. The born agains think that the Catholic Church today still has too much wealth. What do I tell them?"

"Tell them to be fair minded," I replied. "Tell them to look at all the hospitals, hospices, schools and orphanages that the Church supports all over the world. Ask them, for example, about the work of Mother Teresa and the sisters in Calcutta and other cities throughout the world. They minister to those who are living and dying in the most desperate situations. Many of our Catholic schools are giving poor children a very good education. They can do this—and have done this for years—because men and women in religious orders have worked for salaries far below what they could earn in public schools. They make these sacrifices because they have a great love of the poor."

"My friends are always saying the Catholic Church is a Church of the rich."

"Well, at certain times and in certain places throughout history, that's true. Take Cuba, for example. It's now a Communist country under Fidel Castro, who overthrew a government that kept a few rich Catholic families in power. These families owned most of the land. Unfortunately, the Catholic Church in Cuba was closely allied with that oppressive government."

"Bishop, when people see those pictures from the Vatican on TV, wouldn't they conclude the Church today is a Church of the rich?"

"Yes, they could. Some Catholics who have been to the

Vatican think there is too much ritual, too much pomp and ceremony. They're embarrassed by all the attention and deference given to the pope—almost as if he is some superhuman person."

"Are you embarrassed when you go to Rome?"

"Yes, sometimes I am. I think Jesus would be too. I don't like all that shouting, 'Long live the pope!' in seven or eight different languages, but what can I or anyone else do to stop it? This custom has been going on for centuries."

"Bishop, the pope could stop it.

"True enough, and some have tried," I said. "There used to be the custom of not only kissing the pope's ring but also his foot."

"How gross!" screamed Toni. "Do they still do that?"

"No, thank God. It's been discontinued," I said. "There also was the custom of six men carrying the pope on a chair when he came into St. Peter's Basilica. My hero, Pope John XXIII, tried to discontinue this practice, but he met with a lot of resistance."

"Who from?"

"Probably from the six men who carried the chair. They didn't want to be out of a job. So reluctantly he kept them on but increased their salary."

"Why did he do that?" Toni asked.

"Because he had a great sense of humor. He was a very short but heavy man, so he figured they should be compensated for carrying the extra weight of the pope," I said with a laugh.

Toni laughed too. "I like him already."

"So did millions of people, Toni. It's too bad that you and your born again friends didn't live in his time. He said the Church had to open its windows and get rid of all the trappings and wealth that have accumulated since the time of Constantine. He wanted the Church to be a Church of the poor. I think if your friends read about Pope John XXIII, maybe they would have a different take on the papacy."

"Well, maybe. But they aren't too fond of this pope, what they know of him."

"What do they know of him?"

"Probably only what they hear from their ministers or read in the newspapers. They know he has traveled a lot. They can understand why he says that women can't be priests because they agree that women should be silent in church. They quote Saint Paul on that. But they can't understand why guys have to take a vow of celibacy if they want to be priests."

"Neither can I," I said, "but I can't say that publicly."

"Why not?"

I got up, poured a glass of water for myself and one for Toni. I was trying to give myself time to think about an answer before expressing it. I sat down.

"Toni, does your school have any policies that many students don't like?"

"Sure. Like a lotta kids would like to leave school at lunch period and go to McDonalds or Burger King for a hamburger and coke, but we're not allowed to."

"Do the teachers uphold that policy or have any come out publicly against it?" I asked.

"No, they haven't."

"Why not?"

"Well, I mean, they're probably afraid of losing their jobs or maybe being suspended."

"Could it also be that they want to be loyal to the administration and not do anything to undermine it?"

"Yeah, I guess so."

"Do you think some of those teachers think the policy should be changed?"

"Sure," she said.

"You're right, Toni, but they don't go public. They work behind the scenes to get the policy changed."

"So your point is that some in the Church like you do the same thing to get policies you don't like changed."

"Exactly," I said. "The Church is a human organization. The

people in it are human and they work in many ways that are similar to other organizations."

"Bishop, my born again friends want me to ask you why you're not married."

"Well, that's an easy one to answer. I'm not married because years ago right before I became a subdeacon, I took a vow to remain celibate for the rest of my life. And I have kept that vow."

"Some of my friends said you—um, well, like—they said you're probably gay. I don't think that," Toni said, "but what should I tell them?"

I smiled and said, "No, I'm not gay. In fact, in my senior year at Notre Dame, I was very much in love with a young lady at St. Mary's, a college right across the road from Notre Dame University. We nearly got engaged, but I broke it off."

"Why?" she asked.

"Because I felt a strong call to become a priest. I thought that the priesthood, not the marriage state, was my vocation."

"How did she take that?"

"Naturally, she took it very hard and so did I, but not enough to spend the rest of her life pining away. Six months later she met a wonderful young man whom she married a couple of years after she graduated from college. They reared six children in Detroit."

"Do you ever see her?"

"No. She died about ten years ago after a long bout with cancer. I officiated at her funeral at Queen of Martyrs Church in Birmingham, Michigan. Her husband died unexpectedly—it was a heart attack, I think—shortly after she died, but I couldn't get to his funeral because I was in Rome at the time."

Toni paused a while to take in this information about me. It did not overwhelm her, but it did surprise her. Then she asked, "Do you ever wonder what it would be like if you had married her? I mean, are you ever sorry you didn't?"

"Well, I have to confess that when I heard she was going to be married, I spent a lot of time wondering about the decision I made to break off the engagement. I was still a couple of years away from ordination, so I could have changed my mind and contacted her. I thought about doing that, but I didn't. Now fifty some years later I know that it was the right decision, not only for me but for her as well."

"Thanks for telling me about that, Bishop. Would you mind if I shared that with my born again friends?"

"Not at all, Toni, provided that you tell them something from me," I said.

"Sure, Bishop, what should I tell them?"

"Tell them to stop making judgments about whether people are straight or gay. Remind them that Jesus said we should not judge lest we be judged," I said with just a trace of anger.

"That question about you being gay upset you, didn't it, Bishop?"

"No, I didn't take it personally. But what I want to get across to them is that they shouldn't rush to judgment about a person's sexual orientation just because he or she isn't married. Some people don't get married because they don't want to take on the obligations of marriage. Some straight people remain single to support their elderly parents. I know single working women who share an apartment, not because they are lesbians, but to save money. And even if they are lesbians who have a sexual attraction to one another, why should that concern you, me, or your born again friends?"

"Bishop, I mean, doesn't the Bible condemn homosexuals and lesbians?"

"Well, Toni, there are passages in the Old Testament and in Saint Paul in the New Testament which some scholars use to condemn homosexual activity, but we can't find any words of Jesus on the subject."

"My born again friends would be interested in knowing what Bishop Foley says on the subject. What do I tell them?"

"Toni, tell them that there was a time in my life when I was absolutely convinced that homosexual activity was a serious sin, which I condemned. But I never condemned the homosexual person. I did, however, urge them to repent and change their behavior."

"Wouldn't you do that now?"

"No, I wouldn't," I replied. "I've read many studies of psychologists and psychiatrists whose research shows that homosexuals and lesbians, try as they may, cannot change their sexual orientation."

"Bishop, if that's true, then why does the Bible say homosexuality's wrong?"

"A very good question, Toni, and I must confess I don't know the answer. Not too long ago I raised that question with a well known scripture scholar. He told me that I must never forget the Bible was written by the elite for the elite."

"Bishop, you've lost me. What does that mean?"

"He was saying, I think, that the Bible was written by influential people for other influential people who did not like gays and lesbians and wanted to exclude them from God's kingdom. Do you follow me?"

"Yes, I'm no longer lost," Toni answered.

"Good," I said. "This scripture scholar then told me that the reason Jesus was crucified was that he preached that all people, even gays and lesbians, are welcome members of God's kingdom."

"Do you believe that?"

"Yes, I do."

Looking at her watch, she said, "Bishop, I have to leave right now. You've given me a lot to think about and discuss with my born again friends. Thanks for this most honest of our conversations."

"Thank you. Good night, Toni."

CHAPTER 17

Many years ago when I was taking classes at the seminary, I memorized some famous quotations from literature and history. One I liked was from Samuel Johnson who in 1786 said, "Many things happen between the cup and the lip."

Tom's application for a dispensation seemed to be headed for quick Vatican approval, but something happened a few weeks after we submitted the papers that embittered Tom for many years. I tried to get Tom to let it go, but he couldn't. At about ten one morning in July he called me at Haley House.

"Tom, how are things going? Are you calling about the letters I sent to Rome?"

"No, and by the way, I'm not calling from the chancery office, so the phone is secure."

"Good."

"Archbishop, I know on Wednesdays Mrs. Lacey and her granddaughter go out for an early dinner and a movie. Kate's free this afternoon and evening, so how about meeting at Haley House at about four and going out for dinner? I'll make reservations."

"Excellent! Will you and Kate be coming together?"

"No, she'll be driving from the University, and I'll drive from the chancery office."

"Just park in the back near the garages and come in the back door. I'll leave it unlocked. See you at four." When I hung up I told Mrs. Lacey I would be going out to dinner with some friends.

On two other occasions Tom had planned for the three of us to meet for dinner, but both times he was called to attend emergency meetings at the chancery and had to cancel. Finally, I was going to meet Kate.

At about three-thirty, Kate got into her ten-year-old Mercedes coupe, which was parked in the reserved faculty section of the University, and made a right turn on Monticello Boulevard. After driving a half mile, she pulled over to the side of the road to pick up a young girl who was hitchhiking.

"Hey, thanks for giving me a ride," the girl said as she slid into the front seat.

"How far are you going?"

"Euclid Avenue. Know where that is?"

"Yes, I do. In fact, that's where I turn."

"OK, just drop me off at the corner."

They drove for a few miles in silence. Then the girl said, "Nice car. You must have a good job."

Kate laughed. "Well it is a nice car—but it's ten years old and it's got over 150,000 miles on it. But I can't afford to buy a new one right now. I teach English at the University. What do you do?

"I'll be a junior in high school next year, I mean when school starts."

"Good. Any plans for the future?"

"Yeah, I'd like to make enough money as a model so I can go to medical school and become a brain surgeon."

"That's great," Kate said as she pulled over to the curb. "Here's your stop. I wish you well and hope you accomplish your goals."

The girl thanked her and got out, and Kate drove another two blocks down Euclid Avenue and pulled into the Haley House driveway. She parked the car near the garage and rang the doorbell at the back door. I opened it.

"Hello! You must be Kate Green."

"Indeed, I am, and you must be Archbishop Foley."

"Yes, I am." The warmth in her eyes and in her smile won my approval. "A few minutes ago I got a call from Tom," I told her. "He'll be about twenty minutes late, so why don't we go to my office and wait for him?"

"Fine."

"Kate, would you like something to drink?"

"Yes, a diet Coke would be great."

Just then the phone rang. I answered it and put my hand over the receiver.

"Kate," I said, "this call is going to take a few minutes. Would you mind going to the kitchen and getting the coke from the fridge?"

"No problem, Archbishop."

As she went into the kitchen, she nearly collided with a young girl who was coming in the back way. It was the hitchhiker.

"Hello," Kate said, "we meet again. I'm Kate Green, a friend of the archbishop."

"Hi, I'm Toni Vincent. I live here with my grandmother. I hope you won't tell her I was hitchhiking."

"Toni, I don't tell on people. I teach courses in literature. What I do is try to teach students how to realize that life is about making good choices or bad choices."

"So," Toni asked, "You think hitchhiking is a bad choice?"

"Not always. You were probably rushing back here because you had something very important to do, and the fastest way you could get back was to hitchhike, right?"

Toni never got a chance to answer because I appeared at the door and said, "So, you two have met. Good. Toni, what's the movie you are going to see this evening?"

"All week long they're showing old Humphrey Bogart movies. Tonight's movie is *Casablanca.* About World War II. Grandma wants to see it again. I think she's seen it three times. But I haven't."

"It's a great movie, Toni," said Kate. "I think you'll like it. Ingrid Bergman is superb in the film. You'll have a good evening."

"I hope so. Seeya' in the morning, Bishop. Nice to have met you, Kate."

"Thanks, Toni," Kate said. "I'm sure we'll meet again."

After she left, Kate and I went to my office to wait for Tom.

When she was seated, Kate said, “Toni seems like an interesting girl. It’s nice that you have her living here.”

“Yes, she keeps me on my toes. She and I have a question and answer session a couple times a week. She doesn’t buy into a lot the Church teaches.”

Kate smiled. I sensed she was suppressing the urge to tell me that Toni was her kind of Catholic.

“I know something about Toni Vincent, but I know very little about Kate Green. So let’s talk about you.”

“All right. I was born in Dayton, Ohio, attended a Catholic grade school and high school, and got my bachelor’s degree from Miami U in Ohio. After that I earned a master’s in English at Notre Dame and a doctorate in English at Michigan.”

“That’s a very impressive résumé, Kate. You were quite focused, weren’t you?”

“Yes, I was, Archbishop. When I left Miami, some would say I was a feminist. But I don’t like being put in that box. I was–and am–greatly interested in issues that are important to women, but I’m also interested in issues affecting children, health, the environment, the prison system and many other issues that affect all people regardless of gender. I think some people called me a feminist because I resolved that I was going to establish myself in my own right. I wasn’t going to be dependent upon a man for my livelihood. I resolved to earn a doctorate. I considered marriage a couple of times after I earned my master’s degree. But I knew that if I married, the chances of my going on for a doctorate would be slim to none.”

“Seems you made the right choices every step of the way, Kate.”

“So you would have no problem if I were a dyed-in-the-wool feminist?”

“Of course not, Kate! Should I?”

“Certainly not. You have always had a reputation for supporting women’s rights and independence. Thanks to bishops like you, the Church has come a long way."

"Yes, it has, but we still have a long way to go."

"Do you think in the next twenty or thirty years we'll see women ordained as priests?" Kate asked.

"No, I do not. I hope I'm wrong. It all depends on the next pope and the direction he gives to the Church. However, I wouldn't hold my breath."

"What about married priests?" Kate asked.

"That in my judgment will happen before we have women priests. In fact, it's quietly happening all over the world."

"Yes, I've read a few articles making that claim. Tell me about that, Archbishop."

"Well, bishops in some countries are permitting married priests to celebrate Mass on Sunday. They just don't advertise to the people that the celebrant is a married man."

"Would it make any difference if the people knew?"

"I don't think it would make a particle of difference to most people," I replied. "Many people are ready for a married clergy, but the powers in Rome want to pretend that celibacy reigns supreme."

"So the people in Rome are playing charades."

"I think that says it very nicely." After a slight pause, I continued, "If you don't mind, Kate, tell me how you and Tom became an item." I smiled and said, "I saw that term in a gossip column the other day and thought I'd use it."

Kate laughed. "No, I don't mind telling you how we became 'an item,' as you call it. As you know, Tom was a Newman Center chaplain at the University where I teach. He loved working with college kids. Some years ago he asked me to participate in an interdenominational lecture series at the University. He asked me to help recruit speakers from the University who were from other religions: Anglican, Lutheran, Baptist, Jewish, Congregationalist, Unitarian. Tom didn't impose a series of topics that he thought would be interesting. Rather he sent out a survey and asked the students what they thought should be discussed."

"That's not surprising to me, Kate. Tom is great on building consensus. How did the series go over?"

"It went very well. That's partly because Tom had us–the speakers–meet a few times before we launched the series. The group asked me to be moderator of each session. I didn't need the extra work, but I was hooked when I saw how interested the students were."

"Were these sessions open to students from other denominations?"

"Yes, and that's what hooked me." Kate paused. "And I also got hooked on Tom. He was great to work with and the kids really loved him, Catholics and non-Catholics alike. When the cardinal reassigned him to work in the chancery office, the students were stunned and angry. And I was angry too, I guess, because he was really reaching kids—and because I found myself falling in love with him. I knew that Tom was the kind of man I would like to marry. And I sensed that Tom was falling in love with me."

"Well, each of you has made a good choice, but I want to ask you, Kate, how do you feel about Tom having to ask the Vatican to return to the lay state?"

"It's demeaning and absurd. Why can't a regional office in the country handle the matter? Why does it have to be such a big deal?

"Your questions are the same ones that many of us bishops raised repeatedly with authorities in Rome. But we get nowhere," I said. "And that's strange."

"No, it's not strange. It's rather simple. I think it's about punishment and control. I know you have to be the loyal foot soldier, so I won't ask you to comment on that, but that's my judgment."

"It's one that is shared by many," I said.

Just then Tom arrived through the back door. It was obvious that he was upset because his face was red as if he were about to explode. He shook hands with me and kissed Kate. Then he said rather heatedly, "Well, not only does our chancery office leak like a sieve but the Vatican does as well. Someone over there found out I'm applying for a dispensation and leaked the information back to the archdiocese here. The chancellor and his assistant grilled me at length about it."

I was shocked at this information because Bill Hunter at the Vatican promised there would be secrecy until Tom was ready to announce it himself.

"How did you respond?" I asked.

"With surprise and with questions."

"What kind of questions?" I asked.

"Who is your source? Name him. What did he tell you?"

"How did the chancellor respond?" I asked.

"He said it was privileged information."

"And how did you respond, Tom?"

"Well, I kept my cool—believe it or not—and told him that I would not respond to rumors and innuendo. If they had anything to discuss with me, let them put it on the table so we can talk about it straight on."

"Exactly the right approach," I said. "But I think all this is making Kate uncomfortable. Am I right, Kate?"

"Yes, but don't consider my feelings. Consider Tom's. He's trying to do the right thing, using a legitimate channel, and then suddenly someone in the Vatican leaks it to authorities back here. And he's grilled by the chancellor who says he cannot reveal confidential sources. I don't know how this strikes you, gentlemen, but it strikes me as outrageous. I'm sorry Tom and I ever agreed to apply for a dispensation."

"I'm sorry too," Tom said. "I'm thirty-five years old and here I am asking people in Rome for permission to exercise a right that everyone has. I feel like telling them all to go to hell."

I decided it was time to inject some levity into the situation, so I asked, "Where is the condemned man taking us to dinner tonight?" We all laughed and then headed toward Tom's car as he would be driving. "By the way," I said. "I want to ask you not to use my title unless we are in a formal setting. Just call me Ed."

"Sure, Ed. No problem." Tom said. "We've always called you Ed behind your back anyway."

With mischief in her eyes, Kate said, "Well that's very generous of you, Ed, but do you have permission from Rome to do that?"

I laughed and said, "OK, you two. You've had your fun. Now let's get to that restaurant. I'm starved."

Tom had made reservations at Graffinos, one of the best Italian restaurants in the city. It was a Wednesday night and the place wasn't crowded. One or two people greeted me as we passed by tables, but no one seemed to know Tom or Kate.

Tom thought it appropriate to order a bottle of Chateau Neuf du Pape 1968. Both Kate and I appreciated the irony. Then we ordered soup and salad, linguini, and lingered over crème brulé and coffee.

During dinner the matter of the dispensation didn't come up, nor did the grilling of Tom by the chancellor. We talked about their plans for their future and about Tom's doctoral program at Northwestern. Regardless of what Rome did, Tom and Kate would be married by me when Tom's dispensation came through. And just when would that be? In six weeks? In six months? In six years?

I knew Vatican officials could be punitive and vindictive. I hoped I could find out in the morning how the information had been leaked from the Vatican back to the archdiocese. I was aware that Tom's papers would come up for review, but I thought that since I was involved in the process, I would have been notified beforehand. I recalled Tom's—and Kate's—expression of regret over applying for the dispensation and could not blame them. Later I told them how much it embarrassed me to be part of such a system.

It was almost midnight when we got back to Haley House, so I did not invite Kate and Tom to come in for a nightcap. Tom and Kate got into their cars and drove away. I went into the kitchen area and then took the elevator to the second floor.

I felt very happy for Tom and Kate. They are two good people.

I was quietly seething that someone in the Vatican had leaked the information back to our chancery. And I had to suppress feelings of rage that our chancellor had grilled Tom about it. He doesn't know how lucky he is that I no longer am head of the diocese. If that happened on my watch, I would have called him in and given him a tongue lashing he would never forget.

CHAPTER 18

Something else happened to derail Tom's application, which we had both hoped would be quickly approved. It illustrated quite well Samuel Johnson's warning about the slip that can occur between the cup and the lip. It further angered and disillusioned Tom but gave Kate the opportunity to vent her feelings to me about the process. As I review my journal on this particular incident, I think she could have softened her discussion with me. Then again, maybe not. I needed to hear what many women have felt but have never expressed.

One morning Mrs. Lacey came to my office and told me that a Monsignor Bill Hunter was calling from Rome. I had dealt with him before many times and knew him as a hard working, honest man. It was he to whom I had sent Rinehart's papers for a dispensation.

"Ed," he said. "I'm sorry that word leaked out about Tom's application. I was away for a few days and my assistant who is new didn't realize the need for secrecy at this critical time. When I came in today, I learned something that tells me the application is dead."

Intrigued, I asked, "And what would that be?"

"Well, the word is that a new archbishop of your archdiocese will be named in a few days—finally, after all these months. I don't know who it is, but rumor has it that it will be Bishop T. Patrick Graham. Do you know him?"

"No, I don't," I said. "Tell me something about him."

"Well he's been in the Vatican embassy for ten years or more. He also graduated from the Gregorian. He's an academic type." He added, "He's never been in charge of a diocese to my knowledge."

"Well, Bill, what has this to do with Rinehart's application?"

"This may be conjecture on my part," Hunter said, "but I think someone from your diocese told him you had submitted it, and that ticked him off."

"Why would he be angry about that?" I asked.

"Ed, I can only guess. He might believe you were overstepping your authority."

"Well, if he thinks that, the man is really paranoid," I said, not trying to hide my anger and disgust. "What happens next?"

"The Vatican office will send Tom and you letters indicating that the petition for laicization has been refused," Hunter said. "Tom can submit it again after your new archbishop is installed."

"Do you think the new archbishop, whoever he is, will say anything to me about Graham's role in this?" I asked.

Hunter laughed and said, "Ed, you must be kidding. Have you forgotten how the game is played? Graham's fingerprints will never be found in this. It's the Church's equivalent of 'plausible deniability,' remember that term?"

"Yes, I do," I replied. "It was used a lot in the Watergate hearings during the Nixon years. The president's aides wanted to make sure he always had an out."

"You've got it, Ed. Only we both know the popes were into plausible deniability centuries before our country was founded."

"Thanks for the call, Bill. I'll get in touch with Rinehart and give him the 'good news.' He's not going to be a happy camper and neither will Kate. Not that I blame them. *Ciao.*"

As soon as he hung up, I phoned Rinehart and asked him to come to Haley House that evening. Rinehart thought Kate was free, so he suggested inviting her if that was all right with me. It was.

At nine that evening, all three of us met in the kitchen of Haley House. Tom and Kate had driven separate cars. After exchanging a few pleasantries, we went into my office where I told them about my conversation with Hunter earlier in the day. I was surprised that they took the news so calmly. I didn't know Kate very well, but I knew that Rinehart had a volcanic temper and did not suffer fools gladly, especially those in Rome. I could see that under that calm demeanor, however, Tom was trying to hide his anger.

"Let me begin by saying two things," I said. "First, I am greatly disappointed with this turn of events. Secondly, I'm surprised that you're taking it so well."

"Ed, Kate and I anticipated this might happen, so we have rehearsed for this moment," Rinehart said, his voice edged with a trace of anger. "But in case you've been wondering what our next step will be, we want you to know I'm not going to resubmit the application. That's my decision, not Kate's. She'll go along with whatever I decide."

"That's right, Ed," Kate said. "As you know, I'm big on encouraging people to make informed decisions, and I think Tom has arrived at one he can live with. He has played by the Vatican's rules, and obviously that's not good enough for the boys in charge. So both he and I have decided to move on. We are not going to beg for forgiveness and mercy."

"Well, I can't fault you for that," I said. "I'm so sorry it turned out this way. I looked forward to officiating at your wedding, and I plan on being there if I am invited."

"Ed, of course you will be invited," Rinehart said. "When we decide on the time and place, you will be the first to know."

Kate nodded in assent. Rinehart started to get up from his chair, but sat down when Kate said: "Ed, Tom and I are grateful for all you have done for us and we value your friendship. However, I think you should know how an educated Catholic woman feels about all this. Ed, I'm glad Tom and you are close friends and that you have extended that friendship to me. I hope what I am about to say will not damage our friendship."

"Fire away, Kate," I said. "I promise not to take it personally."

"All right, Ed. Let me ask you how Tom's application would have been handled in Rome if there had been some married and unmarried women deciding Tom's case?"

"Good question, Kate. They would have read the case and a few minutes later would give an affirmative decision. But you know that would never happen," I said.

"Yes, I know that because the Vatican would never give women that kind of power," Kate replied. "We are second-class citizens who must accept whatever the Mullahs in Rome decide."

"Kate, you're equating us with the Taliban. Isn't that a bit strong and rather unfair?" I asked, my voice rising slightly.

"Perhaps, it is, Ed, but you are in a very weak position when it comes to the issue of fairness for women. So if the shoe fits—or should I say burkah—wear it. The Church for centuries has been a stronghold for male chauvinism, and it still is today. Is that fair?"

"Kate, I can't deny that in the course of history, the hierarchy and the clergy have treated women very badly," I said, "but I think we have made progress over the past fifty years."

"Progress?" Kate asked somewhat sarcastically. "Women still are not in leadership positions as priests, bishops, or archbishops despite the fact that many, including myself, are eminently qualified. I can become an astronaut, the president of a college or a corporation, a senator, a governor, even president of the United States (in theory) but I cannot aspire to anything but a subservient role in the Church because of my gender."

"That's true, Kate, and I am sorry about that," I said.

"Sorry enough to do something about it when you had the chance?" Kate asked.

"What could I have done?" I asked

"Well, you could have taken a risk," Kate said. "You could have publicly made this announcement: 'If in the next two months, the pope does not permit qualified women to be ordained to the priesthood, then without permission from the Vatican, I will go ahead and ordain a group of women as deacons for my archdiocese.'"

Rinehart was enjoying the dialog, but he winced at Kate's statement. I was enjoying it too. I said, "And if I did what you propose, Kate, what do you think would have happened?"

"Well, all hell would have broken loose," Kate said. "Edicts from Rome and statements from bishops and priests around the world would have condemned your audacity and questioned your loyalty to the Church. The media would have had a field day. Clerical talking heads would have been in demand on CNN and Sunday morning talk shows. Cartoonists would love you because you'd be good copy. People all over the world would take sides over this issue."

"And watch my execution—I mean excommunication," I said with a wry smile.

"Not necessarily, Ed. Once women from all over the world weighed in on the issue, once their voices were heard, I think Rome would back down," Kate said.

"Kate, I'm not as sanguine. Maybe the new archbishop will do what you think I should have done. But don't hold your breath."

"Don't worry, Ed, I won't," Kate said. "The Vatican will send us someone who will parrot the party line—a mullah who will obey orders from the Grand Mullah in Rome. So all male Catholics in the world—especially bishops and archbishops—can sleep easily tonight. There won't be any coup that shifts power to women who make up more than 51% of the Church."

"That's good to know, Kate," I said with a grin never realizing that my off the cuff remark would really tick her off.

"Ed," she said, "I don't claim to know as much theology of the Church as you do, but I have taken a lot of courses in ecclesiology. I remember one of my profs writing on the board two words—*teaching and learning*. Jesus meant us to be not just a teaching church but also a learning church, a listening Church. Well you men in the hierarchy do a lot of teaching but damn little listening, especially listening to women. You could learn a lot from women and their experiences. I have heard about priests who urge women to obey their husbands even if they are temperamental, abusive, sexually demanding drunks. But never once have I heard about a priest who encouraged a woman to divorce a husband who demeans her, ridicules her, abuses her. We women have heard too damn much from the teaching church but not enough that shows you guys have been a listening and a learning Church."

Sensing that this conversation could get heated, Tom interrupted and suggested we continue the discussion at dinner later in the week. He said he was tired and that Kate had a full schedule of classes tomorrow. So we said our cool goodbyes.

Later that evening I reviewed the events of the day, especially my encounter with Kate. She has a temper but controls it much better than Tom controls his. Wow! She really let me have it. Her words stung me, and I began to ask questions of myself:

Is the pope our Grand Mullah? I hope not, but we often treat him as if he is. The popes in the last two hundred years have made concerted efforts to centralize more power to Rome, and priests and people have let them do that.

Have I been part of the Church's Taliban whose headquarters are in Rome? I certainly hope not, but I must admit that when I had authority, I was often afraid to exercise it, fearing that Rome was looking over my shoulder. Yes, there's a network operating in the Church, although it's not a violent one like Al-Qaeda. But Rome has sycophants in every country who keep the pope informed.

Has our treatment of women been as oppressive as Kate says? Are we perceived by women as being a teaching Church but not a listening Church? Maybe it's not as bad as she says, but God knows we have a long way to go. Intelligent, educated women like Kate, and especially women in religious orders, have been the backbone of the Church in America, but we seldom acknowledge it. They have continued their education, more so than the majority of the clergy, who seem to think the seminary taught them everything about theology they will ever need to know. These are the guys who patronizingly refer to the sisters as "the good nuns." What a travesty.

CHAPTER 19

On July 31, a couple of weeks after Hunter called Foley from Rome, the Vatican announced that Bishop T. Patrick Graham, a Vatican diplomat, would become the new archbishop of Forest Park. Graham, who had arrived in the city a couple of days before the announcement, faced the media a few hours later and answered questions from reporters and journalists in the area.

Graham invited me to be on the dais with him, along with the chancellor of the archdiocese. Graham came across as personable, intelligent, and thoughtful.

One of the first questions reporters asked Graham was whether the cathedral renovation, scheduled to begin in August, would be canceled. Graham assured reporters that the renovation would proceed as scheduled. Architects, project managers, and others involved in the process had been meeting for months, and Cardinal Mohr's plans would soon be realized.

Asked when and where his installation would take place, he said, "There's no hurry. Perhaps we'll have two celebrations in one—my installation and the completion of the renovation, both in November."

Reporters asked him questions about his stand on such issues as a married clergy, women as priests, abortion. Graham handled their questions with openness and humor. They knew he could not deviate from official church teaching, but they asked him about these controversial subjects anyway. They were telling him they were not going to give him a free pass. Graham liked that. It was obvious that members of the media liked him and that he liked to interact with them. He was the consummate diplomat.

After the press conference, Graham went to Saint Joseph

Cathedral, where most of the area clergy had assembled to meet their new archbishop. Some drove from distances of seventy miles because they wanted to see and shake hands with their new boss. A few of the younger priests had met Graham when they were graduate students in Rome, but most knew him only through newspaper accounts about his appointment as archbishop.

There was much speculation about his view of church. Some said Graham was a conservative, others that he was a moderate. No one said he was a liberal, but then no one called him a reactionary. A search of the Internet failed to reveal any books or articles he had published. T. Patrick Graham was a mystery man. He had been ordained for thirty years, but he left no paper trail, not unlike most of the priests he was going to lead.

Since the death of Cardinal Mohr six months earlier, the archdiocese had been without an archbishop. Naturally, priests and people of Forest park speculated on who Mohr's successor would be. Some hoped the Vatican would choose someone from the archdiocese while others believed that Mohr's successor should be someone from the outside. A small but vocal group of priests whose unofficial spokesperson was Father Paul Hartman thought the clergy and the people should be consulted about Mohr's successor. They wanted to ask Graham where he stood on the issues of birth control, abortion, married priests, women priests, accountability, and the decision making process in the archdiocese. Because this was not done, they were not enthusiastic about Graham's appointment.

Nevertheless they joined in the standing ovation for Graham when he entered the sanctuary of the cathedral to greet them. His remarks were friendly and informal. He spoke no more than ten minutes, but in that time he spoke of me in glowing terms and told the priests he wanted to meet personally with each one of them over the next year. He said he did not want his administration to follow a top down model of the church. He preferred, he said, in building consensus. He ended his remarks by suggesting that we all leave the cathedral and move to the assembly room of the cathedral for cocktails and hors d'oeuvres. That suggestion was greeted with another standing ovation.

In the assembly room Graham came over to me. "Ed, I've heard a lot about you and your tenure here as archbishop and it's all good. We need to meet quite soon because I want you to tell me about your experience here as archbishop. I can learn a lot from you."

"Thanks, Pat. You give me too much credit, but let's talk more about this after the dinner we're having for you this evening at Haley House. Some officials from the chancery will join us. And Mrs. Lacey, our housekeeper, told me not to forget to remind you that you have been invited to stay overnight at Haley House."

"You can tell Mrs. Lacey I'm looking forward to having dinner at Haley House, and I will stay overnight."

Graham made the rounds, easily entering into the banter of the cocktail gathering.

Later that evening at dinner, an appropriately elegant catered affair, I acted as master of ceremonies. I told a few humorous stories about my own coming to Forest Park and then introduced the chancery officials, who welcomed the new archbishop.

Rinehart, who had been invited to the affair, was introduced but did not speak. He was keeping a low profile after the Vatican tipped off the Forest Park chancery office that he had applied for a dispensation to be laicized. Rinehart was sure Graham knew about the leak. In fact, he suspected that he might even be the source of it; but he could not prove it. Graham greeted Rinehart warmly, indicating in no way that he was aware of Tom's plans to leave the active ministry. As Rinehart said later, "Roman diplomacy at its very best!"

The dinner was over by nine-thirty. After Graham and I thanked the visiting clergy for coming to the dinner, I led Graham to a suite of rooms on the second floor. Mrs. Lacey had made sure everything was in order.

"Pat," I said, "you must be dead tired, so I'm going to get out of your way. My rooms are just down the hall, but knowing Mrs. Lacey, she has provided everything you will need. And by the way, there's good liquor in the cabinet."

"Thanks, Ed. I don't need anything to drink, but what I would like is a good book, a murder mystery that I can read to get my mind off the events of today. I heard there's a good library in Haley House, so just point me in its direction."

"Just take the elevator to the first floor and walk straight ahead," I said. "I'll be glad to go down with you."

"Ed, that won't be necessary. I'll find it."

Graham put on the lounging robe that he found hanging in the closet and headed for the elevator. As he was entering the library, however, he nearly collided with Toni, who was just leaving with a book of poetry.

"Hello," said Graham. "You must be Toni Vincent. Archbishop Foley told me that you live here with your grandmother. I'm Pat Graham. I'll be staying here overnight. I was just looking for something good to read. Any suggestions?"

"Well, I guess you're looking for theology or philosophy? Those are against the back wall. They sure would put me to sleep! On the other side, there are some great novels and short stories. A lot of them are on loan from the public library."

"Who keeps the library holdings current?" Graham asked.

"Miss Valentine from the public library," Toni said. "She comes in a couple times a week with books and newspapers and magazines and stuff for Bishop Foley. He encourages me to use the library, and I can even invite my friends in. It's a great place to study."

"I'm sure it is," Graham said. "Have your friends taken you up on your invitation?"

"A few have, but most of them prefer to use the library down the street. But I think they'll probably come around—eventually." She laughed. "They think coming here is too much like going to church—and some of my friends want no part of church."

Graham liked this young kid. Her friendly openness was refreshing.

"Well, Toni, suppose you are the librarian tonight. What would you recommend that will make me laugh or smile as I'm trying to fall asleep?"

"Well, just yesterday Miss Valentine brought in some paperback books—eight in all I think. They're called the Brother Cadfael Chronicles written by an English woman— Ellis Peters, I think her name is. Miss Valentine said they're written in the form of mysteries. She said they're very humorous and entertaining."

Toni led Graham to the shelf where they were located.

"Good," Graham said. "Let me take this one–*A Morbid Taste for Bones.* Interesting title. I'll sign out for it."

He said goodnight to Toni and headed toward the elevator.

CHAPTER 20

Once or twice a week Toni would take a bus to the University to do some odd jobs for Kate and mostly just visit with her. After only a few conversations with Toni, she knew that she was dealing with an unusually intelligent and savvy young girl with great potential. Kate wanted to help her in any way she could and didn't mind having her "hang out" in her office, to use Toni's words. She realized that Toni was beginning to regard her somewhat as a surrogate mother.

Kate made it clear to Toni, however, that she was hired at Haley House to help her grandmother, so her duties at Haley House should always take precedent over her volunteering at the University. Toni assured Kate that she had cleared it with Mrs. Lacey.

One day when she was dusting the book shelves in Kate's office, Toni remarked that many of the pictures on the wall were women and that quite a few books on the shelves were by women authors writing about women.

"Kate, you have an awful lot of books written by women on topics that relate to women. Why is that?"

"I'm interested in women's rights, Toni. I suppose most people would call me a feminist."

"I hear people use that word," Toni said, "but I'm not sure I know what it means to be a feminist. Doesn't it mean you hate men?"

Kate laughed and said, "Well some people think that, but that's not what it means. I don't particularly like the word 'feminist,' Toni, because I like to think that I care not just about women's rights but all people's rights. But the term is here to stay, I guess, for lack of a better one. Being a feminist means being actively interested in issues that enable women to achieve their dignity and freedom as human beings. I'm not a single issue person, but issues affecting women really get my attention."

"Issues like what?"

"Like the freedom to be married or unmarried, like the freedom to be an equal partner in marriage, like the freedom to have children or not have them. Let's start with those."

"Haven't women always been free to be single or married?"

"No, Toni, they haven't been entirely free. Not too long ago women had very few careers open to them. If they didn't marry, they could become school teachers, nurses, librarians or social workers, but many careers were closed to them. That limited their earning power. Also, women who didn't marry were called spinsters and old maids."

Toni pointed to a portrait hanging on the office wall. "Who's this?" she asked.

"That's Susan B. Anthony. Ever hear of her?"

"I might have, but I forgot. Who's the lady in the next picture?"

"That's Elizabeth Cady Stanton. Ever hear of her?"

"Nope," Toni replied.

"That's all right, Toni. Few women in this country could identify their pictures. But they are two of the most important women in American history."

"Really?"

"Really. These two women started the Woman's Suffrage Movement in the 19th century. They believed it was un-American and undemocratic for men to deny the right of women to vote. That movement eventually changed the course of American history. But they and their followers had to endure fierce opposition and ridicule from civic and religious leaders, from journalists and even from women themselves."

"Wow. Kate, when did women get the right to vote?"

"In the presidential election of 1920. But not without a bitter struggle against a male dominated society that wanted to keep them in their place."

"Where have I been? I didn't know that."

"Most girls your age probably don't either, so don't think you're alone, Toni. You have a lot of company."

Toni pointed to another picture. Kate, who's that?"

"That's Eleanor Roosevelt, the wife of President Franklin D. Roosevelt—one of the most important women of the 20th century. She's one of my heroes. She was a feminist who cared about poor women in the Great Depression, but she also fought for the rights of all working men and women."

"Sounds like someone I should know about. Got any books on her?"

"Yes, here's one by Doris Kearns Goodwin called *Franklin and Eleanor*. It's a very good read."

"Thanks, Kate. I'll get it back to you real soon." Toni started paging through the book, then looked up and asked, "How did you get interested in feminism, Kate?"

"Well, my mother was something of a feminist, and my father was very supportive and respectful of her views. They both wanted me to have many career choices. They thought that was very important especially for a young woman like me."

"Didn't they want you to get married?" Toni asked.

"I'm sure they did, but they wanted me to be independent so that I could have choices about what I wanted to do. They made me understand that I didn't need marriage to be fulfilled."

"You're lucky, Kate. I wish my dad hadn't died so young. And I sure wish my mother hadn't married that stupid ass jerk Randy. You know they're both in prison?"

"Yes, I do, Toni." Kate paused and added, "What's that like for you?"

"Well, I have a lot of anger toward my mom, but I'm trying to forgive her."

"I bet that's hard." After a brief pause, Kate said, "Toni, you remember the night we first met, I'm sure. But do you remember what we talked about?"

"Sure, it was about my hitchhiking. I got the message–you disapprove of it."

"Hmm. I remember our conversation a little differently, Toni. I think I told you that I use my literature classes to teach my students the importance of making good decisions. Do you remember my saying that?"

"Yeah, now I do."

"I think I also said that sometimes the decision to hitchhike might be a good one, but generally I think it is not a good decision. Remember my saying that?"

"Yeah. I mean yes."

"Well, Toni, sometimes good people like your mother make bad decisions because they panic. Life at times overwhelms them. Your mother may be a classic example of that."

"How do you mean?"

"Well, your father's sudden death probably unraveled her — and hurt her deeply. I know your grandmother provided a home for you while your mother worked. But she still must have had a very difficult time."

A very thoughtful and pensive Toni said, "I guess she did, but– you know—I guess I never thought about it–from her point of view, I mean."

"That's all right, Toni, most kids your age wouldn't. So don't beat yourself up. Just try to understand that your mom might have done the best she could."

"Kate, I'm sorry, but that's bullshit. How could she get mixed up with that drunk—Randy. How could she do drink and drugs? How could she agree to be a lookout while he robbed that Convenience store?"

Kate respected Toni's anger and was glad she was expressing it. She paused for a moment before she answered.

"Toni, you've asked some very good questions that are hard for me–or for anyone–to answer. But they're legitimate questions. Your mother is in trouble because she did not know how to make good decisions affecting her life and yours. She panicked. She probably thought Randy was a ticket to happiness for her–and for you. Countless women have made similar decisions, often with the same disastrous results."

"I just hope I don't do the same," Toni said, brushing away tears from her eyes.

"So do I, Toni," Kate replied as she threw her arm around Toni's shoulder. "And I don't think you will if you work hard to get a very good education that will enable you to be independent. But education is just one factor. Self reflection is another. I think education and self reflection will teach you that you can be happy and productive without having to depend on a husband."

"Like you are right now?" Toni asked.

"What do you mean by that?"

"Well, you know, I guess you don't intend to marry. You seem happy as an English professor and you probably want to stay that way," Toni said.

Kate laughed. "Toni, I haven't been clear. If the right man came along and asked me to marry him, I would. But if Mr. Right doesn't appear, I can live with that. I'm not going to get married because I think I need a man to make me happy."

"You've given this a lot of thought, haven't you, Kate?"

"Yes, I have. It's something I need to do if I am to make a good decision."

Checking her watch, Toni said, "Kate, I have to go. I promised my grandmother that I'd be home before five. If I miss the next bus, I'll have to hitchhike." She smiled mischievously and waited for a reaction.

Kate gave her a good natured shove toward the office door. "Get on that bus, Toni. We'll talk again. Thanks for coming."

CHAPTER 21

A week after Kate, Tom, and I met at Haley House to discuss the disposition of Tom's request for laicization, I went to the University to look over the list of the fall continuing education courses. I turned a corner and came face to face with Kate Green. She was quite gracious and friendly. Neither she nor I made any reference to the rather sharp discussion we had the last time we met.

Since there were students in the hallway, I decided it would be more professional to greet her rather formally.

"Hello, Professor Green," I said. "I'm here to find some interesting continuing education courses for the spring session. Any suggestions?

"Why, yes, Archbishop," she said. "If you're interested in a course in literature, Professor Moira Callan is offering a course on James Joyce. She's excellent on Irish literature, especially the works of James Joyce."

"Good, when I was in college years ago, I tried to read *Ulysses*. I think I read about a third of that novel and then gave it up. Never went back to it."

"Well," she said, "I had trouble with it too until I took her course."

"That settles it. I'll sign up before I leave."

"Good, you won't be disappointed."

When we passed the cafeteria, I suggested we get some coffee. Kate looked at her watch and said, "Good. I'm supposed to meet Toni here in about five minutes. I want her to pick up some books from the library for me before she comes up to my office. So she can join us and keep you company when I have to leave for a three o'clock appointment with a student, which is exactly twenty minutes from now."

I got a tray and two large cups while Kate found a place where we could have some privacy while we talked.

"Ed, the idea of your having honest conversations with a 16-year-old girl intrigues me. Those conversations level the playing field, don't they?"

"That's a good way to put it, Kate. Yes, I think those conversations put us on an equal footing."

"The same with me when Toni comes to my office," said Kate. "She's very helpful—running errands and straightening up my perpetually disorganized desk—but what I enjoy most are the conversations we have. She asks very insightful questions. What seems curious, I guess, is how she can relate to both of us. You have to admit we're worlds apart in some ways." Kate smiled mischievously – obliquely referring to our last meeting.

"I suspect that our worlds are more alike than not—in many ways," I said with a smile. "About Toni, though—she's not easily intimidated by age or authority. The other day I asked her if she had met Archbishop Graham, who had just moved into Haley House. She said she had met him one evening when he came down to the library looking for a good mystery story to help him unwind after he had his first press conference and met the priests of the diocese. She said he seemed very nice. She even helped him select a book. I told her I thought she and Graham would get along just fine."

"I'm sure they will," Kate said. "Oh, here comes Toni now." She waved Toni over to the table.

Toni's exuberance was delightful. She greeted both of us warmly. "Hey, this is a surprise, Bishop. I didn't expect to see you until I got home—I mean, Haley House."

"That's home, Toni, for both of us. And seeing you here is an unexpected pleasure."

Kate stood up. "Well, you two, you'll have to continue without me. I don't want to be late for my appointment." Turning to Toni, she said, "Take your time visiting with Bishop Foley. And before you come up to my office I'd appreciate your picking up two books from the library. Just ask anyone at the main desk for them. I told them you would be picking them up. By the time you get to my office, I'll probably be finished with my appointment, but if not, you won't have to wait long, OK?"

"Sure, Kate." She seemed pleased that Kate gave her instructions in my presence.

Kate apologized to us for having to rush off.

"No problem at all, Kate. Toni and I'll have a little chat, then I'll wander over to the bookstore and get a paperback copy of *Ulysses*," I said.

"While you're there, pick up a copy of *Nora: The Real Life of Molly Bloom* by Brenda Maddox. It's a book about Joyce's mistress and wife, whom he treated very badly," she said.

"OK, I will, Kate. Let's chat again very soon."

We said goodbye, and I said to Toni, "Can I get you a coke?"

"No, thanks, Bishop. I just drank some water. I carry it in my book bag. Maybe later."

We sat in silence for a few minutes.

"Toni, I know you have some very negative thoughts and feelings toward your mother, but basically she could be a good woman and a good mother. I think both you and I can help her in that halfway house to make a good decision about her future and yours too."

"Sounds like you've been talking to Kate Green."

"Why do you say that?"

"Because she's also talking about the importance of making good decisions. She uses her literature classes to make that point."

"That sounds like a good course," I said. "Maybe I'll ask Kate if I can sit in on some of her classes some time. But Toni, let's not talk about Kate right now. Let's talk instead about your mother, whom we both can help."

"OK, Bishop, but you know I'm not happy with her for what she and Randy did."

"Yes, Toni, I know that. Don't you think your mother regrets what happened? Don't you think she wants a better life for herself and you?"

"How can I know that unless she proves it? Who's to say she won't fall for the next Randy who comes along?"

"Well, Toni, let's remember that we can give her two things she needs right now."

"What are they?"

"The first thing is respect," I said. "That's something we all need and something that a lot of people never get. Some wives never get respect from their husbands and vice versa. Some children never get respect from their parents. Some students never get respect from their teachers. Some parishioners never get respect from their pastors. Some workers never get respect from their bosses. And on and on it goes, leaving people feeling used and devalued and depressed. We can't let that happen with your mother. She's probably feeling worthless for what she's done. We have to respect her for who she is and for what she can become."

"You said there were two things everyone needs. OK, one thing is respect. I always thought you were supposed to earn respect. What's the second thing?"

"Hope is also something we need. We all have to be able to imagine a better future for ourselves and others. That's especially true of your mother. She has to have the hope that after she serves her time you will be there waiting for her and forgiving her."

"That's too much. You can't ask me to do that. And I don't even know how to do that."

"Well, you could write to her," I said. "You could call her on the phone. You could visit her with your grandmother and me whenever there is a visiting day. You could talk to her about the future and not the past.'

"But, Bishop, what about me? I need to talk about the past."

After listening to Toni complain about her mother and Randy and realizing that I was making little headway with her, I decided to take a different tack. I went to the refreshment stand in the cafeteria, ordered two large Cokes and brought them back to the table where Toni and I were sitting. A few professors recognized me and came over to say hello. I introduced Toni to them. They asked Toni what year she was in, and she informed them that she was still in high school. They told her they hoped she would come to the University after high school, and Toni told them she was thinking about it.

After they left, I told Toni that the three persons she met were all history professors and that they make up the history exam that all incoming freshmen take.

"Well," Toni said, "history is a favorite subject of mine, so that exam should be a piece of cake."

"I'm glad to hear that, Toni. Professor Ramani, the very tall professor you just met, told me recently that one of the essay questions the committee included in last year's test went something like this: Write a short essay indicating who you think is the most imaginative person in history. Support your answer with examples."

"Bishop, I'll bet they got the names of at least fifty people."

"They did," I said.

"Well, what was the correct answer?"

"Well, as you guessed, many historic figures were named. And the judges accepted many names—like Columbus, Magellan, Shakespeare, Madame Curie, Thomas Edison, Henry Ford, Thomas Jefferson, Mother Teresa—the list is almost endless."

"Sounds like they didn't want to make a decision," Toni said.

"No, they really wanted to see how the students made their decision."

"So, Bishop, who do you think is the most imaginative person who ever lived?"

"Jesus Christ," I said.

"Jesus Christ!" She shouted this so loudly that many people in the cafeteria stopped eating and stared at her. They thought she and I were having a heated argument. When I laughed at how incongruous the situation was, so did she. We went back to our conversation.

"Sorry about my outburst before about Jesus, Bishop. It just sorta surprised me. But I should've known that you would bring him into our conversation."

I smiled and said, "Why don't you think Jesus might qualify as the most imaginative person who every lived?"

"I guess because I never thought of the imagination of Jesus."

"That's true for most of us, Toni. But consider what Jesus did. He singled out twelve uneducated fishermen and sent them out to preach a message of love, goodness, gentleness, mercy, compassion, and generosity. No one was to be excluded. He did this at a time when the Roman Empire ruled by the sword. But, Toni, in 300 years the Roman Empire ended, but Christianity has spread throughout the world."

"So you're saying, Bishop, that because Jesus had a great imagination, he saw something in those twelve uneducated men that no one else saw."

"Yes, Toni, and if we are followers of Jesus, then we should try to see in others the good and the potential Jesus sees in them. The trouble is that most of us have put limits on our own imagination."

"I think you're sending me a message here, aren't you? You're telling me to start imagining what Jesus imagines my mother could be. Bishop, that's going to be tough. After a long pause she added, "But I'll give it a try."

"Good, Toni. And just remember that your grandmother and I will be trying with you."

"Thanks, Bishop, I'll try to remember that." She sat quietly for a moment, then got up from the table. "I'll see you later. Right now I should get to Kate's office."

CHAPTER 22

Before his appointment to the Vatican diplomatic corps T. Patrick Graham had lived most of his clerical life in chancery offices and seminaries in the archdiocese of Palmer where he had been ordained.

Graham's full head of gray hair matched his steel gray eyes, which still gave him excellent vision, although he always kept a pair of reading glasses handy. Tall, handsome and somewhat on the slim side, Graham's athletic body showed that keeping physically fit was important to him. Two or three times a week he jogged, and some days he swam and exercised at the fitness club that he joined shortly after he arrived at Forest Park.

Graham played sports in the seminary, but unlike some clerics he didn't fanatically follow professional sports. He was an avid reader of books on theology, scripture, and history, especially works on the papacy. He loved art, and most evenings he listened to classical music. He was fluent in Italian, Greek, French and German.

Graham told me to continue living at Haley House. He himself had decided to live at a city parish because, he said, he wanted to be close to his people. He chose Saint Michael parish near the heart of the city. It had seen better days, as did the neighborhood, but it was on a major street, about three miles from the chancery office. City buses stopped in front of the old Gothic style church. Graham planned to walk to his office or take a bus so he could see and be seen by the people.

But, he told me in September, after about two months into his tenure that he also had another plan. Because some night meetings at the chancery office ran late, he decided to make Haley House his second home. Accordingly, he took over most of the second floor, merging three suites of rooms into one, and sparing no expense in the process. I couldn't help thinking—somewhat uncharitably, I admit—that he wanted to be admired by the faithful for living in the Spartan surroundings of an inner city parish house but at the same enjoy a more comfortable lifestyle. His years as a diplomat had conditioned him to live like a diplomat and act like a politician when necessary.

The oak paneled dining room in Haley House delighted him, and he let Mrs. Lacey know that he would be doing a lot of entertaining. She had his permission to hire the extra help she would need on those occasions.

Graham, I felt, was somewhat imperious, yet I wouldn't call him a snob. I suspected, however, that for all his statements about wanting a collegial style as archbishop, he was somewhat of an autocrat. Too much of a Roman.

The priests of the diocese were learning that Graham was charming and gregarious with a smooth style he had polished in the diplomatic corps. They also learned, however, that he did not believe in consensus if the thinking of the group ran counter to his own. He believed his decisions would be accepted provided there was at least the appearance of consultation. When, shortly after he arrived in Forest Park, he closed a high school for girls whose enrollment was primarily African American and non-Catholic, the opposition he encountered surprised him. Why would the clergy and people not accept his decisions? Wasn't there consultation? Didn't they respect his credentials? After all, he is a Roman.

Late one night I was in my suite on the second floor of Haley House. Graham was in his almost renovated suite across the hall. Suddenly I heard loud voices coming from Graham's suite. Wondering whether Graham was being attacked, I opened the door to the hallway, ready to call for help.

"If you cut off my salary, I'll expose you for the fraud you are," I heard the intruder say.

"Ron, please lower your voice. You don't scare me," Graham said. "You are not going to be my chauffeur, and I am not going to pay you any money. Your blackmail scheme is not going to work, so please leave and don't come back again. You're not welcome here."

"You'll regret this," the intruder said. "I'm going to hound you for as long as it takes. You'll never be rid of me. People will soon know what you were doing in Rome."

I heard the door to Graham's suite open. Graham said, "Ron, leave now or I will call the police."

"That won't be necessary, your Excellency," the intruder said, his words dripping with sarcasm. "Just remember, I'll be back!" He slammed the door and walked down the corridor toward the back stairs.

I was sorry I heard this. I closed the door and went back to my sitting room. I had a lot of thinking to do about this man named Ron who was blackmailing Graham and probably had been doing so for some time. Should I confront Graham about what I heard? Our relationship had been civil but rather guarded and reserved.

At breakfast Graham told me he would like to see me about a private matter. We went to my office. Graham instructed Mrs. Lacey that we were not to be disturbed.

"Ed, you have a sterling reputation," Graham said. "Priests and parishioners know they can trust you. Secrets are safe with you, something that is not always true with some men in our profession, but you know that, don't you?"

"Yes, Pat, I do. What I hear in confidentiality stays right in this room—unless for some reason you give me permission to discuss what was said."

"That's reassuring, Ed, because I'm going to tell you something about myself that may shock you."

"Pat, in my fifty-five years as a priest, I think I've heard everything. I'm shock proof."

Graham smiled and began to relax. Then he asked, "Did you hear that argument coming from my suite last night?"

"Yes, I did. I didn't know what was happening. I thought you were being robbed or attacked, so I opened my door and heard part of the conversation. A man was blackmailing you, threatening to expose you as a fraud for what you did in Rome. You told him that he was no longer your chauffeur and ordered him to get out and not come back."

Graham looked at me and said, "Ed, you have good hearing. You would have made a good reporter. The man who was threatening me is Ron Hackett, who was my chauffeur in Rome."

After a brief pause, he said, "Ed, do you know what I was doing in Rome that was so terrible?"

"No, I don't, but I can guess. It's about one of three things—money, sex, or drink. Am I right?"

"Yes, you are, Ed, but it's not about money or drink. It's about sex."

"You had a relationship with a woman in Rome?"

"No, but I did have a male friend—Pierre is his name—with whom I was involved for about eight years. We were partners who had made a commitment to each other, but of course, we lived apart. He had an apartment about two miles from my living quarters. A couple times a week, I would visit Pierre at his place near the Spanish Steps. Sometimes, I would stay with Pierre overnight and would take a cab or walk back to my place in the morning."

I took all this in without any facial expression or body language that showed I was surprised by this revelation. Then I said, "Pat, tell me about Pierre. Is he a priest or a bishop?"

"No, Ed, he's a layman, a diplomat in the French Embassy. He's Catholic but he's never studied for the priesthood."

"How did you meet?"

"I met Pierre at a dinner at the French Embassy on the Via Veneto. I was introduced to him at the cocktail party before the dinner. I told him about my background—that I was French on my mother's side and that I was interested in finding out something about her parents, who were killed in World War I. They lived in the small village of Berzy, and in the battle at Verdun they were killed by artillery fire. My mother, their only child, survived. She was about two or three at the time. Some nuns who operated an orphanage near Verdun took care of her. When she was sixteen, she left the orphanage and emigrated to the U.S. with a French couple for whom she had worked while she was in the orphanage. They were very good to her. Eventually she married, and I'm the product of that marriage."

"Is she still living?"

"Yes, she's a widow living in New York City. My father died about ten years ago. She now lives in an assisted living home. The nuns who operate the retirement home give her excellent care. Daily I thank God for them."

Graham was silent for a minute. Then he said, "Let me tell you more about my relationship with Pierre. Some homosexual relationships are about power, and I detest them. They are ugly and degrading. Our relationship is not that kind."

"What do you mean, Pat?"

Graham said. "As a young boy, I knew I was gay and had a friend at school named Frank who was gay too. But Frank and I managed to hide our homosexuality. After high school we both went to the seminary where we continued the relationship. I don't think anyone suspected we were gay. We were into sports, we smoked and drank, told dirty jokes, and even dated during the summer months although that was forbidden. And we ridiculed guys who were effeminate or what we called 'queer.' What we did was cruel, but we were accepted as straight, and to us that's all that mattered. The seminary didn't keep guys who were suspected of being homosexual."

"That certainly was true in my day," I said. "In fact, if we visited another student's room, we had to keep the door open. If you were in someone's room and the door was closed, you could be expelled if someone in authority saw this and reported it."

"That also was true in my day," Graham said, "but let me continue my story of Frank and me. We stayed out of each other's rooms, but at least once a week we managed to have secret meetings in the dead of night in one of the laundry rooms in the seminary basement."

"What happened to Frank? Was he ordained with your class?"

"No, he wasn't. Frank left the seminary right before we entered the theologate. His dad died quite suddenly and left the family in a lot of debt, so Frank dropped out and went to work in a steel mill."

"That must have been really hard on you, Pat."

"Yes, it was. I was depressed for months. A priest at the seminary who was vice rector noticed this and suddenly took a great interest in me. He was in his early fifties and had the title of dean of discipline. He invited me to come into his room for 'spiritual guidance.' At first he didn't put any moves on me. After a year or more, however, he started to become more affectionate. He would put his arm around me, and even kiss me."

"How did this affect you at the time?"

"Well, I was startled. I hadn't suspected he was a homosexual. I was very uncomfortable. After all, he was my superior. As I look back on it, I should have reported the bastard. I was a vulnerable young man and he was taking advantage of it. But I didn't report him to anyone and started returning his advances. That was a big mistake."

"Did the relationship continue until ordination?"

"Yes, and even beyond. He took a great interest in my career, as he called it. I must say he opened doors for me. He was instrumental in my being sent to Rome for graduate studies. Oh, yes, he had big plans for me."

"I don't get it, Pat. If he was in love with you, why would he send you three thousand miles away?"

Graham laughed and said, "Good question, Ed, one I asked myself when I got to Rome. Then it dawned on me that the dean of discipline had a new boyfriend in the seminary, some young theology student who was four years away from ordination. I was being jilted. I think that was his modus operandi for years."

"That must have been a painful experience for you," I said.

"Yes, it was, Ed, but it was also something of a turning point in my life as a gay man—or gay priest."

"What do you mean by that, Pat?"

"Well," Graham answered, "it goes back to that power issue. That seminary dean had power over me and used it in a way that I now find despicable. So I resolved that my life as a homosexual would never go that route. I would never use a position of authority to coerce or entice another male to be my lover. And I would never get involved with another homosexual unless we were equals."

"Like you and Pierre," I said.

"Exactly," Graham replied. "We were both diplomats, he for the French embassy and I for the Vatican embassy. He had no control over me, and I had no control over him. And that's the way it has been with relationships I have had with other men before I met Pierre."

"Pat, you obviously care a lot about Pierre. Wasn't it hard to leave him and come back to the U.S.?"

"Yes, it was. In fact, I wanted to refuse the appointment to become archbishop of Forest Park, but Pierre persuaded me to accept it."

"Had your relationship cooled?"

"Not at all, Graham said. "Pierre now has some serious health problems. He's not a practicing Catholic, but he is a deeply spiritual man. In the last year he's been doing a lot of thinking about death." He paused for a moment and then added, "And he's been thinking about judgment. He's been meditating on that sentence of Saint Paul about all of us having to die and all of us having to be judged."

"As an eighty-year-old man, I think of death and judgment too," I said. "It helps me put my life in order."

"The same with me. Pierre and I decided that my appointment as archbishop of Forest Park would be a good time to end our relationship."

"How do you feel about that?"

"Well, Ed, naturally I'm sad. This might seem strange to say, but I thank God every day that I met and loved Pierre. I don't regard our relationship as mortally sinful. Neither he nor I wanted to be homosexual, but that's what we are. That's the way God made us. Pierre has been very good for me and I think I've been very good for him."

"I'm sure that's true," I said.

"Ed, you are probably wondering if I intend to enter another partnership now that I am back in America. The answer is no. I intend to live as a celibate archbishop."

"I'm glad to hear you say that, Pat. I have no problem with the fact that you're gay. But, to be frank, I do have a problem that you didn't honor our common vows. I have no problem working for a bishop or archbishop who is gay, but I would have a big problem working for a gay bishop or archbishop who doesn't observe the vow of celibacy on the theory that celibacy is only about sex between a man and a woman. Some gay priests seem to think that they are observing their vow of celibacy because they are having sex with a man, and not intercourse with a woman. That's an insult to me, a betrayal of me and others who have observed the vow since we were ordained. And let me say also that I would have trouble working for a bishop or archbishop who is straight but has a relationship with a woman on the side."

"Ed, you are right. For the past few years I have been struggling with the celibacy issue and whether my behavior has been a betrayal of our common vows. If you have any doubts about me, let me solemnly assure you that I intend, with God's grace, to live a celibate life. I intend to throw myself into my work and become a role model to the priests and people of Forest Park, as you were and still are."

He paused for a moment and then said, "The time has come for me to develop my prayer life and be serious about imitating the Lord Jesus."

"Hasn't that always been your intent?" I asked.

"Not really," Graham said. "In retrospect, I have to admit that one reason I entered the seminary after high school was not so much to follow Jesus but to have a place where as a gay young man I could be safe and be respected. It was the perfect closet where I could hide and be accepted."

"Do you think our seminaries today are still closets?"

"Yes, Ed, for some they are. But the men in these closets are coming out of them, and in my opinion, that's not good for the Church," Graham said. "By that I mean, if the priesthood is looked upon as a gay profession, then a lot of young men who are straight are not going to join the priesthood, and that's going to cause a real crisis."

We were both silent for some time. Then I said, "There's something else that will exacerbate that crisis and I think you know what it is, Pat."

"Yes, I do," Graham said. "The larger the pool of gay priests becomes, the more likely it will be that a large percentage of bishops in the future will be gay. Right now the number of bishops who are homosexuals is not very large, but it's an issue that looms on the horizon."

"Exactly," I said. "Church leaders need to confront this issue. Many are so fixated on the celibacy issue that they can't imagine a married clergy or women as priests or homosexuals as priests or bishops. Nobody wants to talk about the elephant in the living room. But, Pat, now is probably not the time to discuss that issue."

"Right," Graham said, "but we should discuss it sometime in the near future."

"We will, Pat. But what about that man Ron who was your chauffeur in Rome? He threatened to expose you if you didn't hire him as your chauffeur here in Forest Park. How much did Ron know about your relationship with Pierre?"

Graham said, "He knew very little. Pierre sometimes drove us to Berzy near Verdun so I could do research on the history of my mother's family. He also drove us to the orphanage where my mother lived after her parents were killed. Pierre and I sent money to support it. At times Pierre's chauffeur would do the driving and Ron would stay in Rome. But Pierre and I were very guarded and reserved in Ron's presence and in the presence of Pierre's French Embassy chauffeur. This is not to say that Ron didn't have his suspicions about out relationship, especially since we always took our vacations at the same time. We traveled separately and would meet at a villa we rented on the Adriatic Sea. But we never told our chauffeurs where we were going or that we were going together. As diplomats we certainly were not going to discuss our personal lives with our chauffeurs because we both knew we could be blackmailed."

"So you're not worried that Ron might now go public?"

"Well, I don't relish that kind of publicity," Graham said, "but I think I should call his bluff. If I hired him, that would look as if I had something to hide. Furthermore, I don't need a chauffeur here in the states as I did in Rome. Driving on the streets of Rome is a wild experience."

I laughed and said, "I can attest to that. When I was there, I always had someone do the driving."

"Ed, this conversation has been good for me in many ways," Graham said. "Thanks for being such a good listener. Now, there's something else I would like to discuss with you."

"And what would that be?"

"Let me come right to the point," Graham said. "When you resigned at age 75, many bishops, including me, thought the pope had made a mistake to accept your resignation. He should have let you continue for five more years. But some of your enemies here and in Rome, like Bishop Maytin from Forest Park, convinced him that it was time for you to go. You were too liberal for them, right?"

"So I am told."

"Ed," Graham said, "I don't want to keep you on the sidelines any longer. You can be of great help to me. As you know, I haven't got off to a good start here. During my first two months as archbishop of this diocese, I have made too many important decisions without consulting others like yourself. I can't offer you a position in my administration, but I would like very much for you to be my guide and mentor. You've seen a lot of history in this archdiocese. And you have made history here, too."

"Pat, thanks for your vote of confidence. I am pleased, of course, and I will do everything I can to help you as the new archbishop—with one proviso."

"And what would that be?"

"I don't want you to defer to me," I said. "I don't want to be an albatross around your neck. You need to have the freedom to be your own man and to say no to suggestions I make. Just because I have more seniority and experience, I don't want you to think I'm looking over your shoulder, being critical of decisions you make. I'll be brutally honest with you, Pat, and I want you to be brutally honest with me. And I don't want any type of announcement saying that I will be an advisor to you. Let's keep this very fluid and very informal. Just between the two of us."

"That works for me, Ed. Once again, thanks for being so understanding and nonjudgmental." Graham rose from his chair and shook hands with me. As he left my office, I wondered whether he could resolve the weighty problems he had discussed with me.

Shortly after Graham left my office, Toni stopped to see me.

"Bishop, if it's none of my business, please tell me, but I'm really worried about something I saw last night."

"What was that, Toni?"

"I was reading a book in bed when I heard shouting from your floor. I ran down the stairs to see what was happening. I was afraid someone had broken in and was attacking you or Archbishop Graham. I was about half way down the stairs when I got scared and stopped. I was going to go back up and call the police. I heard Archbishop Graham call someone Ron, then I saw this mean looking guy running down the stairs to the first floor. He didn't see me, though, and was I glad. Who was that man?"

"I'm sorry you were frightened by the incident, Toni. You'll understand, I know, that I can't discuss it. It's a private matter between Archbishop Graham and the man—Ron."

Toni nodded and said, "OK, Bishop. I understand. But I sure won't forget the mean look on that guy's face."

"By the way, Toni. No school today?"

"I decided to take the day off."

I frowned.

She laughed and said, "Gotcha! There's a teachers' conference today."

Before I retired that evening, I went to the liquor cabinet and poured some Dewars Scotch into a glass filled with ice. I needed to reflect upon the day's events, especially Graham's confession that he is gay. Graham, I thought, is very shrewd. He had to know I overheard Ron trying to blackmail him. He could have chosen to ignore the subject but instead he laid it all out.

Why? Is it because he knows that Hackett will probably spread stories of his partnership with Pierre? Graham wants to control this, so he tells me about Pierre before I hear it through the rumor mill. Then he asks me to be his mentor, his confidante. I am now on his side. That's the way he wants it.

Is Graham really serious about cutting off his relationship with Hackett? Was that shouting incident staged to make me believe that he is through with Ron? And why is he maintaining another residence in the inner city? Is that where he intends to meet Ron, who may be his lover despite what he says about avoiding power relationships?

I poured a little more Scotch in my glass, raised it as if giving a toast and thought, "Here's to power and to those who know how to use it."

CHAPTER 23

On a rainy morning in October, Rinehart took an elevator to the top floor of the Chancery Building for an appointment with Archbishop Graham, a meeting requested by Graham. Gen Campbell, an intelligent woman in her early fifties whose diplomatic skills exceeded those of most of the clerics she worked for during her thirty years in the chancery, greeted him warmly. Rinehart accepted her offer of a cup of coffee.

"Is it still regular with just a touch of cream, Tom?" she asked. Gen had addressed him as Tom since the day they met at a staff meeting when she was secretary to Cardinal Mohr. He felt uncomfortable calling her Gen—a woman old enough to be his mother—and having her address him as Father. He had told her then that if she continued to call him Father Rinehart he would call her Mrs. Campbell.

"Yes, Gen," he said with a smile, "it's still regular with just a touch of cream. You didn't forget."

When she returned with the coffee, she reported that the archbishop had just phoned and said that he would be about ten minutes late. This news did not upset Rinehart. In fact, he expected it. He knew the drill. Unnerve your adversary by keeping him waiting. Gen knew the drill as well but showed no sign that she did.

"Perhaps I'll see you on your way out," she said as she left the room.

At ten minutes after nine, Graham entered the office and greeted Rinehart.

"Tom, I'm sorry I'm late. Got a call from the National Conference of Catholic Bishops office in Washington. Some bishop wants me to serve on a committee. And I don't want to do it. Too much to do here. I'm just getting my feet wet. Well, that's my problem, not yours, so let's go into my office and get to know one another."

"Fine, Archbishop, I'd like that."

In his office, Graham said, "Tom, I've been looking over some letters between you and the late Cardinal Mohr which were in his file. You really didn't want the job of being his secretary, did you? You made it quite clear that you preferred to stay in Newman Center work at the University."

"That's right, Archbishop. I could think of four or five qualified persons from the laity who could perform the same job just as well and even better because my heart wasn't into it. I really missed working with the young people at the University."

"Well, despite that," Graham said, "Cardinal Mohr has some letters in his file that highly praise your work. Evidently he saw you as a future bishop and wanted you to get accustomed to the environment of a chancery office."

"Well, I wouldn't want to have a bishop's job either. I'm not cut out for that. I'm not good at playing games. That's not my bag."

"What is your bag, Tom? I need to know so that I can give you a new assignment."

Rinehart laughed, "Archbishop, let's not play games. You must know that I applied for laicization through Archbishop Foley."

"When I was in Rome, I heard rumors to that effect, and again, since coming here. What's happened to your request?"

Rinehart smiled. "It's been denied. But you know that, don't you?"

"Tom, how would I know that?"

Rinehart felt anger boiling within him, but he resolved to speak softly. When he was sure that his temper was under control, he smiled and said, "Archbishop, I told you before that I'm not good at playing games, so let's not start. My contact in Rome told me you were in the Vatican office when my application was being processed. I suspect it was you who blocked it."

This remark took Graham off guard, so he went to a window and stared at the traffic below. After a minute, he asked, "Tom, why would I block your application?"

"I don't know. It could have been an ego thing or a power thing. Maybe you were angry that I went through Foley instead of you. I can only speculate. Only you know what you did in the office that day. I don't have time for the equivocation game."

"Tom, I am not equivocating. I heard that someone in the Vatican leaked the news about your application to the chancery office here. Then a couple of men in the chancery office grilled you about it for an hour or more. That should never have happened. I'm sorry they treated you so badly."

He paused for a moment, looked up and asked Rinehart, "Would it help if I resubmitted your application?"

"I'm not asking for that," Rinehart said. "My fiancée Kate and I are meeting today with the Lutheran chaplain at the University. We think he will agree to officiate at our wedding the third Saturday in November."

Graham was silent for a moment or two. Then he said, "Tom, I wish you would reconsider. Your wedding by a Protestant minister will get you excommunicated and will affect your bride's standing in the church as well."

"Yes, I know that, but I no longer care. And neither does Kate. We tried to observe the rules, but it wasn't good enough for the Vatican. Archbishop, I'm sorry to say that you are an integral part of a very dysfunctional church."

"That's pretty strong, Tom."

"It is, Archbishop, and I apologize if those words offend you. So let me put it another way. I think God must be amused. The Church is going to excommunicate someone who tried to follow the rules. God must be wondering who will excommunicate those who refused to grant the dispensation."

Just then Gen Campbell interrupted the conversation to tell Graham that his call from San Francisco had come through.

Graham excused himself and took the call in an adjoining office.

After five minutes he returned and said, "Tom, I ask you to reconsider your decision to be married by a Protestant minister. It's not a good one."

"With all due respect, Archbishop, Kate and I think it is. We have thought long and hard about it. And prayed about it too. And we read some literature to confirm us in the decision."

"I'm intrigued," Graham said, "about your reference to literature. Tell me more."

"At the University Kate uses fiction to show students how some fictional characters made good decisions and others made bad ones."

A somewhat skeptical Graham asked, "What piece of literature helped you and Kate to make this decision?"

"An American classic that you have read," Tom answered. "*Huckleberry Finn.*"

"Of course I read it, Tom, and really enjoyed it; but that was probably forty years ago. What part of the story helped you and Kate? It's been a long time since I read it."

"Archbishop, I'm sure you recall the scene where Huck and the runaway slave Jim are on a raft floating down the Mississippi. Huck is having conscience problems because he's hiding a runaway slave, which is against the law. So he has written a letter telling Jim's owner where she can find Jim. But then he thinks about Jim, what a great friend he is and what a fine human being he is. So he rips up the letter, and says, 'All right then, I'll go to hell.'"

"Yes, now I recall it," Graham said. "I remember our English professor saying that passage is one of the greatest in all literature. Huck sees slavery for what it really is. He will disobey the law that supports it even if he has to go hell."

"Yes," Tom said, "and he almost made a bad decision by choosing it over his best friend Jim."

"Tom, I'm somewhat confused here. I fail to see how this passage has helped you and Kate."

"Well, when Huck looked at that note he had intended to send to the authorities, he suddenly had an awakening. He saw what a horrible system slavery is. He saw how the white power structure used chains, fear, informants, and even lynching to keep it in place. And when Kate and I looked at the paper I signed asking for emancipation from celibacy, we were awakened to the fact that the Church had taken away our right as man and woman to marry and would use techniques of fear, isolation, humiliation, and even excommunication to keep us and the system in place. Like Huck Finn we said, All right then, we'll go to hell."

Graham was silent for a long time. Finally, Rinehart said, "Archbishop, I know my leaving and my marriage will embarrass some in the Church, but we aren't going to invite more than forty people. Also, we're not going to use our wedding as an occasion to blast the Church. There'll be no press conference. It's not going to be a media event. We are going 'gentle into that good night,' and we are not going to 'rage, rage, rage against the dying' church."

A smile came across Graham's face as he said, "Dylan Thomas would be proud of you, Tom. I hope I will meet Kate some day. She must be an unusual woman."

"That she is, Archbishop." He rose from his chair, shook hands with Graham and left.

Graham got up from his desk and stared out one of the windows and reflected on the meeting with Rinehart. It was obvious that the encounter had upset him.

Tom Rinehart is quite a man. I'm sorry he's leaving. That business of asking Rome for laicization is absurd. Why must a man living in the U.S. have his application reviewed by someone in the Vatican who doesn't even know him? Yes, it is about punishment and control. How sad. So Tom has a contact in the Vatican who knows that I was in the office in Rome when Tom's case was being reviewed. When I was asked by a monsignor there if I knew Rinehart, I said I didn't. He must have interpreted that as a sign that I wanted the application to be squashed. What naiveté on my part. I need to learn how to deal with personnel in the Vatican.

That Kate must be a great teacher. Imagine, using literature to show students how fictional characters make good and bad decisions. And that Huck Finn scene where Huck tears up the letter and says he'll go to hell rather than obey the law and turn in Jim. That really tore me up.

Are we in the Church into another kind of slavery? One that keeps gays and lesbians in the closet out of fear? One that keeps priests enslaved to a celibate life they once loved but now hate? One that keeps women enslaved to an abusive, destructive marriage? Or married men enslaved to arrogant, self-centered wives? Control and punishment. It was institutionalized in the days of slavery. Is it institutionalized in the Church today?

CHAPTER 24

I once suggested to Kate that some afternoon she should take Toni on a tour through the archdiocese. Most kids her age hear the word "archdiocese" but have no idea how much territory the archdiocese of Forest Park covers. So on a crisp fall afternoon Kate decided to take Toni for a ride to show her the beauty of the autumn leaves and to show her that that the archdiocese of Forest Park was quite extensive, much more than the neighborhood surrounding the cathedral and Haley House. Twenty-five miles south of the city, Toni was astounded to see horse-drawn buggies on the highway.

"Is there a race track near here?" Toni asked.

"No," Kate said, "the race track is north of the city. Those horses and buggies on the road aren't going to a track. Those are Amish people in those buggies going to their homes."

"Amish? I've never heard about the Amish. Tell me something about them."

"Well, they belong to small Christian communities that strive for simplicity in life," Kate replied. "They don't own cars, radios, television sets, washing machines, computers and other gadgets we think are so important. They make their own clothing and are not worried about keeping up with the latest fashions. The elders do permit farmers to have gasoline tractors on their farms. The Amish try to lead lives of prayer. Many of their prayers are said together or in common."

"Kate, how do you know so much about these people?"

Patient teacher that she is, Kate asked Toni, "Do you remember the first day we met?"

"Sure do," Toni said. "I was hitchhiking and you gave me a ride. You said something about making good and bad choices.

Usually you don't approve of hitchhiking, but sometimes it can be a good choice. You said that if the only way I could get to my grandmother who was very sick and needed me, then hitchhiking could be a good choice."

"That's right," said Kate."

"But why are you bringing this up again? I mean about making choices."

"Because, Toni, it has something to do with the Amish. In this country, our government gives us lots of choices, even the choice of living a very simple life. That's why many groups like Amish came to the United States. In some countries in Europe they were persecuted and harassed because they chose a different life style."

"Just because they don't use modern gadgets?" asked Toni.

"Not just because of that. The Amish believe that carrying arms violates the words of Jesus about peace. Our country gives Amish young men the right to avoid military service. Some countries won't honor their beliefs."

"What about their young girls?" Toni asked. "Any restrictions on them?"

"Yes, they're required to attend only eight years of schooling, but the Amish had to go to court to get that ruling."

"Only eight years! Why wouldn't the Amish want their young girls to have more than an eighth grade education?"

"Because they believe that God intends young girls to become wives and mothers," Kate said. "If girls went to high school and then to college, many wouldn't return to the Amish community. They would marry men who weren't Amish and live in the cities where their husbands worked. Gradually the Amish community would die out."

"So, the young girls have no choice."

"Well," Kate said, "they certainly don't have the choices that other girls your age do."

"How do these young girls make a living?"

"They cook, bake, make jellies, and sew and mend clothes,"

Kate said. “They also learn how to make quilts that are very beautiful. On the weekends especially in the summer and the fall, tourists from all over the State come to Amish Town to shop. They can also buy rocking chairs, tables and all kinds of furniture that the Amish men have made. The furniture is very handsome and is reasonable priced.”

They drove on a little while and then stopped. Kate said, “Let’s drive over to Amish town. Today is Wednesday and there won’t be many shoppers, but you can get a flavor of Amish life.”

“Great idea,” said Toni. “Maybe I can get an idea for a term paper I have to do on immigrants.”

“I promise you, Toni, the Amish will give enough for a book.”

Five minutes later they were in the heart of Amish Town. Horses and buggies were parked on one side of the road. The men wore overalls and had beards. Young girls were walking along the sidewalk with their mothers. They wore bonnets and long plain simple dresses. Kate and Toni greeted them. The women and girls smiled but did not attempt to engage them in conversation.

Most of the shops along the street were closed, but a furniture store was open so Kate and Toni entered it.

“Guten Tag,” said a ruddy faced, bearded man as he greeted them.

“Guten tag,” replied Kate.

“May I help you?” he asked in his heavy German accent.

“I’m Kate from the University and this is my friend Toni, who is in high school. She wants to know more about this Amish community.”

“Gut,” he said. “My name is Jakob Mueller. You are quite welcome to walk around. Feel free to ask me any questions. I’m making this rocking chair for a man in Forest Park. It’s almost finished.”

“It’s beautiful,” Toni said.

“Danke,” Jakob said.

Kate noticed the puzzled look on Toni’s face and said, “Jakob is thanking you for the compliment."

"Oh, you're welcome," Toni said.

Jakob bowed his head and smiled.

Kate and Toni stepped into the store, looking at the chairs and tables. Kate hadn't told Toni about her forthcoming marriage. She wanted Tom to come with her some Saturday to Amish Town to choose furniture for the home they planned to buy after their marriage. Kate thought that the dining room table, the chairs and the king-sized bed would appeal to Tom as they did to her. She found hard to believe the reasonable prices on these hand-crafted items.

Toni went into a room where wooden coffins were being made. Most were six feet in length, but one was about four feet long.

Toni asked Jakob if the coffins came in different sizes.

"No," he said, "this one is for an eight-year-old girl who died a few days ago. She will be buried on Friday afternoon."

"What happened to her?" Toni asked.

"Well," Jakob said with tears in his eyes, "we were coming back from a prayer meeting when a car tried to pass us on a hill. But another car was coming down the hill and forced us off the road. The horse and buggy tipped over. I was thrown clear, but the young girl—my only daughter—was killed."

Kate and Toni were so moved by this story that they found it hard to speak. It was as if all the air had been sucked out of the room.

When she recovered control of her emotions, Kate said to Jakob, "I'm so sorry for your loss. And thank you for your hospitality. You and your family will be in our prayers. I will be back soon to buy some furniture. Danke shőn und aufwiedersehen."

He smiled and said, "Aufwiedersehen."

Both Kate and Toni were silent as they drove out of Amish Town. They were both thinking of Jakob making a coffin for his only daughter, who had died so tragically.

CHAPTER 25

The next day Kate called Toni and asked her if she would like to take another ride after school. Toni cleared it with her grandmother, and at 4:00 PM they met at Haley House and drove into the country. The ride, Kate thought, would give Toni an opportunity to talk.

Kate decided to take a different route rather than the shorter route they had traveled yesterday. As the two settled into an easy conversation, Kate found herself in a rather rundown section of the city. She saw a dilapidated church and rectory and what appeared to be an unused school building she had never seen before.

"Is that a Catholic church?" she asked Toni.

"Kate, how would I know?"

"Well, you know a lot about this city," Kate said. "I was wondering who the pastor is. I thought Archbishop Foley might have mentioned the church."

"Sorry, can't help you. Why are you so interested in it?"

"Well, the church, the rectory, and the school look rather substantial even though they are now in disrepair. This must have been a very nice neighborhood at one time."

"Couldn't prove it by me," Toni said.

Kate parked the car, and she and Toni got out and headed toward the church. To the right of the church doors was a weather-beaten sign—Saint Mary Church. They tried the doors of the church, but they were locked.

As they were walking back to the car, the door to the rectory opened and a man appeared. He was over six feet tall, had gray hair, and was solidly built. He was wearing blue jeans, a plaid shirt, and a faded denim jacket. Kate thought he looked like Paul

Newman, the movie star. He was that handsome.

"May I help you? I'm Mike Brown, the new pastor of Saint Mary's. I was appointed about a week ago. I'm supposed to be installed in a couple of months."

"We're just looking around. I'm Kate Green from the University, and this is my friend Toni Vincent."

"Are you members of a local parish?"

"No," Kate said, "I grew up in a parish in Dayton. Now I worship at the Newman Center chapel at the University. Toni lives at Haley House with her grandmother, who is the housekeeper for Archbishop Foley."

"He's a good friend of mine," Brown said. "Tell him I said hello." Toni said she would.

"What happened to the pastor who was here?" Toni asked.

"He died six months ago," Brown said. "The chancery people thought the parish should be closed. The archdiocese was subsidizing the place for about three thousand dollars a month. Catholics in the neighborhood kept moving to the suburbs."

"So the chancery people never appointed a new pastor?" Kate asked.

"Well, Kate, with the death of Cardinal Mohr, everything was on hold. Now that Graham is the new archbishop, he's making appointments. That's why I'm here."

"When did the school close?" Toni asked.

"About six years ago," Brown said. "Enrollment had dipped to about one hundred for all eight grades. As far as I know, I don't think the chancery people want the school to reopen. The new archbishop, however, may have a different idea."

"Well, Mike," Kate said. "You have a lot of work to do. Do you mind my calling you Mike?"

"Hell, no. Excuse me, I still have some rough edges. Sure, call me Mike. That goes for you too, Toni."

"Cool, Mike," Toni said.

"Mike, I meant it when I said you have a lot of work to do,"

Kate said. "Do you have anyone coming to help you get this place ready?"

"No, I don't," Mike replied. "I have a lot of friends at Saint Boniface, the place where I've been assistant pastor for the last ten years. But that's about seventy-five miles from here. Too far for them to come."

"You're probably right," Kate said, "but why not ask them to help? We have five or six weekends before you take over, so if we can get a work crew here on a Saturday and Sunday for three or four weeks, I think we can help you get this place in reasonable shape for your installation. I'd be willing to recruit some students at the University where I teach."

"And I'll get some kids from the high school to help," Toni said.

"Wow!" Mike exclaimed. "I'm beginning to believe in guardian angels again."

"Well, these aren't angels, but flesh and blood kids with big appetites," Kate said. "So, Mike, get a ton of food ready! Hot dogs, hamburgers, baked beans, cold cuts, pickles, catsup, mustard, relish. And have plenty of coffee, tea and pop on hand. And get some mops, rags, rakes, lawn mowers, gloves, paint, and paint brushes. Do you need any money?"

"No, the people at Saint Boniface had a send-off for me and gave me $4,000 for a trip to Europe so I could visit my relatives in Ireland."

"Mike, they really must have liked you," Toni said.

"Yes, they did. And I really liked them. We hit it off just fine. And Jack Wagner, the pastor, was great too. He slipped me five C-notes from his savings."

"Mike, don't you think you'll disappoint those people if you don't take that trip?" Kate asked.

"I suppose so, Kate. But they didn't say when I had to take it. I'll get to Ireland eventually. Maybe next year or the year after. Those people want me to use the money any way that will make me happy. They won't object if I use all of it or part of it to rehabilitate this church."

After pausing to light a cigarette, he asked Kate and Toni if they had ever been to Amish Town.

"Yes," Kate said, "we were there just yesterday. We were in Jakob Mueller's store. The furniture those Amish make is beautiful."

"You got that right, Kate. I'm going to have Jakob Mueller make a dining room table and some other furniture for the rectory. And he isn't charging an arm and a leg. Some of the Amish have even volunteered to help me clean up this place."

Kate and Toni were delighted. "That's super!" said Toni.

Mike added, "Kate, maybe Jakob Mueller told you about the tragic death of his young daughter. She'll be buried this Friday afternoon. I'm going to the service. Would you and Toni be interested in going, too?"

"Will it be all right?" Kate asked.

"Sure will. They'll be touched that you want to share their sorrow."

Kate looked at her watch. "Mike," she said, "I have an appointment at five, so Toni and I will have to leave. But tomorrow we'll be back at four, and I'll give you a list of the things we'll need. And we'll try to get there for the Amish funeral service. Nice meeting you, Mike. Come on, Toni, we have to run."

"Goodbye, Kate. Goodbye, Toni. Thanks."

Toni waved and followed Kate to the car.

On the way to the University, they talked about their meeting with Mike.

"I'm glad we met him. Seems like a nice guy. What do you think, Toni?"

"He's really handsome. I'll bet he broke a lot of girls' hearts when he decided to be a priest."

"I'm sure he did," Kate said.

Toni hung out in Kate's office while Kate was at the meeting.

It was after 6:00 P.M. when Kate drove her to Haley House in time to help her grandmother put dinner on the table. Tired, but happy with their trip to Amish Town, Kate quickly punched in Tom's cell phone number to tell him she would arrive about a half hour late at the University, where they had arranged to meet for dinner.

Tom was settled at a table when she arrived. After they went through the cafeteria line and got settled at their table, Kate looked at Tom and said, "Tell me what you know about Mike Brown. He's about fifty, and his first pastorate is a rundown parish in the inner city. Doesn't make sense."

"No, it doesn't, but about twelve years ago there was an unfortunate incident in Mike's life that made the headlines."

"What happened?"

"One rainy night Mike was driving home smashed. A deer darted out in front of his car. Mike hit the brakes, skidded on the wet pavement, sending the car into the path of an elderly couple driving home from church. Both cars were totaled. Mike was not seriously hurt, but the elderly couple was hospitalized for many months. Both still need therapy."

"How tragic!" Kate said.

"Yes it was. It made headlines for a few days. The police arrested Mike on a DUI charge. It was his first offense, so he didn't do any jail time, but he had to get into AA. Archbishop Foley sent him to a treatment center for alcoholics and then assigned him as an assistant pastor at Saint Boniface about seventy-five miles to the south. Jack Wagner, a recovering alcoholic, is pastor there. Real good guy."

"So, the chancery is testing the waters about Mike Brown."

"You've got it, Kate." Tom replied. "If Mike stays sober, he'll get a better parish. If he screws up, it's not a great loss. It's only a rundown parish. The chancery has other recovering alcoholics they can put in there should Mike fail."

"What a rotten system," Kate said.

"Agreed. But no different from a lot of corporations."

"I know. But I want to ask something else that's gnawing at me," Kate said.

"Shoot," Tom said.

"I want to know why Mike was driving smashed. Was he an alcoholic, or did something happen that got him into drinking to excess that night?"

"Good question, Kate. No, Mike was not an alcoholic then, and Jack Wagner tells me he's not an alcoholic now. He hasn't had a drink since the night of that terrible accident."

Kate listened, shaking her head.

"About fifteen years ago," continued Tom, "Mike fell in love with a very smart and attractive woman. He wanted to marry her, but he could never get up enough courage to tell his widowed mother he was leaving the priesthood. After three years his woman friend got tired of waiting. She broke off the relationship and married someone else. That threw Mike into a tailspin. That's when he began drinking—to excess. Well, you know what happened."

"What a sad story, Tom. And what a sad, sick system. I'm glad you're getting out of it."

"Well I'm glad I'm getting out too, Kate. But let's be fair. The 'system' showed compassion for Mike. It worked for his rehabilitation and didn't throw him to the wolves. Mike functions very well now, and I am sure he's going to be a great pastor for Saint Mary's."

"I see what you mean, Tom. This celibacy issue has really skewed my thinking about the Church. I know I need to temper my thinking—and my remarks."

"And so do I, Kate."

CHAPTER 26

Kate and Toni drove out to Saint Mary's a few days later, intending to prepare a plan for the volunteer cleanup crew. Kate parked at the side of the road about three hundred yards south of the church, and they got out and started walking.

"Hey, wait for me!" someone yelled.

It was Mike Brown. "Hey, Kate. Hey, Toni. Did you lose something?"

"No, Mike," Kate said. "We're looking for the cemetery."

"Well," Mike said, "It starts about a hundred yards from here. But it hasn't been kept up. I'm embarrassed to have you see it."

"It's not your fault, Mike," Toni said. "You just took over the place."

"I know," said Mike. "But I'm embarrassed for the Church. I understand they have some college kids cut down the weeds about three times a year, but they need a caretaker here to keep the place in good condition. That won't happen, though, because some penny pinchers in the chancery think they can save the diocese some money."

"I'll bet they would think differently if their parents and grandparents were buried here," Kate said.

"What a gorgeous view of the city from this rolling hill," Toni said. "When I die, bury me here."

"I'll try to remember that for the next fifty years. Toni, right now you're too young to be thinking about dying."

"So am I," Mike laughed. "But I'll try to get a crew over here today to cut down the weeds and pick up those headstones that have been knocked down."

They walked around for a few minutes, remarking on some of

the ages carved into the stone. “Look,” said Toni. “This one says ‘born 1916, died 1921.’ Gosh, that means she was only five years old! And you say I’m too young to be thinking about death!” The three talked about what a loss that death must have been to the parents of the child. Looking at her watch, Kate nudged Toni. “Hey, kid,” she said. “It’s time for us to get to the rectory to draw up a plan for the cleanup. Want a ride, Mike?” Mike thanked Kate and said he needed the walk.

“Go right in. It’s unlocked. I’ll be there shortly,” he said.

Instead of going right back to the rectory, Mike stayed and tried to pick up as best he could some of the headstones that had been knocked over. He recognized a few names of old-timers who had been among the first parishioners at Saint Mary’s. He also came across a plot of ground with rows of small headstones that marked the graves of babies who had died without receiving baptism.

When he got back to the rectory, he joined Kate and Toni in the kitchen. Kate had made a pot of coffee. The three of them sat around the table.

Kate said, “Mike, you seem down. You were so upbeat when we saw you in the cemetery a while ago.”

“Maybe Mike’s embarrassed because the head stones have been knocked over and he didn’t want us to see them.”

“No, it’s not that, Toni.”

“What is it then?” Kate asked.

“Well, as I was walking back to the rectory, I came across a small plot of ground with a fence around it. Inside the fence were a couple of rows of small headstones with names like Baby Marie Holmes, died 1912; Baby John Wertz, died 1912; Baby Gretchen Stover, died 1913. I felt sad and depressed.

“Really?” Kate said.

“Yes, Kate, I almost cried,” Mike said.

“You couldn’t have known these kids, Mike. Are you that sentimental?”

“No, Kate, I’m not. What I came across were the graves of

infants who had died without baptism. They were buried in unconsecrated ground."

"Why?" Toni asked.

"Because Jesus had said: 'Unless you are born of water and the Holy Spirit you cannot enter the kingdom of God.' Ever hear those words, Toni?"

"Yeah, the born agains at school quote those words all the time."

"Well, Toni, what do you think happened to those infants who died without baptism?" Mike asked.

"Well, I guess they went to heaven. Why wouldn't they? They never committed a sin," Toni said.

"True, they didn't commit sin," Mike said, "but they couldn't go to heaven because they weren't baptized."

"You're kidding! So what does God do with all those unbaptized babies?" Toni asked.

"The teaching is that He created a special place for them called Limbo, where they are always completely happy, but they never get to heaven." Mike said.

"Why not?" Toni asked.

"Because they have not been baptized," Mike said.

"I don't believe that Limbo crap," Toni said. "I read the Bible almost every day so I can discuss things with the kids who are born agains. But I've never read that word Limbo in the Bible. And even if it was in the Bible, I wouldn't believe in it."

"Neither would I," Kate said. "And neither would Mike. Right?"

"Right! But that's what I was taught in the seminary, and that's what I preached for some years after I was ordained. I remember telling women whose infants died before baptism that their baby would always be naturally happy but they would never see their infants again because it had not been baptized. It was not in the state of grace."

Toni said, "Mike, you had to be out of your mind to teach that shit."

"You're absolutely right, Toni. But at the time I thought it was theologically sound. I thought the Church knew what God wanted and that God would do what the Church wanted."

"Why don't you tell Toni about other people who couldn't be buried in that cemetery?" Kate asked.

"Yeah, tell me," said Toni, obviously puzzled.

"Well, for a long time, the Church wouldn't bury people who had committed suicide or were public sinners or people who had married outside the church."

"Didn't church authorities know that people who commit suicide aren't thinking clearly when they commit such an act?" Kate asked.

"Well, they know it now, thanks to studies of the human mind and human behavior," Mike said. "But fifty years ago or more churchmen often looked at psychologists and psychiatrists as crackpots. Today, I don't think that any priest or bishop would deny Christian burial to any man, woman, or young adult who had committed suicide. Our attitude today is much more understanding and compassionate. Thank God."

"Amen to that," Kate said.

"We had a guy in our school who committed suicide last year," Toni said. "I think he was gay. Some of us went to his funeral Mass. The priest gave a really good homily. He made everybody feel a lot better about what happened."

"I'm glad to hear that, Toni. Most priests, I think, are like that, but there are still a few who think they should give a hell and brimstone sermon on such an occasion. Lord, deliver us from them," Mike said.

"Amen to that!" Toni said.

"Tell me this, Mike, would you bury a public sinner?" Kate asked.

"I'm lost," Toni said. "What's a public sinner?"

"Someone who is a notorious criminal, like the mobsters who

used to shoot up Chicago during the Roaring Twenties. Someone like Al Capone, for example," Mike said.

"Mike, would you bury someone like him?" Kate asked.

"Yes, I would," Mike said, "for the sake of the family. Why punish the family? Why add to their embarrassment? The guy who did these terrible things has left the scene. Let God judge him."

"OK, I buy that," said Kate, "but tell me, what would you do about a young newly married Catholic couple who are married by a minister because they couldn't get a dispensation for the husband—who had been a Catholic priest? Let's say that on their wedding trip they die in a plane crash and their families come to you and ask you to bury them. Would you?"

"Kate," said Mike, "are we talking about a hypothetical case or did this really happen?"

"Mike, it didn't happen. But it could. When Tom Rinehart and I get married later this year, we're going to Europe on our wedding trip. Suppose the plane goes down, killing all aboard. Would you deny us Christian burial knowing that Tom's application for laicization was turned down?"

Both Mike and Toni were speechless. Mike took a deep breath and said, "Kate, let me extend my best wishes. Tom is one hell of a guy and will make a great husband. And—I've known you for only a couple of days, Kate, but you're going to make a great wife. I hope you'll invite me to the wedding. And yes, I'll bury you and Tom, and I will also bury anyone from the chancery who tries to stop me."

"Thanks, Mike," Kate said, as she gave him a big hug.

Toni was speechless, trying to absorb this news. Finally, she said, "Kate, I'm really happy for you, but why didn't you tell me? I thought you were going to teach college for the rest of your life. I didn't know you and Tom were in love."

"Well, Toni, now you know," Kate said. "And there's something else you should know. Tom and I both want you to live with us if anything happens to your mother or to your grandmother.

Our home will always be your home."

Toni burst into tears and hugged Kate. "Thanks, Kate, you and Tom are going to be very proud of me."

"We already are," Kate said. "And we hope you will always be proud of us."

After Kate dropped off Toni at Haley House, Toni asked me if she could see me after dinner. "Of course," I told her, "but I can only give you a half hour because some friends are coming over for a visit. If that's all right, be in my office at 7:30."

Precisely at 7:30, there was a knock on my door. "Come in, Toni," I said. "What's new?"

"Well, Bishop, this afternoon, I found out that Kate and Tom are going to get married. But you knew that, didn't you?"

"Yes, I did, Toni, and I'm happy for both of them."

"So am I," Toni said, "but why aren't you marrying them?"

"Well, they asked me to officiate. But when Tom's request to be returned to the lay state was turned down in Rome, they decided to ask the Lutheran chaplain at the University to preside. Tom refused to ask for permission again."

"Bishop, how does this make you feel?" Toni asked.

"Well, Toni, I feel very sad. I looked forward to officiating at their wedding. They are both very good people."

"Will you be there for the ceremony?" Toni asked.

"Probably not," I said. "I don't want some reporter to use me for a story that could embarrass Archbishop Graham. I do plan to attend the dinner and reception, though."

"You guys—I mean priests—really protect one another, don't you?" Toni asked.

I laughed and said, "Toni, it's not protection, but etiquette, good form. The right thing to do."

"Well," Toni said, "it's bullshit if you'll excuse my French."

"Toni, I'm not going to argue with you. Many people feel the same as you, so let's move on to another subject."

"All right," Toni said, "I also learned this afternoon that if after they get married by that Lutheran minister and they die in a plane crash, they can't be buried from the church. Why not?"

"Because according to Church law, they'd be excommunicated. They knowingly chose to do something that put them outside the Catholic community. That's what excommunication is."

"That's a real tough penalty, Bishop. Mike Brown said he wouldn't enforce it. He would bury both of them. Would you?"

"Well, Toni, I'm not a pastor, but I would try everything to get around the law so I could bury them," I said. "Tom and Kate tried to play by the rules. That would really influence my decision."

"When we were driving back, Kate and I talked about why we even need Catholic cemeteries. She thinks that it's a way the Church continues to exercise punishment and control. Do you think that, Bishop?"

"Well, Toni, there's some truth in what Kate says. But many Catholic cemeteries were started to affirm our belief in the resurrection of the body. A hundred years ago or more the Church's teaching on that subject was under attack. Some people were getting cremated to show their contempt for the doctrine of the resurrection of the body. So people who were cremated were denied burial in a Catholic cemetery."

"My dad was cremated after he died and he's buried in Queen of Heaven Cemetery. How come?" Toni asked.

"Because the law changed," I said. "Catholic people can now be cremated and the ashes buried in a Catholic cemetery."

"Kate also said that Catholic cemeteries are money makers for the Church. Is that true?" Toni asked.

"Well, Toni. Funerals are a big industry, and our Church has helped it grow."

"Bishop," Toni said, "I watched Cardinal Mohr's funeral on television. He was buried in a casket that must have cost $10,000. It was a beautiful casket. But couldn't he have been buried in a plain casket?"

"Yes, he could have, Toni, and probably should have. But he

didn't have that in his will. So when he died so suddenly, some people in the chancery thought that since he was a cardinal, he should have the very best. When I die, just bury me in a plain wooden box. Nothing fancy."

"OK," Toni said, "but make sure that's in your will."

"It soon will be because Bill Danko is rewriting my will. After my death, once the chancery people see his name and my name on the document, they will follow the instructions I wrote in the will. They won't want to get into a legal fight with Danko because they know they will lose. He's much better at playing hardball than they are."

"Hooray for our side," Toni said with a grin.

I laughed, walked her to the door and said goodnight.

CHAPTER 27

At 8:00 AM the following Saturday an energized group of thirty volunteers assembled outside the rectory of Saint Mary parish. The tall maples behind the church had lost most of their brilliant gold and red leaves, covering the yard and the nearby cemetery with a soft carpet. Mike Brown, the pastor, greeted the volunteers and thanked them for coming and then introduced Kate.

"Hi, I'm Kate Green, and this is Toni Vincent, who will be directing the efforts of volunteers from the high school. I'll be directing the volunteers from the university. And Mike will direct the neighborhood volunteers and his friends who came up from Saint Boniface parish to help. Remember that Mike is the person in charge here. He'll tell us what needs to be done. Mike."

"Thanks, Kate. Our task today and tomorrow is to remove the beer and pop cans and other trash littering the yard, rake the leaves, bag them, and load them into the truck that Marilyn Schwartz drove over from St. Boniface. A couple hundred yards south of here is a small cemetery in need of repair. We can't replace the broken monuments and head stones in the cemetery, but we can cut down the weeds and rake the leaves. We also have to clean the inside of the church. That means scrubbing the floors, washing the pews, vacuuming the carpeting around the altar, cleaning the sacristy. Next week we'll start painting anything that doesn't move. One other thing, fill out a name tag and wear it. No titles. We're all on a first name basis. Now let's have coffee and donuts and then go to work. We'll break for lunch at noon. We'll hand out boxed lunches and eat outside if this good weather holds up."

As the group stood around drinking coffee and hot chocolate, a shiny black Lincoln Town Car pulled up.

"It's the Mafia," someone joked. "Maybe we're on their turf."

"Get serious, gang," yelled one of the high school football players, "if it was the Mafia, the guy would have a bodyguard driving a Lexus SUV or a Maserati." Everyone laughed.

Mike Brown came over and welcomed the newcomer. He was stockily built, with thinning gray hair and a tanned rugged face. He was wearing blue jeans, boots and an old letter sweater from the University of Michigan.

"Welcome, I'm Mike Brown, the new pastor of Saint Mary's. Meet Kate Green and Toni Vincent, who recruited most of these people. Who are you?"

"Hi, I'm Alger Kuraitis. I'm an architect. My office is downtown."

"What brings you to Saint Mary's this Saturday morning, Alger?" Brown asked.

"Well, I heard the parish was being resurrected. I felt I had to come and do something to pay this parish back. My brother and I went to school here when my mother brought us from Lithuania. That was in the fifties. My dad was drafted into the Russian army and couldn't come with us. The Sisters of Charity who taught here were very good to us."

"When did your dad join you?" Kate asked.

"He never did. The government over there won't release him even though the Cold War is over. My mother had a nervous breakdown a few years after we came here and has been in a nursing home ever since."

"That's terrible," Kate said. "How did you kids survive?"

"Well, a nun named Sister Thomas Marie took a great interest in us. She arranged for us to live with some people in the parish and gave us money for books and clothes. She was instrumental in my getting a scholarship to the University of Michigan. That's how I became an architect. But I didn't come here to talk about myself. What can I do to help?"

"Well, Alger," Mike said, "I'm going to assign you to work on the inside of the church. Sometime later we can talk about what we can do with that old school building. It hasn't been used in years."

"I certainly would like to do that, but right now I'm interested in getting to that table for some coffee and donuts."

Toni was waiting for him at the table. "Hey, Alger. We met when you drove up. I'm Toni Vincent. Thanks for coming. Want some coffee?"

"Sure do. Black. No sugar."

While she and Alger were talking, Kate walked over to the church, which was empty. She flipped open her cell phone and called Tom, who was preparing to go to the chancery office to remove some of his files. He had sent out a letter to the priests of the archdiocese and to the newspapers that he was leaving the ministry and would marry Kate Green from the University.

"Tom, I'm glad I caught you. Are you planning to come over to Saint Mary's today?"

"Yes, I am, honey, but I probably won't get there until late morning. How are things going?"

"Great," she replied, "but I wonder if you could use your media contacts to get a television crew over here."

There was a long pause before Rinehart answered. "Kate, you're as savvy about the media as anyone. Why would a TV director send out a crew to take pictures of people raking leaves and picking up beer bottles? Is there a human interest story in this?"

"I think there is," Kate said. She told him about Alger coming here as a kid from Lithuania with his mother and brother and finding kindness and love from the nuns who taught at Saint Mary's.

"Tom, this man's story needs to be told, and our cleanup project at Saint Mary's gives him a chance to tell it."

"Kate, you've got my attention. I'll call our friend Mary Teare at KWST."

"Good, Tom, and I'll call that newspaper reporter—the one

who's Toni's neighbor. Toni knows his name. Maybe he would want this story for the Sunday paper."

"What time is lunch over there?" Tom asked.

"At twelve noon sharp."

"Good, I'll try to get the TV people there by noon. I'll call you back if I can get a commitment from them."

For the next few hours, the place was humming. Toni kept bugging Mike to play some music that she and her friends liked. "Mike, my friends from school aren't going to hang out here if you don't play their kind of music."

"You're right, Toni. I've got a CD player and a speaker system I brought with me. They're in a box in the living room that I haven't unpacked. It's marked in big black letters—CD. Why don't you and a couple of your friends unpack it and select whatever you want? Better still, can your friends supply the music?"

"OK, Mike," Toni said. She called a couple of her friends over, and in no time found the CD and the speaker system. One of the university students volunteered to set it up and brought out a stack of CD's he kept in his car. Soon their favorite music was blaring across the yard.

"Mike," Toni asked, "is this music too loud? We don't want to disturb the neighbors."

"Don't worry about it, Toni. I think the neighbors will be happy that we're doing something. This property has been an eyesore too long."

He was right about the neighbors. Within a few minutes, several strolled over to investigate—a white guy with his two sons, two black women whose husbands joined them later, and a Latino and his girlfriend. Mike Brown greeted them and offered them coffee and donuts. None, however, volunteered to work, which was OK with Mike. He told them about the box lunches at noon and said they were welcome to come. One promised to return.

At noon, Mike asked Toni to give out a loud whistle. He gave a referee's timeout sign and told the group it was time for lunch.

Fifteen minutes later the television crew from KWST arrived. Mary Teare hopped out of the truck and looked for Tom Rinehart, but he had not yet arrived. Kate went over to her and assured her that Tom would be along shortly.

"Mary, I'm Kate Green. I'm the one who asked Tom to call you. There's a good human interest story here."

"If it's a good one," said Teare, "we'll use it. Tell me more."

Kate told her about Alger coming to this country as a kid from Lithuania, the hardships he and his mother and brother experienced, and how they would not have survived were it not for the sisters who taught here. Teare said she wanted to meet Alger.

"Is he willing to be on camera?" Teare asked Kate.

"Yes, he is," Kate said. "At first he didn't want to go on camera. But when I told him that his story could do more for this parish than his raking the leaves around the church, he agreed. He's a rather quiet guy, as you'll find out."

Just then Tom arrived and greeted Kate and Mary Teare. Kate excused herself to look for Alger, and a couple of minutes later brought him back and introduced him to Teare and Rinehart.

Teare huddled with Alger and Mike Brown. A short time later, the crew began shooting, planning to have something ready for the six o'clock and eleven o'clock news. Teare seemed genuinely pleased to have been called.

Later in the evening, Toni, Kate, and Tom met me in my office at Haley House. I was the only one of the group who had been free to watch the six o'clock news program.

"I saw what you people are doing at Saint Mary's," I said. "Great publicity! Whose idea was it to get the interview with that architect?"

"It was Kate's idea," Tom said. "When she called me and asked me to have Mary Teare send a camera crew to the parish, I dismissed it. Why would a TV station send a crew to take pictures of volunteers cutting grass and pulling up weeds? Then she told me about Alger. What a story."

"Indeed," I said. "And I knew that Sister Thomas Marie he talked about. What a great lady. Where is she now?"

"I asked Alger that question, and he told me that she's in her nineties and lives at their Motherhouse," Kate said.

"Well, I'm glad she's getting recognized for the great work she did."

"So you were pleased with the coverage, Ed?"

"Pleased? Ecstatic is a better word. For once people could turn on their televisions and not see pictures of sick priests who molested kids. I'll bet that television station was swamped with phone calls. And, mark my words, you're going to be swamped with volunteers tomorrow—and maybe even some contributions to help with renovations."

"Ed, I hope you're right," Kate said.

"Me, too!" Toni said excitedly.

There was a knock on the office door. It was Archbishop Graham.

"Hi, everyone. Stay seated. I saw that television newscast about Saint Mary's. What a shot in the arm for Mike Brown and his new parish. The story that architect told really touched me, and I think it will touch a lot of viewers. I called Mike Brown and told him I saw the program. He told me he has a lot of plans for Saint Mary's. He also told me that he got a call from Hank Kolar, the columnist for the newspaper. He's going to do a story on Alger and those nuns next Sunday, and he'll write about what Mike Brown is doing as the new pastor."

"You couldn't have made a better choice for that parish, Archbishop," Rinehart said. "Just watch him. He'll resurrect the parish and the entire neighborhood."

"That's good news, Tom," Graham said. "A resurrection would be great for all of us."

"Indeed, it would," I said. "And speaking of resurrection, did you see the small cemetery that's about 500 yards south of the church? It belongs to the church and to the diocese, but I don't think anyone has been buried in it for twenty years or more. It's been badly neglected, and that's a disgrace."

"Yes," Toni said, "Kate and I checked it out this morning with Father Brown. It's at the top of a rolling hill and gives a great view of the city."

"Bishop," said Kate, "Toni has fallen in love with the place. She's already picked out the place where she wants to be buried."

I laughed at that, and Graham said he hoped the cemetery would still be there when it came time for her to die.

"It will be," Toni said.

CHAPTER 28

After dinner on a Thursday night, I was surprised to find Toni waiting outside my office. When she didn't appear at dinner, her grandmother explained that Toni was still at school for basketball practice.

"Well hello, Toni, how did basketball practice go?"

"OK. We have a game this Saturday, but the coach isn't too pleased with our performance as a team. He says too many of us are selfish. I think he has a point. We stink."

I sensed she was not interested in talking about the team but about the newspaper she was carrying, so I dropped the subject.

"Well, young lady, what are we going to discuss tonight?"

"Sickos and creeps. I mean priests molesting little boys. This newspaper is filled with it, and my born again friends at school have been on me all day about it. Jeez, it's embarrassing."

"I'm sure it is," I said. "I'm embarrassed too." I asked Toni if I could look at the newspaper, and she handed it to me. After I scanned the article, I said, "This story is about pedophile priests on the Eastern seaboard. No priests from our diocese are mentioned."

"Has it happened here?" Toni asked.

"Some years ago we did have a few cases of priests who had abused altar boys. On the advice of a very competent priest psychiatrist we removed them from their parishes immediately and notified the police, who arrested them. I met with the parents of the boys and apologized."

"Did they sue—like some of the people in this article did?"

"Yes, they did. The jury ruled in favor of the parents and their sons, and the diocese was fined a substantial amount of money."

Toni excused herself and went to the kitchen. She came back

carrying a glass of coke. She looked puzzled. "Bishop, why would a guy who is ordained molest a little kid? It's gross."

"You're right, Toni. Priests who do that are pedophiles, which means that their sexual development has been arrested. They're still adolescents as far as their sexual development is concerned."

"Is that common, Bishop?"

"Unfortunately, it is. And they're not just priests. They are lawyers, doctors, accountants, teachers, salesmen, truck drivers, or construction workers who abuse children in their own families and try to convince the child that this must be kept secret. 'Mom must never know,' they say. 'She wouldn't understand the deep love I have for you.'"

"Yuk, that's really sick!"

"Yes, it is. But these are very sick people."

"Can they ever be cured?" Toni asked.

"There was a time when professional people in medicine thought so," I said. "They can be given drugs that help control their urges, but psychiatrists and psychologists and social workers now think they can never be cured. What has to happen is that they must never be alone with children. And they must never be ordained to the priesthood."

"So how does the seminary keep out these homosexuals?"

"Hold on, Toni. You've just made a mistake that many people do, namely, that a homosexual is a pedophile. Not true. A married man who is a father of a small child can be a pedophile. A father sometimes crawls into bed with his young son or daughter. And sometimes the mother suspects that the child is being sexually abused but says nothing."

"Bishop, that's really disgusting."

"Yes, it is, Toni. I only mention it to help you be better informed. There's a lot of gay bashing going on over this scandal in the priesthood. Gays are being targeted as pedophiles, and it simply is not true."

"Are there gays in the priesthood?"

"Yes, there are. And there are gays in every profession. I know some gays who are very good priests. They are on the job every day. They work on their homilies, they are dedicated to the poor, and they keep their vow of celibacy. Of course, some don't. But that's also true of some priests who are straight. They get involved in affairs with women in their parishes, some of whom are married."

"Bishop, weren't most of the apostles married men?"

"Yes, Toni, most scholars believe all the apostles were married except John," I said.

"So when did the Church make the rule that priests couldn't marry?"

"I think it was at the end of the eleventh century, something like 1097, but don't hold me to that date."

"What happened that made the Church change the rules and not let priests marry?" Toni asked.

"Money and property, I am sorry to say," I replied.

"What do you mean?"

"The church feared that married priests would think of the church buildings that were part of their ministry as their own property that they could will to their sons. So the pope ordered that all priests had to be celibate. They could no longer marry, and if they did, they were excommunicated."

Toni was silent for a minute trying to take all this in. Then she said, "Well, I heard this talk show the other day, and one of the priests on the panel said that celibacy was a precious jewel that Christ gave to the Church."

I laughed and said, "I think I heard the same program. I think that priest was trying to make points with the Vatican. If celibacy is such a jewel, why did it take a thousand years before it became the law?"

"Bishop, you're celibate, but you don't seem to think it's such a great thing."

"Toni, I think you're jumping to conclusions. I have found that celibacy has a real value in my own life. As I look back over my years in the priesthood, I probably could not have accomplished the things I did if I had a wife and children. But it made for a lonely life. I believe that a young man aspiring to the priesthood should be given the option of marrying or being celibate."

"Do you think that will happen soon?"

"Certainly not in the lifetime of the present pope. Maybe not even in the lifetime of his successor. But eventually it will happen, and that will be a good thing."

"You know, Bishop, this conversation has really helped me personally. And I think it will help me explain things to the born agains who are all over me."

"Before you go, Toni," I said, "I would like you to suggest to your born again friends that they do a survey of hospital emergency rooms in our city. They might be surprised to learn that in the vast majority of cases of children treated for sexual abuse in emergency rooms, the perpetrators are not priests but relatives such as a father, brother, uncle, cousin."

"Cool! I'll run it by them tomorrow. Good night, Bishop. Thanks."

"Always good to talk to you, Toni. Good night."

CHAPTER 29

Early Friday morning, the doorbell rang at Haley House. Mrs. Lacey answered it and was surprised that the visitor was Bill Danko, my lawyer.

"Good morning, Mr. Danko. I suppose you're here to see Archbishop Foley."

"Yes, I am, Mrs. Lacey, but I don't have an appointment. Is he in?"

"Yes. He's having breakfast, but I'm sure he'll be glad to see you. You know the way to the dining room, don't you?"

"I certainly do. Thanks."

When Danko got to the dining room, he could see that I had finished my breakfast and was having coffee as I read the morning newspaper.

"Bill! What a pleasant surprise. Come in, sit down, and have a cup of coffee."

"Thanks, I will."

"Bill, I can see something is bothering you. You look agitated. What's happening?"

"Well, Archbishop, I was just at the court house. The place is buzzing with the news that a priest of this archdiocese is going to be charged with sexually molesting a woman who once worked in the chancery office twenty-five years ago."

"Well, that was on my watch. Who is she accusing?"

"Archbishop Edward Foley!"

"Me? Bill, this has to be some kind of sick joke." I was visibly upset, but I quickly controlled my emotions and said, "I shouldn't be surprised. In today's climate, priests and bishops, even retired ones, are fair game for some persons hoping to capitalize on all this negative publicity about priests accused of sexual abuse."

"You're right, Archbishop. What can I do to help you handle this with the media? They're going to be all over this place in a couple of hours."

"We'll get to that in due time, Bill. But first tell me who is accusing me and when did all this happen?"

"Well, the papers have not yet been filed with the court, but a Mrs. Sally Reed claims that when she worked in the chancery, she was romantically involved with you and that she left the employment of the diocese because of your sexual advances. Do you know her?"

I didn't answer right away. I was trying to remember the woman and what incident could have occasioned her making such a charge. Then I said, "Yes, I do know her, Bill. She was a secretary in the diocesan tribunal. She was divorced and had two high school age children. She was an attractive woman, always professionally dressed, and she had good secretarial skills."

"Was she ever your secretary?"

"Not officially, but occasionally my own secretary would be absent because of illness or a doctor's appointment, and the office manager would assign Sally Reed to my office if I had some urgent material to get out."

"How often would that happen?"

"That's hard to say, but I think it was once or twice a month. Until she was dismissed."

"Why was that?" Danko asked.

"She had a drinking problem."

"How do you know that?"

"Well, secretaries in the tribunal would go out to a bar for a drink with her after work. It became obvious to them that after a couple of drinks she talked too much, especially about divorce or annulment cases pending before the tribunal. They reported her to Mrs. Carol Jackson, the office manager, who called her in and confronted her with this unprofessional behavior."

"Did Sally Reed deny the charges?"

"No, she did not," I said. "As I recall, she and her husband were in a nasty custody dispute putting Sally under a lot of tension."

"Did Jackson fire her?"

"No, she didn't. Not at that time. We had a policy in place that offered a person a chance to work at another job within the organization. We also offered counseling services for a person seemingly overwhelmed by domestic problems."

"Well, that's very humane and civilized," Danko said.

"And also very Christian. You know as well as I that the Church doesn't pay the high wages many women earn in corporations and law firms. But at least we can provide some job security and a safe workplace environment for them."

"So, did Sally Reed get counseling?"

"Yes, she did. But unfortunately, she continued to reveal confidential information, and ultimately, she was dismissed."

"She claims you made sexual advances. What do you say to that?"

"Simply that's it not true. She and I both know that."

"What do you intend to do about it?"

"Well, my first thought is to go on television and really blast her. That would be very human but maybe not Christian. So, Bill, I have to do some thinking about this and some praying. I also think that I should have a press conference in the late afternoon."

"Would you like me to prepare a statement saying that you will meet with reporters in the afternoon?"

"Bill, I hope you don't take offense. I do want someone to write a statement, but that someone should not be you."

"No offense taken, Archbishop, but could you tell me why you don't want your lawyer to meet with the press?"

"Bill, if I have my lawyer out front, some in the media and in the public will think that we're circling the wagons and preparing to fight this woman in court. The people are sick and tired of lawyers acting as mouthpieces for bishops. They'll think I am trying to hide something. I have nothing to hide. Do you understand?"

"Yes, I do, Archbishop. I don't agree that I should not be involved, but I respect your decision," said Danko, waiting to see whether I would argue the point. When I didn't, he stood up and said, "Well, Archbishop, I have to get back to the office. I'll be in and out during the day. But if you need to talk to me, just call my secretary and she'll page me. Thanks for the coffee."

"And thanks for the heads up, Bill. I'll be in touch." Danko left Haley House through the back door.

A few minutes later I called Tom Rinehart. "Tom, something urgent has come up. I need to see you right away."

"I'll be over in ten or fifteen minutes," said Tom, hearing something in my voice that telegraphed the importance of what we had to discuss. In the meantime, I took out my Bible and began to read the Psalms.

When Rinehart arrived, I told him what Danko had said. Rinehart started to curse, but I asked him to just calm down and listen for a moment.

"Tom, I understand that at noon a lawyer for Sally Reed will notify the media that Mrs. Reed is charging me with sexual harassment and gross sexual imposition. He will then answer questions from media people. What I want you to do is get on television shortly afterwards and hand out a statement announcing that I will have a press conference at five o'clock to respond to the charges that this woman has leveled against me."

"Don't you think Archbishop Graham's media relations person would be a better choice?"

"No, I don't. This is my problem, not his. I called Archbishop Graham a few minutes ago and told him what I intend to do. He wanted to get involved but said he will respect my wishes."

"Well, suppose this case goes to trial and a jury rules against you. Don't you want the archdiocese to make the financial settlement?" Rinehart asked.

"No, Tom, I don't."

Rinehart was not about to try to get me to change my mind. From years of experience he knew that once I had decided on a course of action, nothing could deter me. It took Tom about twenty minutes to draft a statement. After I made some minor changes, the brief statement alerted the public that I would hold a press conference in the library of Haley House at 5:00 PM.

Pointing the remote at the television, I said, "Well, Tom, let's hear what the lawyer for Mrs. Reed has to say."

I listened intently. Rinehart barely managed to control his anger. What particularly galled him was the fact that the woman bringing the charge was identified only as Mrs. Jane Doe and her face was not shown. "God dammit! You are identified by name, but she's referred to as Jane Doe. What a crock of legal bullshit!"

"Tom, settle down. Don't have a heart attack over this. This will pass. And please don't let the media people see your anger and know how upset you are. Just answer their questions and be as courteous as you can possibly be."

"You're right, Ed. I'll be on my best behavior. I'll FAX this information to the media, and if it's OK with you, I'll ask Kate to be here, too."

"And make sure Toni is also here. I don't want her turning on TV and learning about this. Also, Tom, I would appreciate your answering the phones. The media will deluge us with calls. I don't think it's fair to put Mrs. Lacey front and center on this."

"You're right, Ed. I'll fill Mrs. Lacey in on what's happening. I'll tell her I'll take over the phones and doorbells before the press conference."

I nodded in agreement. "Good idea, Tom."

Noting my weary expression, Tom added, "Ed, why don't you disappear for a while? I'll introduce you at the press conference at five."

"Thanks, Tom. I'd like to do some praying and thinking after I take a rest, which I'll do as soon as I get to my room."

I know Rinehart felt sorry for me and was having difficulty controlling his temper. I think Tom wanted me to use the press conference to blast her.

A short time later, Kate and Toni arrived. After an exchange of kisses, Kate said, "Tom, when I got your call, I came as soon as I could. On the way, I stopped at Toni's school and collected her. When I told the principal what was happening, she sent for Toni and told her she was free to go with me. On the way over, I filled Toni in on what was happening."

Toni, visibly upset, asked Rinehart, "What's the bishop going to do?"

"All I know is that he's going to have a press conference at 5:00 PM, and he wants you to be there. Says it's part of your education."

He went over to her, gave her a hug and said, "Toni, the archbishop is going to do just fine. I think that woman and her lawyer are going to be in for a big surprise. This is going to backfire."

"Oh, Tom, I hope so," Toni said, tears spilling down her face. "This must be causing him a lot of pain."

Kate asked Tom what she and Toni could do.

"Let's see—the press conference will be in the library, so make sure there are enough chairs in the room. The television people will be here about an hour before to set up their cameras, so welcome them. Be cheerful and smile, but the only question you answer is if they ask where the rest rooms are. They might try to ask you how the archbishop is taking this. Just tell them you haven't seen the archbishop since the news broke."

Kate and Toni began to arrange the chairs. Afterwards, they went to the kitchen for a coke and to talk to Mrs. Lacey, who was visibly upset. Toni gave her a big hug and so did Kate. They assured her everything would turn out fine. In the meantime Tom answered the constantly ringing phones. Local and network media people were trying to get background information on the story. Obviously, this was going to be a big story on the evening news, not only in Forest Park but across the country.

Precisely at 4:00 PM, armed with cameras, spotlights and other equipment, a television crew rang the doorbell. Toni let them in, and showed them to the library. She returned to her post at the door, and over the next hour admitted several newspaper reporters, who vied for chairs near the table where I was to be seated.

A couple of minutes before five, I entered the room preceded by Rinehart. We took our seats at the table. Cameras were running.

At exactly 5:00 PM, Rinehart said, "Good afternoon, ladies and gentlemen, I am Tom Rinehart. Archbishop Foley has asked me to be his spokesperson for this event. You heard a statement at noon today by a lawyer for a woman identified only as Mrs. Jane Doe, who worked in the diocesan tribunal of this archdiocese twenty-five years ago. She was not Archbishop Foley's personal secretary, but she did fill in occasionally when his secretary was absent because of illness. As you know, she has made some serious charges against the archbishop, who has called this press conference. Most of you know Archbishop Foley, so I am going to turn the mike over to him. Archbishop Foley."

"Thank you, Tom. Good afternoon, ladies and gentlemen of the press," I began, "and thank you for coming. As you know, a Mrs. Jane Doe has leveled some serious charges against me. You heard them in the press conference her lawyer conducted earlier today. Let me state that I categorically and emphatically deny them. She and I both know they are not true.

"I would be less than honest if I did not tell you that these charges have angered me, and that I thought about using this press conference to respond to each and every accusation made against me. This is not the time and place for that. This case will probably go to trial and I will be asked to respond to these accusations then. This, of course, I will do.

"Mrs. Doe's lawyers may suggest that there be a financial

settlement so that the case does not go to trial. I will reject this. None of my personal savings or diocesan money will be used to avoid a trial. Nor will I counter sue this woman for her libelous remarks.

"I decided on this course of action after I read a marvelous sermon on forgiveness which was sent to me by a Unitarian minister who once worked here in Forest Park before answering a call to minister to a congregation in North Carolina.

"Reverend Grigolia told the story of Gregg Levoy, who wrote the book *Callings.* Levoy had gone to see an exhibit called, 'Wisdom and Compassion: The Sacred Art of Tibet,' during which a group of monks traveling with the Dalai Lama were creating a six-foot-wide circular mandala—a spiritual rendering of the cosmos—made of colored sand ground from gemstones. 'For nearly a month,' Levoy wrote, 'they worked silently, bent over the low platform that cradled the growing sacrament. They laid out their intricate geometry of devotion by hand, surrounded constantly by onlookers who stood sometimes for hours, as I did, simply watching: our busy lives were uncharacteristically forgotten. . . .'

Lavoy continues, 'Just as the monks finished the work of art, a woman broke through the crowd waiting to witness the final ritual and trampled the mandala shouting something like 'Buddhist death cults.'

"Lavoy was outraged by this act of violence. His rage, however, turned to disbelief when he learned that the monks had forgiven her. 'We don't feel any negativity,' said one of them.' We don't know how to judge her motivations. We are praying for her for love and compassion.'"

I paused for a moment and then continued.

"Ladies and gentlemen of the press, for over 50 years I have been building a mandala, the story of my life. And suddenly when the work is almost complete, a woman named Jane Doe comes forward and tries to destroy it.

"From Lavoy's story," I told the press, "I have taken some

grains of wisdom, and I hope you and the television audience do, as well. Again, thank you for coming. This is all I have to say at this time. Tom Rinehart will answer your questions."

I left the room. Reporters shouted questions at me, but I did not respond. Rinehart stayed and passed out copies of my statement. Rinehart was controlled and courteous in answering questions from the media people. He stressed four things: 1) the charges are false; 2) no money will be given to the plaintiff to drop the charges; 3) if the case comes to trial, Archbishop Foley will answer the specific charges in detail; and 4) Archbishop Foley forgives the woman and will not counter sue.

CHAPTER 30

Late the next afternoon when Toni returned from school, she went to the kitchen for a snack and spent some time chatting with her grandmother, who was preparing dinner. Mrs. Lacey wanted to know what happened in school that day and Toni was only too happy to tell her that many kids at school and their parents watched my press conference. Very few of them believed the charges against me. All were surprised that I did not verbally attack the woman but thought that what I said was more like what Jesus would have done.

Mrs. Lacey was happy to hear that. She told Toni that I had an outstanding reputation and she thought the woman and her lawyer would drop the charges before they went to court. In fact, television commentators reported that telephone calls were running five to one against the woman named "Jane Doe."

"So, Toni, don't worry about Archbishop Foley. Tell me what else happened at school today."

Toni told her that she got an A on her book report on the novel *To Kill a Mockingbird.* Naturally her grandmother was pleased. Toni gave her grandmother a hug and went to her room, changed into a sweatshirt and levis, and went down to the Haley House library to do her homework.

When she sat down, she noticed a stack of papers that someone left on the table. She picked them up and saw there was no name on the top sheet, so she began reading the first page. It had a lot of words in it that she did not understand like "ecclesiastical" and phrases like "invested me with the awesome responsibility of governing this archdiocese." Then it dawned on her that this must be a draft of the speech that Archbishop Graham would give at the

Mass at the Cathedral on Saturday. These papers belong to him, she thought, so I'll give them to my grandmother when I leave. She can put them next to his place at the dining room table. Toni put the papers aside and went back to her books.

A few minutes later someone tapped her on the shoulder, and said, "Hello, Toni. Sorry to interrupt." It was Archbishop Graham.

Toni looked up, and said, "Hi, Archbishop. You must be looking for the speech you left on the table. It's right here."

"Yes, I am, Toni. Thank you. Have you read it?"

"Only the first two pages. There was no name on the first page, so I had to read it to find out who it belonged to. Hope that's OK," she said casually. Authority figures—parents, teachers, priests, bishops, even policemen—didn't intimidate Toni.

Graham smiled. "Of course it's OK. What do you think of it?"

She thought he might ask that, and she didn't want to tell him she couldn't give it an 'A.' She parried his question with one of her own: "Who's going to hear it?"

"The people in the cathedral and people who will be watching on television."

"Well, I only read two pages, but what you wrote really didn't grab me. Like, I mean, it didn't get my attention. Kids my age probably wouldn't listen to it."

"Well, I'm glad to know that, Toni. Young people like you are really important. I want to reach them. What do you think my speech needs?"

"How about a story, Archbishop? Our speech teacher says everybody loves a story. Jesus knew that better than anyone. That's why he talked to people and told them stories or parables."

"You're right, Toni. Do you have any good stories I can use?"

Toni thought for a moment and asked Graham, "Have you ever heard of a writer named Diane Ackerman?" She showed him the book she had been reading before he came in.

"No, I haven't. Tell me about her."

"OK, Archbishop. Not too long ago our librarian brought in

this book that Ackerman wrote, *A Slender Thread.* She told me about it because she knows I'm kinda interested in psychology. She said Ackerman usually writes books on nature, but she also volunteers at a crisis center. In the book she tells how people at the crisis center really have to listen to people who call in. I just finished reading the story of Jack Lewis, an 80-year-old Protestant minister who volunteers at the crisis center. Maybe you can use it. That story really grabbed me. Maybe it will grab the people when they hear you tell it. I'm finished with the book if you'd like it."

"Thank you, Toni. I'll sign it out."

"You're welcome, Archbishop. Hope it helps."

Graham left the library with his draft and Ackerman's book, and Toni went back to her studies. She still had an hour before dinner.

CHAPTER 31

Early Friday evening, Toni returned from the funeral of the ten-year-old daughter of Jakob Mueller, owner of the furniture store in Amish Town.

I recognized her light tap on my office door. "Hello, Toni! Pull up a chair and tell me about the funeral service."

Toni was happy to be asked. "Kate drove Mike and me to Amish Town. Tom couldn't come because he had a meeting with Archbishop Graham. We thought the service would be at a church, but when we asked someone on the street where it would be held, he told us it would be in Jakob Mueller's home, not in a church. I guess that's an Amish custom. Did you know that, Bishop?"

"No, Toni, I didn't. I have to admit I know only a few Amish customs and practices, and I'm not proud of that. I know they want separation between our culture and theirs, and I respect that. I'm aware that they don't try to make converts. I didn't want them to think I was trying to convert them to the Catholic religion, so I've always kept my distance. However, I'm glad the three of you went to the service to express your sympathy. How did they treat you?"

"Very well," Toni said, obviously touched by the events at Amish Town. "Mr. Mueller was really glad that we came. We met his wife and children, and they invited us to join them at the dinner after the burial, and we accepted their invitation."

"I'm glad you did," I said. "Before you tell me about the dinner, however, tell me about the funeral service."

"It was real simple. Rebekka was dressed in a long blue dress, and she had a black bonnet on her head to show she wasn't married. She looked beautiful in that wooden casket her father made for her. There weren't any hymns, but there were readings and prayers. And there was no sermon."

"No eulogy?" I asked.

"A what?"

"A eulogy. That's like a homily. The person giving the eulogy gives words of praise for the good things the dead person did in life," I explained.

"Oh. Well, there wasn't any eulogy. As soon as the prayers were finished, they closed the coffin and carried it out of the house, and then they put it on a wagon. Then everybody lined up, and Jakob Mueller slapped the horse on its butt—I mean rump—and the horse pulled the wagon to the cemetery—about a half mile away, I think. Then the pall bearers put the coffin in the grave and piled dirt on it. After that, we all walked back to the Mueller house for dinner."

"How did the dinner go?"

"The food was awesome, and the Amish ladies who served us were real gracious. But you know what surprised me?"

"No, Toni, what surprised you?"

"The dinner was served on long wooden tables, and the men sat on one side of the table and the women on the other."

"Hmm. What happened after the dinner?"

"The women started clearing the tables and doing the dishes. Kate and I offered to help, but the ladies said no, we were guests. Some of the men huddled around Mike Brown. They knew he was buying furniture for the rectory from Jakob," Toni said.

"Those Amish men will do a great job. Most of them are skilled craftsmen. They're a loving, helpful community of people. If a family's barn burns down, the men of the community assemble within a day or so and rebuild it."

"Really?"

"That's right," I replied.

Toni was silent for a few minutes, fidgeting as if she wanted to add something else. I was learning to read her body language. "Toni, is there something else you want to talk about? Remember this is supposed to be an honest conversation."

"Well, Bishop, I have to tell you that Rebekka's funeral moved me a lot more than Cardinal Mohr's. I watched his on television, you know."

"Why the difference?" I asked.

"Well, Rebekka's funeral was so simple, and Cardinal Mohr's was—like, well, all those priests and bishops, and all those Knights of Columbus with swords, and crosses and—you know what I mean."

"You're right, Toni, but remember that Rebekka was part of a very small community and Cardinal Mohr was the head of an archdiocese that has over a million Catholics. Her death affected maybe a hundred people. Mohr's death affected thousands who regarded him as their spiritual leader. Do you object to people showing their respect for him?"

"Of course not. I heard he was a good guy and people really loved him."

"Yes, he was, Toni. But he was also a public figure. Rebekka Mueller was not. Are we agreed on that?"

"Sure, Bishop. But that's not the point I'm trying to make."

"What is the point, Toni?"

"OK, here's what's bothering me. She's buried in a beautiful wooden coffin that probably cost about five hundred dollars. Even less, probably, since her father made it. Cardinal Mohr's coffin was gold plated. It probably cost thousands of dollars. And what for? It'll be put in a huge crypt in the cathedral with a plaque over it with his name on it. Ten years from now, will anyone know who Cardinal Mohr was?"

"But, Toni, he was an archbishop in this diocese."

"So what's the big deal?" Toni said. Then, embarrassed, she added, "Oh, excuse me, I forgot you were archbishop here before Cardinal Mohr."

I laughed. "That's all right, Toni."

"What I mean is, like, I guess I want to say something about the Catholic Church and the Amish community, if that's all right with you."

"Well, of course, it's all right. Didn't we agree that we'd have honest conversations?"

"Yes, we did. So here goes. It seems to me that the Catholic Church has to make some decisions about the kind of church it wants to be, you know what I mean? Like, is it the Church of the poor or the Church of the rich? Are the Amish people more true to the Gospel than most Christian churches?"

I was stunned—and delighted—by Toni's question, which seemed to reach down into my deepest yearning for the Church and my deepest judgment and fears.

I thought about her comments for a minute and said, "Yes, Toni, maybe they are, and in some instances, maybe they are not."

"Could you give me an example of where they might not be true to the Gospel?" Toni asked.

I paused before I said what was on my mind. "Toni, you're very close to Kate and Tom, and you know they will soon be married by a Protestant minister."

"Yes, I know that," and she added with disdain, "I also know they'll be excommunicated."

"Tell me, Toni, are you going to shun them?"

"You mean not have any contact with them? Are you kidding? Why would I do that? Both of them have been very good to me, especially Kate."

"But by marrying outside the church, they're excommunicated. So don't you think you should shun them?"

"No way! Why would I? Is that what the Catholic Church tells me I'm supposed to do?"

"No it does not. But in the Amish community, people who leave the Amish way of life or marry into another religion are to be shunned. They are to be ignored and not invited to Amish gatherings. They are, in a sense, excommunicated, although the term they use is *shunning,*" I said.

"Well, Bishop, I'm sure as heck not going to shun Tom and Kate."

"I'm glad to hear you say that, Toni, and neither will I. What I'm asking you to do is to consider many things before you make a judgment about what religion is more true to the Gospel."

The doorbell interrupted our conversation. It was Jack Raleigh, just passing by.

Toni greeted Father Raleigh and excused herself.

After she left the room, I said, "Jack, that's one bright kid."

CHAPTER 32

Jack Raleigh, my old friend and classmate at Notre Dame University, often stopped at Haley House unannounced. That night after Toni left, he settled into a rocking chair in the living room. Five minutes later, he turned to me and asked, "Ed, aren't you going to offer me a drink?"

"Great idea, Jack. How about some Chivas Regal? Someone gave it to me for my birthday."

"OK, but don't put any ice in it like you did the last time I was here. When I drink Chivas, I like it neat."

"Jack, if I had known you were going to stop by, I would have ordered some Beluga caviar. I know you like everything first class." I liked to needle Raleigh for not alerting me that he was coming.

Smiling, I went to the liquor cabinet and poured our drinks.

We touched glasses. "Sláinte," I said, using the Gaelic toast my father always used, and added, "To your good health, Jack."

When we settled into our chairs, Raleigh asked me if something was bothering me.

"No," I answered, "not that I know of. Why do you ask?"

"Well, you seem a bit down. You're not as upbeat as you usually are."

"Jack," I said, "I'm now 80 years old and so are you. The game of life is almost over. We're down to the two-minute warning. I wish it were only half-time to continue the football metaphor. There's so much more I want to do."

"Ed, now you're getting me depressed. Give me some more of that Scotch," Raleigh said.

"OK," I said, "but go easy on it. We can't handle booze the

way we could when we were younger."

"I'll be all right, Ed. I won't drive if I think I'm smashed. I'll just curl up on that couch and go to sleep."

"Good. Only don't use the couch. There's a bedroom upstairs you can use."

After a brief silence, I asked Raleigh, "Jack, do you ever regret becoming a priest?"

Raleigh thought for a moment and said, "No, for me it's been a very good life. I've met a lot of good people and helped a lot of people straighten out their lives. I believe I helped save a lot of marriages and helped a lot of kids get into college or enter into good marriages."

"But the system didn't enable you to reach your potential, didn't enable you to do the things where you excelled. Isn't that right, Jack?"

Again Raleigh paused before answering. "Yes, Ed. You're right. I loved literature and I could really write. The dean of our university thought I should be sent to a graduate school—maybe an Ivy League college or to Oxford or Cambridge. But when the academic dean suggested that to the bishop, the bishop said he couldn't spare me. When the dean told me that, I knew I was going to be a parish priest until I died. And that's what happened."

"And you were a damned good parish priest," I told him.

"But I could have become a damned good journalist," Raleigh said. "A hell of a lot better than some guys writing for the Catholic press. I could have covered the sessions of the Second Vatican Council and written reports that would have educated our Catholic laity. Instead I became an assistant pastor and too often sat at table every evening with priests—well meaning guys—whose conversation was usually about baseball or pro football and who is going to win the Heisman trophy in college football. Nothing about world events, nothing about theological and scriptural trends, nothing about science and history, nothing about books and articles that could expand their minds."

"But they read the daily newspaper, didn't they?"

"Sure," Raleigh replied. "The front page, the sports section and maybe the stock market page to see if they were outliving their money."

"Nothing wrong with that, is there?"

The Chivas was getting to Raleigh. "Ed, you know damn well what I mean. You know as well as I that many guys have not read a book since they were ordained."

"You're right, Jack. No wonder some guys get involved with booze or women—or even become sexual predators."

Raleigh was really unwinding. "Ed. Let me turn the tables on you. Let me ask you whether you have any regrets about becoming a priest?"

Without hesitation I replied, "No, I don't, but I might have if I hadn't had the opportunities I had. The diocese let me use my skills as a pastor of a black storefront church and then made me archbishop here. I've met a lot of famous people, dined at the White House a number of times, traveled to Rome for committee meetings. It's been a great life."

After pausing to take a sip of Scotch, I added, "But it also has been a lonely life, and Jack, I have to admit that the older I get the lonelier I become. Mandatory celibacy has done a great disservice to the Church. That policy has produced a lot of old curmudgeons who don't radiate the joy and happiness of Jesus."

"I've heard you say that, Ed, in our private conversations. But I never read that in your weekly column. Why?"

I thought about that for a few moments and said, "Because I knew the Vatican lackeys read my column every week and I didn't want to get in their cross hairs. I was afraid to take a risk. The risk of being punished. The risk of losing the archdiocese. The risk of losing favor with the pope. The risk of losing the power I had."

"Well, Ed," Raleigh said, "don't be too hard on yourself. It's tough to go against the institutional Church or any organization that is large and powerful. Look at some of the big corporations that cooked their books to deceive the public and their stockholders. Many executives knew what was happening, but they didn't want to risk their jobs by blowing the whistle."

I was ready to call it a night, but Raleigh wanted to continue the discussion. He was in residence at a large parish with a pastor and an assistant who were both avid followers of the city's professional baseball and football teams. Raleigh was more interested in politics and current events, but the two men who lived in that rectory had little interest in those topics. That's why he welcomed his visits with me.

"Tell me, Ed," Raleigh asked, "as you look back over your fifty-five years in the priesthood, who were your best teachers?"

"John, let's go back only five years. Otherwise, we'll be talking all night There are five who come to mind: Mike Brown, Jim Kelly, Kate Green, Tom Rinehart, and Toni Vincent."

"I know them all," Raleigh said. "Tell me why you chose them."

"Well, Mike Brown made a nice recovery after that unfortunate accident where he seriously injured two people when he was driving drunk. Too many in the clergy are judgmental about a priest who's driving drunk without knowing all the circumstances. Mike's done one terrific job in rehabilitating himself and he's doing great work at St. Mary's.

"Jim Kelly, the Jesuit priest psychiatrist I told you about, taught me how to deal with priests who are pedophiles. There should be no cover-up, he said, and their victims should be compensated and the perpetrator should be given counseling. But never under any circumstance should he be in contact with children. If he violates that provision, he should be dismissed from the priesthood.

"Kate Green, as you know, is a professor of English at the University. She taught me how to use literature in the decision-making process. She's not a hard-core feminist, but she is interested in issues affecting women. She has made me realize that while the institutional Church has made some progress in recognizing the rights of women, we still have a long way to go. She really zapped me on one occasion and compared the Roman Curia to the Taliban in its treatment of women. She made me think, and that's what a good teacher should do.

"You know of course that she and Tom Rinehart will soon be married. Tom applied for a dispensation, but it was denied. I still think Archbishop Graham was instrumental in killing it. Graham told Tom he could apply again, but he and Kate will have no part of that. They won't play Vatican games. Rinehart has told Graham they have asked the Lutheran minister at the University to preside at their marriage. Tom has taught me that when dealing with powers in Rome, you have to be your own man. Something I have not always been.

"And then there is Toni Vincent. What a great kid! She's only sixteen, but she's very wise—streetwise, too, but just plain wise. Her dad died suddenly when she was only four, and some years later her mother married a man named Randy who is into drugs and alcohol. Life was tough for Toni. Some kids at her school—born again Christians—have given her a hard time. Some kids would get angry. But Toni's tough—and smart. She doesn't hold grudges. She meets the born agains on their own turf. She reads the Bible to find answers to their arguments. Nothing disingenuous about her.

"When we were discussing her living here at Haley House, she spoke right up and said she would leave if it meant she had to go to Mass on Sundays. She has taught me the importance of being in touch with the thinking and attitudes of young kids. She's taught me a lot about being honest and open."

We sat quietly for a few minutes finishing our drinks. Finally, Raleigh said, "Ed, I think I'm going to be co-opted by this Scotch. If it's OK with you and Mrs. Lacey, I think I'll stay here tonight."

"Good. Take the first suite on the right. You'll find a robe, slippers, pajamas, tooth brush and toothpaste, and razor and shaving cream. I'll follow you upstairs after I turn off the lights and let Mrs. Lacey know you're staying and will be with us at breakfast."

When I got to my room, I undressed, put on my pajamas, robe, and slippers and sat in a comfortable chair next to my bed. I wasn't ready to sleep. I wanted to think about my meetings with Toni and with Jack Raleigh.

Toni was right to wonder why Cardinal Mohr was buried in that expensive casket. She didn't buy that line that Mohr was a prince of the Church and deserved the best casket. Prince of the Church? He's a corpse, a stiff, who at that moment was going through stages of decay in a precious metal casket. Why not decay in a simple wooden casket like Rebekka's? I resolved to look over my last will and testament the next day and perhaps get Jakob Mueller to make me a wooden casket. The funeral director might not be happy, but so what? It's my funeral.

What Jack Raleigh said tonight really hit home. When I had the power to do something in favor of optional celibacy, I didn't do it. Why? Because I was afraid authorities would give me a desk job over in Rome and, of course, announce to the public that I was being promoted. I could have come out in writing and said mandatory celibacy should be abolished, but I didn't. I danced around the subject, asking my readers to imagine what the Church would be like with a married clergy and women priests. But I never let my readers know that I was willing to be a leader on these issues. I think Raleigh was implying I'm a coward. He's right.

I was beginning to feel drowsy, so I removed my slippers and robe and went to bed. Even cowards need sleep, I thought. A few minutes later I was asleep.

CHAPTER 33

At noon on November 1, the feast of All Saints, the cathedral was packed with civic and church dignitaries, the public, and the news media for the installation of T. Patrick Graham as Archbishop of Forest Park. The governor of the state was there, and also the mayor, judges, some members of Congress, and all the members of City Council. The clergy was there in great number. Priests in black cassocks and surplices, monsignors in red cassocks, bishops in black cassocks with pectoral crosses around their necks and red bands around their waists. Two of the nation's eight cardinals were there, attired in their ermine robes.

Graham insisted that Toni, Toni's mother Helen, her grandmother Mrs. Lacey, Tom, and Kate be seated in one of the front pews. Seated with them were Hank Kolar, the newspaper columnist and his wife. Toni wanted them there because they had been so kind to her when her mother and Randy were arrested. At Graham's request, Toni's mother Helen was permitted to leave the halfway house for the installation, accompanied by a woman deputy from the Sheriff's office dressed in plain clothes rather than a uniform. Also in attendance were some of Graham's friends from Rome including Pierre Beaucaire, who had come from France for the ceremony despite his ill health.

Toni was not intimidated by the pomp and splendor, but she felt uncomfortable in that setting. She was dressed in a fashionable dark blue suit, but she would have preferred a sweat shirt and blue jeans.

She became visibly uncomfortable when she saw Ron Hackett in one of the front pews near the pulpit. She had seen him only once, the night he had a violent argument with Archbishop

Graham.

"Kate, why is that man here? I've seen him before, and I think he's up to no good. Can't you or Tom have the security people remove him?"

"Toni, that wouldn't be appropriate. He was probably invited by the archbishop and we have no right to ask him to leave."

"I don't think he was invited by the archbishop. His name is Ron, and he's bad news. Please get someone to ask him to leave."

To make Toni feel more comfortable, Tom suggested that he and Toni switch places with the Kolars, who were seated in the row in behind Hackett. That way, he said to Toni, they could keep an eye on the man. Toni agreed, and the Kolars readily made the switch. Toni sat nearest to the aisle, immediately behind Hackett. Both seats were near the Cathedral's side door, which was open.

The fifty-member choir sang "Ecce Sacerdos Magnus" as the clergy marched in. I was second last in line, followed by my successor, the new archbishop, T. Patrick Graham. After the investiture that gave Graham authority over the archdiocese, the solemn Mass began with Graham as principal celebrant. After the reading of the Gospel, Graham ascended the pulpit to deliver his homily.

After thanking the pope for the appointment, praising the people of the archdiocese, acknowledging the presence of the dignitaries and the laity, and thanking me for my fifty years of service to the archdiocese, Graham began his homily:

"My friends, let me begin by saying that I wrote two speeches for this occasion. I spent much time developing the first one, which I thought was quite good because I said all the right things and thanked all the right people. One day when I was in the library of Haley House, I absentmindedly left a draft of the speech on a library table. I went back to the chancery office to compose some letters. When I was ready to leave the office, I looked around for the speech, which I thought was a masterpiece. It was nowhere to be found.

"When it dawned on me where I had left it, I went back to retrieve it. It was still on the table where I had left it. A young high school girl was seated next to it. She greeted me cordially and said that I must be looking for my speech. Since there was no name on the pages, she had read a few pages to determine who had written it. After a couple of pages she could tell it was a speech that only an archbishop could write. (Laughter)

"Then I ventured to ask her what she thought of it. Big mistake. (Laughter) This girl didn't even try to spare my feelings. (Laughter) She said it did not grab her and that it certainly would not grab the attention of kids her age. Bishops and especially archbishops rarely get that kind of response.

"When I asked her what was wrong with it, she told me it needed a story. Then she reminded me of something I forgot, namely, that Jesus told stories. He spoke in parables.

"When I asked her if she knew any good stories, she handed me a book that had just come into the library. Its title is *A Slender Thread* by Diane Ackerman, who is a writer, a naturalist, and a volunteer at a crisis center in upstate New York.

"In her book she tells the story of Jack Lewis, an 80-year-old Protestant minister who volunteers at the crisis center. One morning Lewis got a terrifying call that a man was holding a gun on his wife and children, threatening to kill them and anyone who got in the way. Lewis walked straight into the man's house, sat down beside him, and said quietly, 'Tell me your story.' Ten hours later the man gave him the gun.

"Ackerman then writes, '[E]ach of us has a loaded gun that we aim at ourselves. After hours or years of talking, the story can at last be told in its fullness, and the gun can be laid down. The story has both happy and sad chapters and parts of it may be forgotten. Sometimes it takes an outsider to help remember or clarify it. Lose your story and you lose the pageant of your life.'

"My friends, that story helped me to realize what my role is as archbishop of Forest Park. It is not to tell you my story but to listen to yours. That high school girl, however, had it only half right. Jesus did tell stories, but he also listened to stories people told him. He told people, "Come to me all who are burdened and I will refresh you." In other words, "Tell me your stories. Tell me what is holding you hostage. Tell me what is keeping you from being the beautiful creative person my heavenly Father wants you to be.

"So that is my mission too. I need to hear your stories. And our priests and religious do, too. You don't need to hear our stories about how we need more money to repair the roof on the rectory or how we need to build a new school or a new gym. We need to hear your stories of how you do not have enough money to keep your home, keep the roof over your head, or keep food on the table.

"Jesus told the parable of the woman with the lost coin. We need to hear the story of the woman who has lost a job, lost her health care coverage, and needs more money to live.

"Jesus told the story of the shepherd whose sheep is lost. We need to hear the stories of parents with children who are lost because of drugs, because of sex, because of peer pressure from classmates and friends.

"Jesus told the story of the father who went out daily looking for his wayward son. We need to hear stories from today's fathers who are longing to be united with their sons.

"Jesus told stories about fishermen casting their nets all night into the sea without success. We need to hear stories of unemployed men and women who are exhausted and discouraged from sending out their résumés to the job market without success.

"Will it help? Maybe, maybe not. But these stories you tell will help me as they helped a nun in Outer Mongolia in a place called Ulan Bataar. Sister Nellie read an article a friend of mine had written about telling one's story. She wrote to him from that distant place where Christians are a small minority and said she found affirmation of what limited things she can do simply by being an empty vessel into which the street children, single mothers, unemployed youth, the poor, the lonely elderly can pour in their stories.

"She writes, 'Into my empty vessel has entered the story of a 17-year-old girl who after two years in the streets where she contracted a sexually transmitted disease, finds the courage to return to her parents and continue her education . . . . The 22-year-old girl who found the courage to stand up against her family that wants her to abort her pregnancy . . . . Somehow my vessel empties into God's loving heart and I am again ready to receive.'

"An empty vessel. My friends, that is what any priest, bishop, or archbishop is. I ask you to pour into those empty vessels your stories. Maybe we can't do something about all of them. But maybe we can, in the words of Diane Ackerman, clarify them and remember them and help you hold on to the pageant of your lives. Thank you for your attention."

What was first only polite applause from the congregation grew into a loud crescendo. Everyone rose to give Graham a standing ovation that lasted for several minutes. Graham's speech had captivated all his listeners except two—Ron Hackett and Toni Vincent.

As Graham was descending the steps of the pulpit, Hackett stepped into the aisle.

"You goddamned faggot!" he shouted, pointing a small revolver at Graham.

In one swift motion, Toni leapt from her pew, grabbed Hackett's arm, and wrestled with him for the gun. For one brief moment the two seemed locked in an embrace. Then a shot rang out, and Toni slid to the floor.

As Hackett ran toward the side door, Tom, who had reached out to Toni when she left the pew, knocked Hackett to the floor and began beating him with his fists, uttering every ugly and obscene word he knew. When Hackett tried to escape his grasp, Tom grabbed Hackett's head and pounded it on the marble floor. He would have killed Hackett had not two security officers overpowered him.

"Let me go!" Tom shouted. "What happened to Toni? Is she hurt?"

"Who's Toni?" asked the guard who helped subdue Tom.

"She's the young girl who spoiled this creep's aim," his partner answered, as he locked Hackett's wrists in cuffs.

"She was some brave kid," said the guard to Tom. "But I think she's hurt bad. The shooter missed the archbishop, but his bullet hit her in the chest."

When Tom heard those words, he looked and saw Kate kneeling over Toni and talking to her. Blood was gushing from a wound above her heart."

Kate tried to cradle Toni in her arms. Tom took a white surplice offered by a priest who was kneeling beside Kate and tried to stop the bleeding.

"Toni, dear, you're going to be all right. The paramedics will be here in a minute," Kate said.

Toni opened her eyes and asked, "What happened, Kate? Why am I bleeding?"

Kate said, "Hackett tried to shoot Archbishop Graham. You grabbed his arm but his shot hit you."

"I think I'm going to die," Toni said, with an expression of surprise.

"Toni, dear," Kate said, "let's not talk about dying. Let's talk about living."

"Kate, I'm not afraid to die. Just ashamed."

"Toni, why should you be ashamed?" Kate asked.

She whispered, "Because I wanted to ask forgiveness of my mom and I wanted to tell her I forgive her. Please promise me you will do that for me, Kate."

"Toni, she needs to hear that from you. Your mother is right here. Why not tell her that yourself?"

Kate reached out to Toni's mother and made a space for her. Helen knelt down beside Toni and gently rocked her in her arms as if she were the baby she once sang to sleep. As I looked upon that scene, frustrated that I could do nothing to help, I saw a new Helen—not a woman enslaved by drugs—but a loving mother—beautiful, strong, silent, setting aside her grief to comfort her daughter. Toni relaxed in Helen's arms and with one last effort said, "Please forgive me, Mother."

Tom and Kate sobbed uncontrollably. I barely managed to control my own emotions. Helen, a portrait of grief, made room for the priest whose surplice was red with Toni's blood to administer the last rites. Paramedics arrived and worked feverishly to save her. They placed her on a gurney and rolled it to the ambulance near a side door of the cathedral. I suggested to Kate that she drive in the ambulance with Toni's mother and Mrs. Lacey, Toni's grandmother. I would follow in Tom's car.

At the emergency room entrance of the hospital nurses and doctors were waiting and quickly took Toni into the emergency room where doctors, nurses and paramedics worked feverishly to save her. One of the doctors said through clenched teeth, "We're going to save this kid, dammit!" But he knew it was too late.

Kate, Mrs. Lacey, Toni's mother, Tom, Kolar and his wife and I were ushered into a visitor's room where we waited for news about Toni. A half later one of the doctors confirmed our worst fears. "I'm sorry—we couldn't save her," the doctor said. Kate reached out and put her arms around Toni's mother and grandmother. Tom and I did the same. We all were so overwhelmed by grief that we could not speak. The doctor who introduced himself as Dr. Thompson approached me and kindly suggested that we all gather in the chaplain's room. He said an autopsy would soon begin, as required by law.

Before we left the emergency room, we could see a crowd of journalists gathering outside. I told Tom to take Kate, Mrs. Lacey, and Helen out through another entrance. Kate suggested that rather than going to Haley House we should all meet in her suite of rooms at the University.

I prevailed upon the doctor who had told us that Toni was dead to announce her death to the reporters. I told him that later in the afternoon I would hold a press conference to answer their questions as best I could about what happened in the cathedral.

Dr. Thompson agreed to meet with the reporters. He explained that Toni had died from a bullet wound to her chest and that he would see that they would receive the results of the autopsy.

"How's Archbishop Graham?" a reporter asked.

"He's in a coma," Dr. Thompson said. "Two excellent brain surgeons are preparing to operate on him in an hour. We will keep you updated on his progress."

I couldn't believe what I was hearing. I had been so involved with Toni that I had no idea that Graham had been injured. "Graham in a coma!" I asked. "Was he hit too?"

Dr. Thompson turned to me. "I'm sorry, Archbishop. I thought you knew. As Archbishop Graham was descending from the pulpit, he heard the shouts and the shot, and saw the young girl slide to the floor. In his haste to reach her he tripped on his robe. He fell headlong down the steps and hit his head on the marble floor. His condition is very serious."

Some journalists surrounded me and asked me to comment. I told them I was still trying to sort things out. I told them that the Chief of Police would probably have a news conference later, in time for their evening news deadlines.

While I was talking to the media people, Tom and Kate led Mrs. Lacy and Toni's mother out another door. On their way to the parking lot, they met Mike Brown, who was barely able to control his emotions. His eyes filled with tears as he expressed his sympathies to Toni's mother and grandmother. "Toni was a real hero today. I'll never forget her. What a great kid. She will be in my prayers and so will both of you. God bless."

He walked with the group to Tom's car and whispered to Kate that he was driving out to Amish Town to tell Jakob Mueller what happened. They said goodbye, and Tom drove to the University, just a few miles away. I told them I would meet them there.

When they arrived at the University, Kate led them through a side door and to the elevator to her suite of rooms. The first thing Kate did when she entered her suite was to call the campus nurse. She quietly explained to the nurse what had happened and how Toni's mother and grandmother were in a state of shock. The nurse said she would call Dr. Henry Mason, who would contact Kate shortly. Kate thanked her, and she and Tom went over to Toni's mother and grandmother. They held hands as Tom offered a prayer for Toni and for Archbishop Graham.

A few minutes later, I entered Kate's apartment. I held out my arms to Mrs. Lacey and Toni's mother and hugged them. With tears in my eyes, I looked at them and said, "I know you are both going to miss Toni, and I will too. Many important people have influenced my life. But Toni's influence on me has been profound. We have had many conversations about the church. She listened well and asked some great questions. She has been one of my best mentors."

Dr. Mason tapped on the door and entered Kate's suite. After he expressed his sympathies, he attended to Mrs. Lacey and Toni's mother. He gave them something to relax them and help them sleep.

"Anyone else I can help?" the doctor asked as he turned to leave.

"No, I think we're all right," Tom said. "Thanks for coming, Doctor."

"If you need me, the nurse knows where to reach me."

For a long period there was only silence in Kate's suite. Anticipating my meeting with the press, I reluctantly left the group whose comfort I needed as much as they needed mine.

CHAPTER 34

The more I thought about dealing with the media, the more I wanted to avoid it. I was too drained to think clearly. I decided to call Hank Kolar, the columnist for the Forest Part Sentinel, whom I had learned to trust and like during the interviews we had earlier. He would advise me about what information to release to the media and how to do it.

Kolar graciously made arrangements to meet me at Haley House as soon as he could finish a column he was working on.

"Bishop, I'm glad to help out," he said as we got settled on either side of a table in my office. "You realize, I'm sure, that my first obligation is to my own newspaper. I'd like to file my story about these events before you give the information to the other media, OK?"

"Certainly, Hank. I understand that."

"OK, I have quite a bit of information about Toni—having lived next door to her and knowing how she came to live here, so let's start with Archbishop Graham. The shooter called him a faggot. Is he gay?"

"Before we get into that," I said, "let me share with you a letter that Graham gave me several days ago. This will explain some issues—and raise a few, I suppose. Graham asked me to use the letter at my discretion in the event that something happened to him."

Dear Ed,

Shortly after I came here I was living in a suite of rooms on the second floor of Haley House. Late one night I had a visitor named Ron Hackett, who had been my chauffeur in Rome when I was a diplomat at the Vatican Embassy. When I accepted the opportunity to become archbishop of Forest Park, Hackett assumed he would come to the U.S. with me as my chauffeur. I told him that was out of the question because I intended to drive my own car here. I told him I would help him sign on with one of the other diplomats, but he would not accept that. He demanded that I pay him $100,000. If I did not, he threatened to reveal that I was gay and was involved in a romantic relationship with a diplomat from the French Embassy. Because the diplomat and I were close friends, Hackett concluded that we were both gay.

I told Hackett that under no circumstance would I pay him any money. If he wanted to claim publicly that I was gay, he could do so. But he would have to prove it.

I ordered him to leave Haley House that evening because he became loud and boisterous when I refused to give in to his outrageous demands. Others in the house must have heard him.

As the time grows near for my installation, he calls me almost daily and leaves messages on my voice mail threatening to publicly reveal my supposedly gay life style. I have continued to ignore him, which angers him. He has sent notes stating that I will regret it. You will find these notes in the safe. What he means by these threats I do not know, but knowing Hackett has a violent temper, I fear for my life. I am resolved, however, that I will not give in to blackmail.

Ed, in case anything happens to me, you can use the material in this letter. You are also free to reveal the substance of the conversation we had in my office the day after Ron verbally attacked me in my suite.

You are a man of integrity who will, I am confident, use this information with great prudence.

Sincerely yours,

T. Patrick Graham
Archbishop of Forest Park

Kolar read the letter carefully, then asked, "May I have a copy? This will become public, as you probably know, in the police investigation."

"I intend to turn the letter over to the police. I see no reason why you can't have a copy now. Graham intended it to be used as I see fit. I'll make a copy for you before you leave."

Kolar set the letter on the table. "Well, Hackett thought Graham was gay. Was he?"

"I couldn't say. He gave no indication by mannerism or association that he was. Furthermore, it seems to me that the Vatican would have vetted him carefully and would not have sent him here if they thought he was gay."

"Would you have had a problem if he were gay?" Kolar asked.

"Only if he did not live a celibate life," I replied. "If he were gay but living a celibate life, I could accept that. Let me add, Hank, that I could not accept a straight guy, bishop or priest, having a sexual relationship with a woman."

"Bishop, do you agree with some bishops, particularly one in Rome, who has been vocal on the subject, that gays should not be ordained?"

"No I do not," I answered. "In my years in the priesthood, I have known many gay priests who kept their vows and rendered great service to the church. I totally disagree with that high official in Rome who said recently that gays should not be ordained."

"If the archbishop isn't gay, why was Hackett asking for one hundred grand to buy his silence?" Kolar asked.

"Hank, I don't know. You will have to ask Hackett that question when the police let him talk," I said. "Right now he's recovering from the beating that Rinehart gave him in the cathedral."

"Archbishop, you are going to be asked if Rinehart gave Hackett a severe beating to keep him from talking. How will you respond?" Kolar asked.

"All I can say, Hank, is that Rinehart and Kate loved Toni as if she were their own child. When Hackett killed Toni, Tom did what any loving father would do. He was in a rage—and nearly killed Hackett."

"Bishop, I'm wondering what made Toni react so quickly when Hackett made his move. Did she know that he had threatened Graham?" Kolar asked.

"Toni heard the commotion the night Hackett was shouting at Archbishop Graham, and she did see his face when he was leaving. She told me that Hackett's demeanor really scared her. She was very upset when she saw him in the cathedral and was convinced that Hackett meant to do Archbishop Graham harm."

"I see," said Kolar. "She had her eye on Hackett. She was the only one who was ready for his move."

"That seems to be the case, Hank. To appease her, Tom Rinehart suggested that the two of them change places with you and your wife so they could occupy the pew immediately in back of Hackett."

Kolar sat silently for a few moments. "Bishop, were you consulted about Graham's appointment?"

"No, I was not. Remember that I had resigned and was no longer in charge of Forest Park, so the Vatican did not need to consult me about Graham's appointment. I read about it in the newspapers."

"Have you had any updates on Graham's condition?"

"He's in surgery now. I've been told that his condition is very serious. I'm sure I'll get a call when he's out of surgery."

"Bishop," said Kolar, "I hope you can persuade the public affairs people at the chancery to be as open as you have been. Being secretive will only make them look bad when all the facts come out in an investigation."

"Hank, the job of the media is to ferret out the truth, so why hide anything? I've believed for years in full disclosure. If a priest or bishop has abused a child, that act should be reported to civil authorities. If a policeman stops a priest who has been driving under the influence of drugs or alcohol, he should take the priest to jail, fingerprint him, and fine or send him to jail until his trial."

Kolar smiled. "You're the exception, Bishop. Another question—why didn't you request, or suggest that more police protection be provided for Archbishop Graham—since you had possession of this letter," he said as he pointed to the letter on the table.

"Graham asked us not to increase the police presence. I don't believe he thought Hackett would attempt to murder him in the cathedral in the presence of a thousand people."

"But Toni believed that he would," Kolar countered. "And you—and Rinehart and Kate—will probably be asked if you know why she did." Kolar paused. "Another question will come up, Bishop—that business about the woman who worked in the chancery office making some serious charges against you. What's the status of that case?"

"The woman's lawyers haven't even filed a suit," I answered.

Kolar rose, shoving his notebook in his pocket. "Now, before I leave, let's make a quick summary of points you will want to make when you're contacted by the media. You can give a copy to whoever will be handling this from the chancery, too."

Together we worked on a fact sheet, Kolar advising me about how to answer some of the anticipated questions. As he rose to leave, he said, "I'll get this down to the paper right now. I'd appreciate it if you let me have an exclusive on Graham's letter—until you hand it over to the police. If the TV stations get it tonight, I won't be first with it for the morning edition."

"I understand, Hank. I won't do anything with it tonight. Thanks so much for your help."

He had much to do to meet his deadline. As I walked with him to the door, the phone rang.

"Do you mind if I wait?" Kolar said. "It might be word about Graham."

"No problem. I'll be right back."

Minutes later I returned. "Your intuition served you well.

Graham is still in surgery, but the prognosis is not very good. He may never regain consciousness, but he could live for a long time. Physically, he has always kept himself in good condition. Hank, I'm not a doctor so I would appreciate it if you kept this latest information off the record. Check with the hospital."

"I certainly will, Archbishop. It's been a long, tiring day for both of us. So I'm going to say good night."

CHAPTER 35

Later that evening, I received another call. A man with a heavy French accent identified himself as a close friend of Archbishop Graham and said, "Archbishop Foley, this is Pierre Beaucaire. I am calling from the hospital where Archbishop Graham had surgery. May I come to see you? I would like very much to talk with you."

I knew immediately that the caller was the French ambassador who was Graham's partner in Rome.

"Of course," I said. "Mister Ambassador, may I send a car for you?"

He did not need a car and was at Haley House minutes later. He dismissed his driver, telling him that he would call when he was ready to be picked up.

He already had dinner and politely refused my offer of an after dinner drink. When we were settled in the den, he told me that Graham had spoken well of me and trusted me. He knew that I was aware of their relationship.

"Archbishop," he began. "I—I am just overcome with shock and grief."

"Please," I said. "Call me Ed. And if you don't mind, I'll address you as Pierre." He nodded his approval.

"Ed, I was able to get some information about Patrick—Archbishop Graham—but since I am only a friend, and not family, I have not been allowed to see him. Of course, he is not conscious at this time, but—I am at a loss as to what to do. I was booked on a flight to Paris later tonight, which I have canceled. I have prostate cancer, and my surgeon has scheduled me for surgery a few days from now. He did not want me to come here for the installation ceremonies, but I promised that I would return right after the ceremony. But now, surgery or no surgery, I just can't leave with Patrick's condition so grave."

We discussed what we knew about Archbishop Graham's condition. Pierre was well aware that his friend could die at any time, or that he could live for some time.

"Do they think he will die soon?" Pierre asked.

"It's possible, but often people who are as good physical condition as he is live for some time."

"What do you think I should do?" Pierre asked.

"If you want input from me, Pierre, I would advise you to get back to Paris as soon as possible and have your surgery. That's what Patrick Graham would want you to do. You're not going to help him—or yourself—by sitting around here waiting for him to die."

My advice had a calming effect on him. He said. "Ed, that's what I will do. Now, if you don't mind, I'd like to accept that drink you offered."

Pierre stayed for quite some time. We talked about some of the issues he was dealing with as an ambassador, and a great deal about his relationship with Graham and their mutual decision to end it. They would always remain friends, he said, but anything more than that had ended.

Before we parted, I promised that I would try to arrange a visit with Graham before he left for Paris, and that he could count on me to keep him posted about Graham's condition.

CHAPTER 36

The following morning, I drove to the University to meet Kate and Tom, where they were waiting for me in the parking lot. I was surprised to see a horse and buggy pull into the lot. Kate immediately recognized Mr. Mueller, the Amish man whose daughter had died. He had come to see her.

"Guten Morgen, Fraulein Kate," Mueller said as he got down from the buggy.

"Guten Morgen, Herr Mueller, I'm glad to see you again. You must have heard about Toni?"

"Ja," he said. "Mike Brown drove to my store yesterday and told me what happened. What a terrible tragedy. She was a fine young girl like my Rebekka. I am so sorry for your great loss and have come to express the sorrow of our community. We remember how you and she and Mike Brown came to Rebekka's funeral."

Kate introduced Mueller to me and to Tom, who shook his hand warmly. We asked him to come in, but he said he had to start back to Amish Town to do some work he had promised a client.

"Mr. Mueller," Kate said, "could you make a pine coffin like the one you made for Rebekka? Toni thought it was so beautiful. And it was."

"Fraulein Kate, I started to make it right after I heard the news about Toni's death. It will be finished in two days. Is there anything else we can do?"

"Yes, we would like the coffin to be placed on a wagon and taken to the grave site about two hundred yards from the doors of Saint Mary Church. Could you do that?"

"Ja, I can do that. Anything else?"

"About the time, Herr Mueller," Kate said, "the Mass—the

service—will be Friday evening. We will need you there on Saturday morning. The burial will be at eleven."

"Gut. I will be at your church a little after nine."

"Danke shőn und aufwiedersehen," Kate said.

"Bitte und aufwiedersehen."

Mueller said goodbye to Tom and me, climbed into his buggy, said something to the horse, and the buggy clattered down the highway.

"When I die," I said, "ask Mueller to make my coffin and bury me on that hill next to Toni. And don't let anyone play 'Amazing Grace' on bagpipes. I hate that song and that instrument."

Tom and Kate laughed for the first time since the tragedy. Tom finally said, "Ed, please put all of this in writing and have it notarized. Otherwise Kate and I will have a real battle with the chancery guys."

"Don't worry, Tom, I'm going to have my lawyer Bill Danko do this right after Toni's funeral. Those guys in the chancery office are smart enough to know not to mess with Danko."

CHAPTER 37

The following Saturday was a crisp autumn day for Toni's burial in the cemetery behind Saint Mary Church. Earlier there had been a light mist, but it had dissipated. The sun appeared occasionally so the autumn leaves could be seen in all their beauty. The Mass of Resurrection was celebrated the evening before in the church, which overflowed with clergy, classmates, media, friends, citizens, and the curious.

Classmates of Toni—four girls and four boys—placed the pine coffin on the Amish wagon. The horse neighed gently, seeming to sense the solemnity and sorrow of the occasion. It was obvious that he was no stranger to the grief and sorrow that can grip a community.

Toni's classmates were there in great number. So were reporters and television camera crews and commentators. The newspapers of Forest Park and the national newspapers had been filled with stories about the attempt on Archbishop Graham's life, the grave injuries he suffered, and the heroism of a 16-year-old girl named Toni Vincent.

Hank Kolar's stories appeared in the local and national press. His coverage was superior to that of other reporters, not only because he was an excellent journalist but because he had intimate knowledge of the event. Toni Vincent had lived in his home for a short time, and he and his wife witnessed the shooting. Speculation was rampant among reporters that Kolar could get a Pulitzer for his outstanding coverage of the event.

Reporters were curious about the relationship of Ron Hackett, the shooter, to Archbishop Graham. News organizations scrambled to determine whether Hackett was something more than Graham's chauffeur.

I refused to give any interviews at this time. Kate reluctantly went on camera on a few occasions but only to talk about the simplicity and wisdom of this little girl who had become her dear friend. Archbishop Graham was still in a coma. Neurosurgeons remained guarded in their comments about his recovery.

Hundreds of citizens from Forest Park gathered for Toni's burial. Tom, Kate, Mrs. Lacey and Toni's mother Helen, temporarily released from the halfway house, lined up behind the horse and wagon carrying the wooden pine box with Toni's body. Occasionally sobs escaped Toni's mother and grandmother, who were silently comforted by Kate and Tom. Clergy persons in cassocks and white surplices were present in great numbers. The few bishops blended in with the other clergy because, honoring my request, instead of wearing their red robes, miters and pectoral crosses, they dressed simply in black cassocks and white surplices. Those with the title of monsignor left their red robes at home.

The Knights of Columbus, the Knights of St. John and the Knights of St. Gregory offered to send honor guards. I graciously thanked them but asked them not to come in their uniforms. I explained that Toni's family and close circle of friends wanted the focus of the ceremony to be on that pine box and the courageous girl whose remains they were burying that autumn day. Left unsaid was the fact that I wanted no signs of the church triumphalism and pageantry that had been so prominent in the past, including the funeral of Cardinal Mohr.

When everyone was assembled, Jakob Mueller tapped the horse on its rump and the procession of people, numbering about four hundred, slowly made its way to the burial plot, high on the cemetery hill. When the crowd had formed a sort of semi-circle around the plot, Kate Green stepped forward to the microphone to deliver a eulogy:

Hello, I am Kate Green from the University. When I first

met Toni Vincent, she was hitchhiking. We both agreed hitchhiking was not a good choice for a young girl of her age unless there were very special circumstances. I told her that at the university I try to show that writers of fiction give us characters who make choices, some of which are good and others not so good, even disastrous. In the cathedral last week, Toni made a choice which most of us will never be asked to make, namely giving up her life to save another.

Before she died, she made another choice—where she wanted to be buried. In exploring this old parish of Saint Mary, Toni discovered on a hill behind the church the parish cemetery. Although it had not been kept in good repair, its magnificent view of the city captured Toni. She told me, "Kate, when I die, this is where I want to be buried." I said that I hoped I could remember that in fifty years. Little did I know then that Toni had only some fifty or more hours to live.

When Toni was living in Haley House, she developed a close relationship with her grandmother. Almost every week they went out for dinner and a movie. They took turns choosing the movie they would see. Usually her grandmother would choose a movie with a rating of PG or one that was suitable for all ages. Toni, however, liked to push the envelope and would choose one that had an R rating, which meant that a teenager could see it provided he or she was accompanied by an adult.

The last movie Toni chose was one called "Four Weddings and a Funeral." Toni liked it, but she was puzzled by the reading of W. A. Auden's poem "Stop all the clocks." What troubled her was the last stanza, which she said depressed her. She had written out the poem and had a copy with her, which she read to me:

> The stars are not wanted now; put out every one,
> Pack up the moon and dismantle the sun,

Pour away the ocean and sweep up the woods;
For nothing now can ever come to any good.

I knew the poem and often used it in my literature classes. Toni and I had had frequent discussions about literature, so I asked her what bothered her about those lines.

"Kate," she said, "you know I'm not exactly into going to church every Sunday and all that stuff, but I do believe that there's something after we die—an afterlife, I mean. That stanza really depressed me."

Toni, I said, I see you're carrying one of your favorite books of poetry. I recognized it because we had discussed several selections in it. Have you found something that would lift up your spirit at the time of the death of a loved one?

"Yes," she said. She found a selection that she had read and re-read so often that the book easily fell open to it. I was not surprised when she read these words of Juliet from "Romeo and Juliet."

. . . . when he shall die,
Take him and cut him out in little stars,
And he will make the face of heaven so fine
That all the world will be in love with night
And pay no worship to the garish sun.
(From Romeo and Juliet Act III Scene ii)

That's how Kate concluded her eulogy. I looked over the mourners and could see that Kate's words had a profound effect on many. When Kate was seated, I went to the podium. This is what I said:

I'm Edward Foley. I was archbishop here until I reached my seventy-fifth birthday five years ago. In the course of those years as head of this archdiocese I have met popes, cardinals, archbishops, presidents, kings and queens, governors, and women like Mother Teresa of India. I have learned much from them.

But the person who taught me the most is the young girl Toni Vincent whom we bury today. I met her a little less than a year ago when she came to live with her grandmother at Haley House. Mrs. Lacey, her grandmother, is my housekeeper. Toni was only 16 years of age, but I have to say she was the person who had the greatest impact on my life. Toni was not your traditional Catholic. And I did not attempt to make her one. I told her that I wouldn't ask her to leave Haley House if she missed Mass on Sundays. She was under no obligation to attend. It was her decision.

Toni was full of life, full of energy and full of questions. She studied the scriptures because some of her classmates would tell her she was going to hell because she was a Catholic. She used the scriptures to counter their arguments, but never in a confrontational way. Some of them were her closest friends.

She had no fear of bishops who wore miters, crosiers, and pectoral crosses. Once a week for the past year she challenged me to give honest answers to questions she had about the institutional Catholic church—questions about celibacy, married priests, women as priests, birth control, abortion, the infallibility of the pope, sexual misconduct of some priests.

Toni was a thinker, and as a consequence, a questioner too. She thought that Catholics should not think they alone have the right answers. She thought it more important that we Catholics ask the right questions such as: Why are women treated as second class citizens? Why did the Vatican consider banning girls from serving at Mass? She was really incensed by this, and in the light of what she did in the cathedral to save an archbishop, I think all of us should be incensed as well. Toni questioned whether our Church is a church of the poor or a church of the rich. She asked, is our Church unfair to gays and lesbians who act according to the nature God has given them?

She believed the Catholic Church is in some ways a dysfunctional system. I strongly disagreed with her on this, but her statement caused me to think and to look back over my more than fifty years of priesthood. I regretted that unlike The Rev. Martin Luther King, Jr. I did not speak out more forcefully on issues of peace and race and justice. I should have been more of an advocate for union membership for men and women who are exploited by corporate greed. I did not speak out forcefully enough against injustices to married people, and to priests and nuns. I should have hammered home the point in my writings and in my sermons that homophobia in the Church is telling gays and lesbians they are not welcome at the Table of the Lord. Although I did speak on these issues, I did not speak and write forcefully enough because I feared my words would alienate wealthy right wing Catholics, causing Sunday collections to drop or fund raising projects to miss their goals.

Recently Toni and her good friend Professor Kate Green discovered this old inner city parish of Saint Mary. It was badly in need of a resurrection. So with the new pastor Father Mike Brown they recruited an army of volunteers—Catholics, Protestants, Muslims, Buddhists, believers, non-believers, college kids and high school kids—and armed them with paint brushes, rakes, shovels, and trash bags. In a few weekends they brought the place back to life. And, may I add, in less than a year Toni Vincent brought me back to life.

To be sure, there will be some who will say that I am exaggerating the importance of this sixteen-year-old girl. How can she be more important to my life than two popes, bishops, and the men and women theologians who have influenced me? I don't know what motivates them, but I do know what motivated her. It was to do what was right. As one college student put it, "There was no strategizing, no calling out to others to wrest the gun from the shooter. She knew the right thing to do and she did it. It is oddly rewarding," he said, "to see an innocent kid do what is right because it is right."

I cannot speak for others. Often I knew the right thing to do but I delayed doing it, or maybe did it only when I knew it was the safe thing to do. So inscribe on my headstone, "Night of forgetfulness," and inscribe on hers "Dawn of Remembrance."

I then blessed the grave. Quietly, the student pall bearers moved forward and lowered the pine coffin into the grave. The mourners filed by silently and slowly. The only sounds were those of dirt being shoveled on to the wooden pine box, and the footsteps of mourners making their way back to their cars and the wind whipping through the brittle autumn leaves.

KATE'S EPILOGUE

Every night I look down from the windows of my apartment on the top floor of the condominium in which I now live and think not so much about the cathedral that is below, but of France and its Cathedral of Our Lady of Chartres, which my husband Tom and I visited on our wedding trip a year after Toni's death over twenty years ago. I think especially of those beautiful stained glass windows that artisans have never been able to duplicate. When the sun is shining on them, they are a glorious sight to behold.

I also think of the thousands of men and women who in less than a century built that structure. They belonged to guilds of stone masons, glass workers, and wood workers, and other guilds of butchers and bakers. Most of the townspeople of Chartres were involved in the building of that cathedral. Their names have been lost to us. But that would not matter to them because they were not building the cathedral as a monument to themselves but as an edifice to the Virgin Mary. Few, if any, who started the building in 1190 lived to see its completion in 1260.

As I think about the Cathedral at Chartres, I look down from my suite and see the cathedral that men and women of faith in my city built almost a century ago. Many of those craftsmen and craftswomen died before its completion, never seeing the total effect of their handiwork, no matter how menial or how exalted.

Archbishop Graham never recovered consciousness and died three weeks after the murder in the cathedral. He is buried in that cathedral along with Cardinal Mohr, who succeeded Archbishop Foley.

But I also look out on the city and see Saint Mary Church and the high hill behind it where Toni and Archbishop Foley are buried. He died at age 85, five years after Toni's tragic death. His Mass of Christian burial was celebrated in the cathedral but without the pomp and ceremony that surrounded the burials of Cardinal Mohr and Archbishop Graham. According to his wishes expressed in his will, his wooden coffin (crafted by Jakob Mueller) was placed on a horse-drawn Amish wagon, which made its way to the cemetery behind Saint Mary's church. The coffin was then placed in the grave next to Toni's. Mike Brown gave the homily at Foley's funeral Mass. That too was written in Foley's will. In choosing Brown, the reformed "alcoholic," Foley was sending a powerful message from the other side of the grave that in the eternal scheme of things reconciliation and forgiveness are what really count.

Two years ago my husband Tom had a fatal heart attack on a business trip to New York. Although Tom and I were married by a Lutheran minister, Tom is buried in that parish cemetery, thanks to Mike Brown, who takes a dim view of the process of excommunication and its denial of Christian burial.

Mike Brown even buried Ron Hackett, who was killed in prison after serving ten years of his twenty-year term for the killing of Toni Vincent.

The graves of Mrs. Lacey and Toni's mother and many people who were there when Toni was buried are well cared for under the watchful eye of Mike Brown, who is still pastor of Saint Mary parish. He has established numerous ministries to the handicapped, the poor and the alienated. Sunday liturgies are so well attended that there is no need for a subsidy from the archdiocese.

Much to the delight of the citizens of Forest Park, Hank Kolar received a Pulitzer Prize for his coverage of the murder of Toni Vincent. He now is editor of a prestigious paper in the East.

Toni and Archbishop Foley are dead, but Mike Brown is still alive and continues his ministry to people from all religions or no religion—to all people who are searching for a spirituality that gives meaning to their lives. They are, in retrospect, I think, building a new church—not a brick and mortar church because there are enough of them and we don't need any more. They are building a church of people dedicated to carrying out the corporal works and spiritual works of mercy. For them the center of the church is not a beautiful stained glass window but the Eucharist consecrated by priests of both genders.

This church is a work in progress, and it may take centuries for it to be fully realized. Most, if not all, of us will not live to see its completion. We know that, but we struggle on, convinced as were those who built the Cathedral of Our Lady of Chartres that in the words of Henry Adams "truth must be known, beauty fashioned, the earth subdued and God truly loved."

About the Author

George Eppley is professor emeritus of English, Cuyahoga Community College, Cleveland, Ohio.

He and his wife, Anita Dixon Eppley, have co-authored three college composition textbooks with Harcourt Brace, HarperCollins, and Mayfield. With a group of other writers, they are co-authors of *College and Career Success Simplified* (Pearson Longman Publishers, 2004).

Eppley has been a parish priest, a high school teacher and principal, a college professor, a graduate school dean, and a consultant/innovator for an inner city public high school. His essays have appeared in several publications including *The New York Times, Newsday, The Plain Dealer,* and *Cleveland Magazine.*

Also by George Eppley
Looking Back and Learning—a three-tape audio cassette in which Eppley tells about ordinary experiences that have shaped his life and challenges people to write about the persons, places and events that have influenced their lives and values.